Murder
on the Short List

PETER LOVESEY
(Photograph by Kate Shemilt)

MURDER ON
THE SHORT LIST

Peter Lovesey

This first world hardcover edition published 2009
in Great Britain and in the USA by
SEVERN HOUSE PUBLISHERS LTD of
9–15 High Street, Sutton, Surrey, England, SM1 1DF.
Trade paperback edition published 2009 in Great Britain
by Severn House Publishers, Ltd.

'*The Field*' was first published in Green for Danger (The Do-Not Press, 2003);
'*Bullets*' in The Mammoth Book of Roaring twenties Whodunnits (Robinson 2004);
'*Razor Bill*' in Sherlock, 2004; '*Needle Match*' in Murder is My Racquet
(Mysterious Press, 2005); '*A Blow on the Head*' in I.D.Crimes of Identity
(Comma Press, 2006); '*The Munich Posture*' in The Rigby File (Hodder &
Stoughton, 1989); '*The Best Suit*' in this edition; '*The Man Who Jumped for England*'
In Mysterious Pleasures (Little, Brown, 2003); '*Second Strings*' in The Strand
Magazine, 2004; '*Bertie and the Christmas Tree*' in The Strand Magazine, 2007;
'*Say That Again*' in The Ideas Experiment (Paw Paw Press, 2006); '*Popping Round
to the Post*' in The Verdict of Us All (Allison & Busby, 2006); '*Window of
Opportunity*' in Sunday Express, 2003; '*The Case of the Dead Wait*' in Daily Mail, 2004.

British Library Cataloguing in Publication Data

Lovesey, Peter
  Murder on the short list
  1. Detective and mystery stories, English
  I. Title
  823.9'14[F]

ISBN-13: 978-0-7278-6746-9   (cased)
ISBN-13: 978-1-84751-108-9   (trade paper)

All Severn House titles are printed on acid-free paper.

Printed and bound in Great Britain by
MPG Books Ltd., Bodmin, Cornwall.

CONTENTS

FOREWORD

Writers get used to being asked where they get their ideas from. If you're a crime writer, as I am, the question is loaded. Do I have personal experience of disposing of bodies and evading the police? And when I give my truthful answer, that my ideas come from numerous sources, I sense the questioner thinking that's a cop-out, a typical piece of evasion from someone up to his ears in crime.

Short stories such as these do sometimes have a clear origin enabling me to give straight answers. "The Field" was inspired by the sight of a crop of oilseed rape dominating the landscape and completely obscuring the ground it sprang from. What else was it hiding, I wondered? Wild life, children at play, lovers in flagrante, or a corpse?

"Bullets" was suggested by an old man who told me he'd once won a large amount of money in a newspaper competition to add up to four witty words to a given phrase. His win had created lifelong jealousy in his family. Intrigued, I started researching these "Bullet" competitions just at the time I was asked to contribute a story with a twenties setting to an anthology.

"Second Strings" jumped out from a newspaper report of the theft of a valuable harp that later turned up in someone's garden. I couldn't believe a harpist would steal someone else's instrument and I couldn't think of anything more difficult to carry off than a harp. It became a challenge to create a story that fitted the facts.

My wife Jax watches tennis on TV by the hour. She sees patterns of play that elude me. I find myself getting more interested in the officials than the players. There's a story in every one of them, the umpire, the line judges and the ballboys. When I was invited to write a tennis story I thought it would be interesting to tell the whole thing from the viewpoint of a ballboy, and that became "Needle Match."

Who hasn't heard the phrase "window of opportunity"? It is a modern cliché, reduced now to just "window," as in, "I'll see if I have a window some time next week." Having heard it once too often from some trendy on the radio, I decided to have fun with the kind of person who uses it, and that gave me a theme as well as the title of a new story.

"Say That Again" was a deliberate exercise undertaken with two writer friends, Liza Cody and Michael Z. Lewin. We took a newspaper cutting about geriatric crooks and each agreed to use it as a trigger for a story. This became a booklet called *The Ideas Experiment* and launched as a panel at a conference called Left Coast Crime. I drew heavily on memories of visiting my mother in her retirement home and listening to the residents discussing each other and the staff. Who would shape such a group into effective criminals? It had to be a military man, eager to lead one last campaign, and of course the motive had to arise from one of the infirmities of old age.

For "Razor Bill," I wanted to give an outing to the two Victorian detectives I used in my first novels back in the seventies. Sergeant Cribb and Constable Thackeray featured in eight books and a TV series but had lain dormant for twenty-five years. Razor Bill is active in 1882, six years before Jack the Ripper terrorised London, and it has to be dear old put-upon Thackeray who acts as the decoy.

In a similar way, I put Bertie, the Prince of Wales, through his paces in "Bertie and the Christmas Tree," a seasonal story commissioned by *The Strand Magazine*. The germ of this one was the widely repeated but mistaken belief that Bertie's father, Prince Albert, brought the first Christmas tree to Britain. I believed it, too, but a little investigation soon informed me otherwise. Still, the notion of using a Christmas tree in a royal murder mystery fired my imagination.

In 2006, the distinguished crime writer H.R.F. Keating celebrated his eightieth birthday and I was asked by his wife Sheila to edit a volume of short stories by members of the Detection Club, of which Harry was President for many years. It was a happy task because his colleagues were delighted to write stories in his honour. Each tale had a link of some sort to Harry. In my letter to would-be contributors I suggested various elements in Harry's life and fiction they might wish to explore. This left me with a problem: what could I write about that I hadn't already suggested? In the end I looked up the great man in *Who's Who* and found that he lists his occupation as popping round to the post and that delivered the gift I needed.

You now know where some of my ideas came from. Not all, you'll say. And I will admit that I can't remember how the others dawned on me. Maybe it was while I was digging a grave in the woods.

THE FIELD

A field of oilseed rape was in flower, brilliant in the afternoon sun, as if a yellow highlighter had been drawn across the landscape. Unseen by anyone, a corpse was stretched out under the swaying crop, attended only by flies and maggots. It had been there ten days. The odour was not detectable from the footpath along the hedgerow.

Fields have names. This one was Middle Field, and it was well named. It was not just the middle field on Jack Mooney's farm. It was the middle of his universe. He had no life outside the farm. His duties kept him employed from first light until after dark.

Middle Field dominated the scene. So Jack Mooney's scarecrow stood out, as much as you could see of it. People said it was a wasted effort. Crows aren't the problem with a rape crop. Pigeons are the big nuisance, and that's soon after sowing. It's an open question whether a scarecrow is any deterrent at all to pigeons. By May or June when the crop is five feet tall it serves no purpose.

"Should have got rid of it months back," Mooney said.

His wife May, at his side, said, "You'd have to answer to the children."

From the highest point at the top of the field you could see more than just the flat cap and turnip head. The shoulders and part of the chest were visible as well. After a long pause Mooney said, "Something's happened to it."

"Now what are you on about?"

"Take a look through the glasses."

She put them to her eyes and adjusted the focus. Middle Field was all of nine acres.

"Funny. Who did that, I wonder?"

Someone had dressed the thing in a raincoat. All it was supposed to be wearing were Mooney's cast-off shirt, a pair of corduroy trousers filled with straw and his old cap.

"How long has it been like that?"

"How would I know?" Mooney said. "I thought you would have noticed."

"I may go on at you for ignoring me, but I'm not so desperate as to spend my days looking at a straw man with a turnip for a head."

"Could have been there for weeks."

"Wouldn't surprise me."

"Some joker?"

"Maybe."

"I'm going to take a closer look."

He waded into his shimmering yellow sea.

Normally he wouldn't set foot in that field until after the combine had been through. But he was curious. Whose coat was it? And why would anyone think of putting it on a scarecrow?

Out in the middle he stopped and scratched his head

It was a smart coat, with epaulettes, sleeve straps and a belt.

His wife had followed him. She lifted the hem. "It's a Burberry. You can tell by the lining."

"I've never owned one like this."

"You, in a Burberry? You're joking. Been left out a few days by the look of it, but it's not in bad condition."

"Who would have chucked out a fancy coat like this?"

"More important," his wife said, "who would have draped it around our old scarecrow?"

He had made the scarecrow last September on a framework of wood and chicken wire. A stake driven into the earth, with a crosspiece that swivelled when the wind blew, giving the effect of animation. The wire bent into the shape of a torso that hung free. The clothes stuffed with straw. The biggest turnip he could find for a head. He wouldn't have troubled with the features, but his children had insisted he cut slits for eyes and the mouth and a triangle for the nose.

No question: the coat had been carefully fitted on, the arms pulled through, the buttons fixed and the belt buckled in front.

As if the field itself could explain the mystery, Mooney turned and stared across the canopy of bloom. To the north was his own house and the farm buildings standing out against the skyline. At the lower end to the south-east were the tied cottages, three terraced dwellings built from the local stone. They were still called tied cottages by the locals, even though they had been sold off to a developer and knocked into one, now a sizeable house being tarted up by some townie who came at weekends to check on the work. Mooney had made a good profit from the sale. He didn't care if the locals complained that true village people couldn't afford to live here at prices like that.

Could the coat belong to the townie? he wondered. Was it someone's idea of a joke dressing the old scarecrow in the townie's smart Burberry? Strange joke. After all, who would know it was there unless they took out some field-glasses?

"You know what I reckon?" May said. "Kids."

"Whose kids?"

"Our own. I'll ask them when they get back from school."

The birdsong grew as the afternoon wore on. At the edge of the field closest to the tied cottages more disturbance of the oilseed crop took place. Smaller feet than Mooney's led another expedition. They were his children, the two girls, Sarah and Ally, eleven years old and seven. Behind them came their mother.

"It's not far," Sarah said, looking back.

"Not far, Mum," Ally said.

They were right. No more than ten adult strides in from the path was a place where some of the plants had been flattened.

"See?" Ally said.

This was where the children had found the raincoat. Snapped stalks and blackened fronds confirmed what the girls had told her. It was as if some horse had strayed into the crop and rolled on its back. "So the coat was spread out here?"

"Yes, Mummy."

"Like somebody had a picnic," Ally added.

May had a different, less wholesome thought she didn't voice. "And you didn't see anyone?"

They shook their heads.

"You're quite sure?"

"We were playing ball and I threw it and it landed in the field. We were on our own. When we were looking for our ball we found the coat. Nobody wanted it because we came back next day and it was still here and we thought let's put it on our scarecrow and see if Daddy notices. Was it Daddy who noticed?"

"Never mind that. You should have told me about the coat when you found it. Did you find anything else?"

"No, Mummy. If they'd wanted to keep the coat, they would have come back, wouldn't they?"

"Did you look in the pockets?"

"Yes, and they were empty. Mr Scarecrow looks nicer with a coat."

"Much nicer," Ally said in support. "Doesn't he look nicer, Mummy?"

May was not to be sidetracked. "You shouldn't have done what you did. It belongs to someone else."

"But they didn't want it, or they would have come back," Sarah said.

"You don't know. They could still come back."

"They could be dead."

"It would still be wrong to take it. I'm going to take it off the scarecrow and we'll hand it in to the police. It's lost property."

A full three days later, Mooney escorted a tall detective inspector through the crop. "You'll have to be damn quick with your investigating. This'll be ready for combining soon. Some of the pods are forming already."

"If it's a crime scene, Mr Mooney, you're not doing anything to it."

"We called you about the coat last Monday, and no one came."

"A raincoat isn't much to get excited about. The gun is another matter."

Another matter that had finally brought the police here in a hurry. Mooney had found a Smith and Wesson in his field. A handgun.

"When did you pick it up?"

"This morning."

"What – taking a stroll, were you?"

Mooney didn't like the way the question was put, as if he'd been acting suspiciously. He'd done the proper thing, reported finding the weapon as soon as he picked it up. "I've got a right to walk in my own field."

"Through this stuff?"

"I promised my kids I'd find their ball – the ball that was missing the day they found the coat. I found the gun instead – about here." He stopped and parted some of the limp, blue-green leaves at the base of a plant.

To the inspector, this plant looked no different from the rest except that the trail ended here. He took a white disk from his pocket and marked the spot. "Careful with your feet. We'll want to check all this ground. And where was the Burberry raincoat?"

"On the scarecrow."

"I mean, where did your daughters find it?"

Mooney flapped his hand in a southerly direction. "About thirty yards off."

"Show me."

The afternoon was the hottest of the year so far. Thousands of bees were foraging in the rape flowers. Mooney didn't mind disturbing them, but the inspector was twitchy. He wasn't used to walking chest-high through fields. He kept close to the farmer using his elbows to fend off the tall plants springing upright again.

Only a short distance ahead, the bluebottles were busy as well. Mooney stopped.

"Well, how about this?" He was stooping over something.

The inspector almost tumbled over Mooney's back. "What is it? What have you found?"

Mooney held it up. "My kids' ball. They'll be pleased you came."

"Let's get on."

"Do you smell anything, inspector?"

In a few hours the police transformed this part of Middle Field. A large part of the crop was ruined, crushed under the feet of detectives, scenes of crime officers, a police surgeon, a pathologist and police photographers. Mooney was depressed by all the damage.

"You think the coat might have belonged to the owner of the cottages across the lane, is that right?" the inspector asked.

"I wouldn't know."

"It's what you told me earlier."

"That was my wife's idea. She says it's a posh coat. No one from round here wears a posh coat. Except him."

"Who is he?"

Mooney had to think about that. He'd put the name out of his mind. "White, as I recall. Jeremy White, from London. He bought the tied cottages from the developer who knocked them into one. He's doing them up, making a palace out of it, open plan, with marble floors and a spiral staircase."

"Doing them up himself?"

"He's a townie. What would he know about building work? No, he's given the job to Armstrong, the Devizes firm. Comes here each weekend to check on the work."

"Any family?"

"I wouldn't know about that." He looked away, across the field, to the new slate roof on the tied cottages. "I've seen a lady with him."

"A lady? What's she like?"

Mooney sighed, forced to think. "Dark-haired."

"Age?"

"Younger than him."

"The sale was in his name alone?"

"That's right."

"If you don't mind, Mr Mooney, I'd like you to take another look at the corpse and see if you recognise anyone."

From the glimpse he'd had already, Mooney didn't much relish another look. "If I don't mind? Have I got a choice?"

Some of the crop had been left around the body like a screen. The police had used one access path so as not to destroy evidence. Mooney pressed his fingers to his nose and stepped up. He peered at the bloated features. Ten days in hot weather makes a difference. "Difficult," he said. "The hair looks about right."

"For Jeremy White?"

"That reddish colour. Dyed, isn't it? I always thought the townie dyed his hair. He weren't so young as he wanted people to think he were."

"The clothes?"

Mooney looked at the pinstripe suit dusted faintly yellow from the crop. There were bullet holes in the jacket. "That's the kind of thing he wore, certainly."

The inspector nodded. "From the contents of his wallet we're pretty sure this is Jeremy White. Do you recall hearing any shots last time he was here?"

"There are shots all the time, specially at weekends. Rabbits. Pigeons. We wouldn't take note of that."

"When did you see him last?"

"Two weekends ago. Passed him in the lane on the Sunday afternoon."

"Anyone with him?"

"That dark-haired young lady I spoke of."

The inspector produced the wallet found on the body and took out a photo of a dark-haired woman in a blue blouse holding up a drink. "Is this her?"

Mooney examined it for some time. He eyed the inspector with suspicion, as if he was being tricked. "That wasn't the lady I saw."

There was an interval when the buzzing of insects seemed to increase and the heat grew.

"Are you certain?"

"Positive."

"Take another look."

"Her with the townie was definitely younger."

The inspector's eyebrows lifted. "How much younger?"

"A good ten years, I'd say."

"Did they come by car?"

"There was always a sports car parked in front of the cottages when he came, one of them BMW jobs with the open top."

"Just the one vehicle? The lady didn't drive down in her own?"

"If she did, I've never seen it. When can I have my field back?"

"When I tell you. There's more searching to be done."

"More damage, you mean."

Mooney met Bernie Priddle with his dog the same evening coming along the footpath beside the hedgerow. Bernie had lived in one of the tied cottages until Mooney decided to sell it. He was in his fifties, small, thin-faced, always ready with a barbed remark.

"You'll lose the whole of your crop by the look of it," he said, and he sounded happier than he had for months.

"I thought you'd turn up," Mooney said. "Makes you feel better to see someone else's misfortune, does it?"

"I walk the path around the field every evening. It's part of the dog's routine. You should know that by now. I was saying you'll lose your crop."

"Don't I know it! Even if they don't trample every stalk of it, they'll stop me from harvesting."

"People are saying it's the townie who was shot."

"That's my understanding."

"Good riddance, too."

"You want to guard what you say, Bernie Priddle. They're looking for someone to nail for this."

"Me? I wouldn't put myself in trouble for some pipsqueak yuppie. It's you I wouldn't mind doing a stretch for, Mooney. I could throttle you any time for putting me out of my home."

"What are you moaning about? You got a council house out of it, didn't you? Hot water and an inside toilet. Where's your dog?"

Priddle looked down. His Jack Russell had moved on, and he didn't know where. He whistled.

Over by the body, all the heads turned.

"It's all right," Mooney shouted to the policemen. "He was calling his dog, that's all."

The inspector came over and spoke to Priddle. "And who are you exactly?"

Bernie explained about his regular evening walk around the field.

"Have you ever seen Mr White, the owner of the tied cottages?"

"On occasion," Bernie said. "What do you want to know?"

"Ever seen anyone with him?"

"Last time – the Sunday before last – there was the young lady, her with the long, black hair, and short skirt. She's a good looker, that one. He was showing her the building work. Had his arm around her. I raised my cap to them, didn't speak. Later, when I was round the far side, I saw them heading into the field."

"Into the field? Where?"

"Over yonder. He had a coat on his arm. Next time I looked, they weren't in view." He grinned. "I drew my own conclusion, like, and walked on. I came right around the field before I saw the other car parked in the lane."

The inspector's interest increased. "You saw another car?"

"Nice little Cherokee Jeep, it was, red. Do you want the number?"

"Do you remember it?"

"It was a woman's name, SUE, followed by a number. I couldn't tell you which, except it was just the one."

"A single digit?" The inspector sounded pleased. "SUE, followed by a single digit. That's really useful, sir. We can check that. And did you see the driver?"

"No, I can't help you there."

"Hear any shooting?"

"We often hear shooting in these parts. Look, I'd better find my dog."

"We'll need to speak to you some more, Mr ...?"

"Priddle. Bernard Priddle. You're welcome. These days I live in one of them poky little council bungalows in the village. Second on the left."

The inspector watched him stride away, whistling for the dog, and said to one of the team, "A useful witness. I want you to take a statement from him."

Mooney was tempted to pass on the information that Bernie was a publicity-seeking pain in the arse, but he decided to let the police do their own work.

The body was removed from Middle Field the same evening. Some men in black suits put it into a bag with a zip and stretchered it over the well-trodden ground to a small van and drove off.

"Now can I have my field back?" Mooney asked the inspector.

"What's the hurry?"

"You've destroyed a big section of my crop. What's left will go over if I don't harvest it at the proper time. The pods shatter and it's too late."

"What do you use? A combine harvester?"

"First it has to be swathed into rows. It all takes time."

"I'll let you know in the morning. Cutting it could make our work easier. We want to do a bigger search."

"What for?"

"Evidence. We now know that the woman Bernard Priddle saw – the driver of the Jeep – was the woman in the photograph I showed you, Mrs Susan White, the dead man's wife. We're assuming the younger woman was White's mistress. We think Mrs White was suspicious and followed them here. She didn't know about him buying the tied cottages. That was going to be his love-nest, just for weekends with the mistress. But he couldn't wait for it to be built. The wife caught them at it in the field."

"On the raincoat?"

"That's the assumption. Our forensic people may confirm it."

"Nasty shock."

"On both sides, no doubt."

Mooney smiled. "You could be right about that. So that's why he was shot. What happened to the mistress?"

"She must have escaped. Someone drove his car away and we reckon it was her."

"So have you arrested the wife?"

"Not yet. She wasn't at home when we called."

Mooney grinned again. "She guessed you were coming."

"We'll catch up with her."

In a tree in the hedgerow a songthrush sounded its clear notes and was answered from across the field. A breeze was cooling the air.

On the insistence of the police, Mooney harvested his crop a week before it was ready. He'd cried wolf about all the bother they'd caused, and now he suffered a loss through cutting too early. To make matters worse, not one extra piece of evidence was found, for all their fingertip searches through the stubble.

"Is that the end of it?" he asked the inspector when the final sweep across the field was made. The land looked black and bereft. Only the scarecrow remained standing. They'd asked him to leave it to use as a marker.

"It's the end of my work, but you'll be visited again. The lawyers will want to look at the site before the case comes to court."

"When will that be?"

"I can't say. Could be months. A year, even."

"There won't be anything to see."

"They'll look at the positions where the gun was found, and the body and the coat. They map it all out."

"So are you advising me not to drill next spring?"

"That's an instruction, not advice. Not this field, anyway."

"It's my livelihood. Will I get compensation?"

"I've no idea. Not my field, if you'll forgive the pun."

"So you found the wife in the end?"

"Susan White – yes. She's helping us with our enquiries, as we like to put it."

"How about the mistress? Did you catch up with her?"

"Not yet. We don't even know who she is."

"Maybe the wife shot her as well."

"That's why we had you cutting your crop, in case of a second body. But we're pretty certain she drove off in the BMW. It hasn't been traced yet."

Winter brought a few flurries of snow and some gales. The scarecrow remained standing. The building work on the tied cottages was halted and no one knew what was happening about them.

"I should have drilled by now," Mooney said, staring across the field.

"Are they ever going to come back, do you think?" his wife said.

"He said it would take a long time."

"I suppose the wife has been in prison all these months waiting for the trial to start. I can't help feeling sorry for her."

"If you shoot your husband, you must get what's coming to you," Mooney said.

"She had provocation. Men who cheat on their wives don't get any sympathy from me."

"Taking a gun to them is a bit extreme."

"Quick and merciful."

Mooney gave her a look. There had been a time before the children came along when their own marriage had gone through a crisis, but he'd never been unfaithful.

The lawyers came in April. Two lots in the same week. They took photos and made measurements, regardless that the field looked totally different to the way it had last year. After the second group – the prosecution team – had finished, Mooney asked if he could sow the new crop now. Spring rape doesn't give the yield of a winter crop, but it's better than nothing.

"I wouldn't," the lawyer told him. "It's quite possible we'll bring out the jury to see the scene of the crime."

"It's a lot of fuss, when we all know she did it."

"It's justice, Mr Mooney. She must have a fair trial."

And you must run up your expenses, he thought. They'd driven up in their Porsches and Mercedes and lunched on fillet steak at the pub. The law was a good racket.

But as things turned out, the jury weren't brought to see the field. The trial took place a year after the killing and Mooney was allowed to sow another crop. The first thing he did was take down that scarecrow and destroy it. He wasn't a superstitious man, but he associated the wretched thing with his run of bad luck. He'd been told it had been photographed for the papers. Stupid. They'd photograph any damned thing to fill a page. Someone told him they'd called his land "The Killing Field." Things like that were written by fools for fools to read. When a man has to be up at sunrise he doesn't have time for papers. By the evening they're all out of date.

An evil thing had happened in Middle Field, but Mooney was determined to treat it as just a strip of land like any other. Personally, he had no worries about working the soil. He put the whole morbid incident to the back of his mind.

Until one evening in September.

He'd drilled the new sowing of oilseed, and was using the roller, working late to try and get the job finished before the light went altogether. A huge harvest moon appeared while he was still at work. He was thinking of supper, driving the tractor in near darkness along the last length beside the footpath, when a movement close to the hedge caught his eye.

If the figure had kept still he would have driven straight past. The face turned and was picked out by his headlights. A woman. Features he'd seen before.

He braked and got down.

She was already walking on. He ran after her and shouted, "Hey!"

She turned, and he knew he wasn't mistaken. She was the woman in the photograph the police had shown him, Sue White, the killer, the wife of the dead man.

"What the devil are you doing here?" he asked.

"Walking the footpath. It's allowed, isn't it?" She was calm for an escaped convict.

Mooney's heart pumped faster. He peered through the fading light to be certain he wasn't mistaken. "Who are you?"

"My name is Sue White. Are you all right?"

Mooney wasn't all right. He'd just had a severe shock. His ears were ringing and his vision was going misty. He reached out towards the hedge to support himself. His hand clutched at nothing and he fell.

The paramedics attended to him by flashlight in the field where he'd fallen. "You'll need to be checked," one of them said, "but I don't think this is a heart attack. More of a shock reaction. The blood pressure falls and you faint. Have you had anything like it before?"

Mooney shook his head. "But it were a shock all right, seeing that woman. How did she escape?"

"*Escape*? Just take it easy, Mr Mooney."

"She's on the run from prison. She could be dangerous."

"Listen, Mr Mooney. It's only thanks to Mrs White that we got here at all. She used her mobile."

"Maybe, but she's still a killer."

"Come off it. You're talking about the man who was shot in your own field, and you don't know who did it? It was all over the papers. Don't you read them?"

"I don't have time for the papers."

"It was his mistress that killed him. She's serving life now."

"His mistress? But the wife caught them at it."

"Yes, and that's how the mistress found out for certain that he had a wife. She'd got her suspicions already and was carrying the gun in her bag to get the truth out of him, or so she claimed at the trial. She saw red and shot him after Mrs White showed up."

His voice shook. "So Mrs White is innocent?"

"Totally. We've been talking to her. She came down today to look at those cottages. She's the owner now. She'll sell them if she's got any sense. I mean, who'd want a home looking out over the Killing Field?"

They helped Mooney to the gate and into the ambulance. Below the surface of Middle Field, the moist soil pressed against the seeds.

BULLETS

"Y ou can remove the body."

"Was it definitely ...?"

"Suicide, I'd stake my life on it," said Inspector Carew, a forceful man. "Single bullet to the head. Gun beside him. Ex-army fellow who didn't return his weapon when the war ended. This must be the third or fourth case I've seen. The world has changed too much for them – the wireless, a Labour Government, the bright young things. All these poor fellows have got is their memories of the war, and who wants to think about that?"

"He didn't leave a note."

"Are you questioning my conclusion?"

"Absolutely not, Inspector."

"I suggest you get on with your job, then. I'm going to speak to the family."

The family consisted of the dead man's widow, Emily Flanagan, a pretty, dark-haired woman not much over thirty; and her father, whose name was Russell. They were sitting at the kitchen table in 7, Albert Street, their small suburban house in Teddington. They had a bottle of brandy between them.

The inspector accepted a drink and knocked it back in one swig. When talking to the recently bereaved he needed all the lubrication he could get. He gave them his findings and explained that there would need to be a post mortem to confirm the cause, obvious as it was. "You didn't find a note, I suppose?" he said.

Emily Flanagan shook her head.

"Did anything occur that could have induced him to take his own life? Bad news? An argument?"

Mrs Flanagan looked across at her father.

"No argument," the old man said. "And that's beyond dispute."

Mrs Flanagan clapped her hands twice and said, "Good one, Daddy."

Inspector Carew didn't follow what was going on, except that these two seemed more cheerful than they should.

"As a matter of fact," Mrs Flanagan said, "Patrick was in a better mood than I've seen him for some time." The ends of her mouth turned up in what wasn't quite a smile, more a comment on the vagary of fate.

"This was last night?"

"And for some days. He was singing *Horsey, Keep Your Tail Up* in the bathroom."

"Bracing himself?" said the inspector. His theory of depression was looking shaky.

"What do you mean, 'bracing himself'?"

"For the, em ..."

"*Felo de se*," said old Mr Russell. "*Felo de se* – fellow's sad day."

"Daddy, please," said Mrs Flanagan.

The inspector decided that the old man had drunk too much brandy. This wasn't a comfortable place to be. As soon as he'd got the essential details he was leaving. "I understand you were both woken by the shot."

"About midnight, yes," the widow said, glancing at her fingernails. She was holding up remarkably.

"You came downstairs and found him in his office?"

She nodded. "He called it his den. And Father came in soon after."

"He'd given no indication of taking his own life?"

"He liked his own life, Inspector."

"What was his work?"

"He was an actor. He was currently playing in *Bulldog Drummond* at the Richmond Theatre. It was only a small role as a gangster, but he did it to perfection. They'll miss him dreadfully."

The inspector was tempted to ask, "And will you?" But he kept his lips buttoned. "*Bulldog Drummond*. I can't say I've read it."

"It has a sub-title," said Mrs Flanagan. "Daddy, can you remember the sub-title?"

"*The Adventures of a Demobilized Officer Who Found Peace Dull.*"

"I knew he'd know it," she said. "Being housebound, Daddy has more time for reading than the rest of us. '*A Demobilized Officer Who Found Peace Dull.*'"

This was closer to Inspector Carew's diagnosis. "Poignant, in the circumstances."

"Oh, I don't agree. Patrick's life was anything but dull."

"So last night he would have returned late from the theatre?"

"About half past eleven usually."

"Perhaps he was overtired."

"Patrick?" she said with an inappropriate laugh. "He was inexhaustible."

"Did he have a difficult war?"

"Didn't every soldier? I thought he'd put all that behind him."

"Apparently not, unless there was something else." The inspector was beginning to revise his theory. "Forgive me for asking this, Mrs Flanagan. Was your marriage entirely successful?"

The lips twitched again. "I dare say he had lapses."

"Lapses," said old Mr Russell. "Like lasses on laps."

This piece of wit earned no more than a frown from his daughter. She said to the inspector, "Patrick was an actor. Enough said?"

"Didn't it anger you?"

"We had tiffs if I caught him out, as I sometimes did."

"You seem to treat it lightly, if I may say so."

"Because they were minor indiscretions, kissing and canoodling."

The inspector wasn't certain of the meaning of "canoodling", but he guessed it didn't amount to adultery. "Not a cause for suicide, then?"

"Good Lord, no."

"And how was the balance of his mind, would you say?"

"Are you asking me if he was mad?"

"When he shot himself, yes."

"I wasn't there when he shot himself, but I think it highly unlikely. He never lost control."

"Well, then," the inspector said, preparing to leave, "it will be for the coroner to decide. He may wish to visit the scene himself, so I'm leaving the, em, den as it is, apart from the, em, ..."

"Mortal remains?" old Mr Russell suggested.

"So please don't tidy anything up. Leave it exactly as it is." He picked up his hat and left.

Mrs Flanagan had barely started her next brandy when the doorbell rang again. "Damn. Who's that?" she said.

Her father wobbled to the door and admitted a fat, bald man in a cassock. He smelt of tobacco. "Father Montgomery," he said.

"Should we know you?" she asked.

"I was Padre to your husband in France. I'm the incumbent of St Saviour's in Richmond. I heard from one of my congregation that he'd been gathered, so I came at once to see what I could do."

"Very little," said Mrs Flanagan. " 'Gathered' isn't the word I would use. He killed himself. That's a lost soul in your religion, isn't it?"

The priest sighed heavily. "That *is* distressing. I know he wasn't a regular worshipper, but he was brought up in the Church of Rome. He professed himself a Catholic when pressed."

Old Mr Russell said in a parade-ground chant, "Fall out the Jews and Catholics."

"Exactly, sir. So I do have a concern over the destiny of poor Patrick's soul. Is it certain?"

"If you call putting a gun to your head and pulling the trigger certain, I would say it is," said Mrs Flanagan, wanting to be rid of this visitor. "We've had the police here and they confirm it."

"His service revolver, I suppose? How I wish the army had been more responsible in collecting all the weapons they issued. May I see the room?"

"Is that necessary?"

"I would like to remove all doubt from my mind that this was suicide."

"You have a doubt?"

His eyes flicked upwards. "I have a duty, my dear."

She showed him into Patrick's den, a small room with a desk surrounded by bookshelves. Her father shuffled in after them.

The body had been removed, but otherwise the room was just as the police had seen it, with the revolver lying on the desk.

"Please don't touch anything," Mrs Flanagan said.

The priest made a performance of linking his thumbs behind his back. He leaned over and peered at the gun. "Service issue, as I expected," he said. "Did the police examine the chambers for bullets?"

"Empty. He only needed the one."

"Where did he keep the gun?"

"In the bottom drawer – but don't open it."

Father Montgomery had little option but to look about him at the bookshelves. There were plays by Oscar Wilde and George Bernard Shaw. "Did he act in any of these?"

"No. He collected them for personal reading. He was a well-read man."

"Well-read," said old Mr Russell. "Oh, essay, essay, essay."

"Father adores his word-play," Mrs Flanagan. "Not one of your very best, Daddy."

The books continued to interest the priest. There was a shelf of detective stories above the drama section featuring works by Conan Doyle, E.W.Hornung and G.K.Chesterton. Three by the author who called himself "Sapper" were lying horizontally above the others. One was *Bulldog Drummond*, the novel of the play the dead man had appeared in. On another high shelf were some volumes the priest wished he hadn't noticed, among them *Married Love*, by Marie

Stopes. But his eyes were drawn inexorably to *Family Limitation*, by Margaret Sanger – not for its provocative title but for the round hole he noticed in the binding.

"Might I ask for a dispensation to handle one of the books?"

"Why?" asked Mrs Flanagan.

"Because I think I see a bullet hole through the spine."

"Jesus, Mary and Joseph!" said Mrs Flanagan, forgetting herself. "Where?"

The priest unclasped his hands and pointed. "Do you mind?" He reached for the book and removed it. Sure enough, there was a scorched round hole penetrating this book and its neighbour, *The Psychology of Sex*, by Havelock Ellis. "Didn't the police remark on this?"

"They didn't notice it. What can it mean?"

"Presumably, that two shots were fired and this one missed. If you look, the bullet penetrated the wood behind the books. Do you recall hearing two shots?"

"I couldn't say for sure. I was asleep. I thought it was one shot that disturbed me, but I suppose there could have been two."

"And this was when?"

"About midnight according to the clock in my room. Daddy, can you recall two shots?"

"Aldershot and Bagshot," said the waggish Mr Russell.

"It's a puzzle," said the priest, rotating his head, his eyes taking in all of the books. He replaced the damaged volume and turned his attention to the floor. "There should be two spent cartridges unless someone removed them."

"Do you think you're a better detective than the police?" Mrs Flanagan said, becoming irritated.

"No, but I work for a Higher Authority." He pushed his foot under the edge of the carpet and rolled the corner back towards the chair. He couldn't be accused of touching anything; his feet had to go somewhere. "Hey ho, what's this?"

Under the carpet was a magazine.

"Leave it," said Mrs Flanagan.

"We're allowed to look," said Father Montgomery, bending low. The magazine was the current issue of *John Bull*, that patriotic weekly edited by Horatio Bottomley. The number seven was scribbled on the cover in pencil.

"Well, I'll be jiggered!" said old Mr Russell.

"Is that your magazine, Daddy?" Mrs Flanagan asked him. "You said it was missing."

"No, mine's upstairs."

"We have it delivered every Thursday. Father does the competition," Mrs Flanagan explained. "What's the competition called, Daddy?"

"Bullets."

"Right." She gave her half-smile. "Ironic. He sometimes wins a prize. They give a list of phrases and the readers are invited to add an original comment in no more than four words. Give us an example, Daddy."

"'Boarding House Philosophy: Let Bygones Be Rissoles'."

"Nice one. What about one for the church? What's that famous one?"

"'Wedding March: Aisle Altar Hymn'."

"That won five hundred pounds for someone before the war. Daddy's best effort won him twenty-five, but he keeps trying. You're sure this isn't your copy, Daddy?"

"Mine's upstairs, I said."

"All right, don't get touchy. We'd best keep this under the carpet in case it's important, but I can't think why." Mrs Flanagan nudged the carpet back in place with a pointed patent leather toecap, wanting to hasten the priest's departure. "Is there anything else we can do for you, Father Montgomery?"

"Not for the present, except ..."

"Except what?"

"If I may, I'd like to borrow your father's *John Bull*."

"I'll fetch it now," said the old man.

And he did.

Father Montgomery returned to Richmond and went backstage at the theatre. It was still early in the afternoon and there was no matinee, but some of the actors were on stage rehearsing next week's production.

He spotted the person who had first informed him of Patrick Flanagan's sudden death. Brendan was painting scenery, a fine, realistic bay window with a sea view behind.

"My dear boy," the priest said, "I'm so pleased to catch you here."

"What can I do for you, Father?"

"I've come from the house of poor Patrick Flanagan, rest his soul."

"We're heartbroken, Father. He was a lovely man."

"Indeed. Would you happen to know if he had a lady friend at all?"

"You mean Daisy Truelove, Father?"

"I suppose I do, if you say so. Where would I find her?"

"She's in the ladies' dressing room."

"And how would I coax her out of there?"

"You could try knocking on the door and saying 'A gentleman for Miss Daisy'."

He tried, and it worked. She flung open the door, a flurry of fair, curly hair and cheap scent, her eyes shining in anticipation. "Hello, darling – oh, my hat." She'd spotted the clerical collar.

"Miss Truelove?"

She nodded.

"The friend of Patrick Flanagan?"

The pretty face creased at the name. "Poor Patrick, yes."

"Would you mind telling me if you saw him yesterday evening?"

"Why, yes, Father. He was in the play, and so am I. I'm Lola, the gangster's moll."

"After it was over?"

"I saw him then, too. Some of us went for a drink at the Star and Garter. Patrick ordered oysters and champagne. He said he'd recently come into some money."

"Oysters and champagne until when?"

"About half past eleven."

"And then?"

She hesitated. "Do you really need to know?"

"Think of me as a vessel."

"A ship, Father?"

He blinked. "Not exactly. More like a receptacle for anything you can tell me in confidence."

"You want to hear my confession?"

"Not unless you have something to confess."

She bit her lip. "We went on a river steamer."

"At night?"

"It was moored by the bridge. It had fairylights and music and there was dancing. So romantic. He ordered more bubbly and it must have gone to my head. We finally got home about four in the morning. I'd better say that again. *I* got home about four in the morning. We said goodnight at the door of my lodgings. There was nothing improper, Father. Well, nothing totally improper, if you know what I mean."

"How was his mood?"

"His mood?"

"Was he happy when he left you?"

"Oh, dear!" she said, her winsome young features creasing in concern again. "I'm afraid he wasn't. He wanted to come in with me. He offered to take off his shoes and tiptoe upstairs, but I wouldn't risk upsetting the landlady. I pushed him away and shut the door in his face. Do you think that's why he killed himself?"

"No, I don't," said Father Montgomery. "I don't believe he killed himself at all."

"You mean my conscience is clear?"

"I have no way of telling what's on your conscience, my dear, but I'm sure you did the right thing at the end of the evening."

Inspector Carew was far from happy at being dragged back to 7, Albert Street by a priest he'd never met, but the mention of murder couldn't be ignored.

"The wife lied to us both," Father Montgomery said as they were being driven to Teddington. "She insisted that the shooting was at midnight, but I have a female witness who says Patrick Flanagan was with her in Richmond until four in the morning."

"So what?" said the inspector. "Emily Flanagan has her pride. She won't want to admit that her wayward husband preferred to spend the night with some other filly."

"She wasn't exactly grieving."

"True. I noted her demeanour. Maybe she's not sorry he's dead. It doesn't make her a murderess."

"There's money behind this," the priest said. "A man who can splash out on champagne and oysters at the Star and Garter is doing too well for a jobbing actor with a wife and father-in-law to support."

"We checked the bank account," the inspector said, pleased to demonstrate how thorough he'd been. "They have a modest income, but two days before his death he withdrew most of what they had, about sixty pounds. And so would I, if I was planning to do myself in. I'd have a binge and a night out with a girl before I pulled the trigger. Wouldn't you?"

"I don't go out with girls and I wouldn't pull the trigger," said Father Montgomery. "Neither is permitted."

They drew up at the Flanagans' house in Teddington. Emily Flanagan opened the door, saw them together, and said, "Holy Moses!"

In the kitchen, the brandy bottle was empty. Old Mr Russell was asleep in a rocking chair in front of the stove.

"No need to disturb him," Inspector Carew said. "This concerns you, ma'am. An apparent discrepancy in what you told me. You said the fatal shot was fired at midnight."

"Or thereabouts," said Mrs Flanagan.

"Our latest information places your husband on a river steamer in Richmond at midnight."

"The heel! What was he doing there?"

"Dancing with an actress until nearly four in the morning."

"I'm not surprised," she said, failing to appreciate what an admission this was. "Which baggage was it this time?"

"Do you admit you lied to me?"

"How could I have known what he was doing in Richmond?"

"The time. You lied about the time."

" 'Thereabouts' is what I said. What difference does an hour or two make to you? I guessed he was entertaining some little trollop on the last night of his life, but the world doesn't need to know, does it? Allow me some dignity when I walk behind his coffin, Inspector."

"Did you know he emptied his bank account and treated his actor friends to oysters and champagne?"

"Did he, the rotter?"

"You don't seem overly concerned."

"He left no will. As his nearest and dearest I'll inherit everything he ever owned, including this house."

"Not if you're hanged for murder, madam."

"*What?*" For the first time in all this sorry business, she looked alarmed.

Father Montgomery raised his hands to urge restraint on both sides. "Before we go any further, Inspector, why don't I show you what I discovered in the den?"

Emily Flanagan, muttering mild expletives, followed them into the room where the body had been discovered. The priest pointed out the bullet hole in the books and remarked that it was unlikely that the victim had held a gun to his head and missed. "I suggest that someone else was holding the gun, someone who waited through the small hours of the night for him to come in and then pointed it at him and brought him in here and sat him at his own desk, where it would look as if he chose to die. I suggest there was a struggle and he deflected the first shot, but the second was fired with the gun to his head."

"A crime of passion, then," said the inspector.

"No. Let me show you something else." He rolled back the carpet and revealed the copy of *John Bull*. "You can pick it up," he told the inspector. "Take note of the number seven scribbled on the top right corner. The magazine was delivered to this house as usual. It was Mr Russell's copy, but Patrick Flanagan grabbed it the day it was pushed through the letterbox and hid it here. Now turn to page thirty-eight, headed *Bullets*, and look at this week's thousand pound winner."

The inspector read aloud, "*Mr PF, of Teddington, Middlesex.* That's Patrick Flanagan. No wonder he was out celebrating."

"But Patrick didn't do the Bullets!" said Mrs Flanagan in awe.

"Right, it was your father who provided the winning entry. Being unable to walk more than a few steps, he relied on Patrick to post it for him. Patrick ripped open the envelope and entered the competition under his own name. I dare say he'd played the trick before, because the old man was known to have a flare for Bullets."

"They're second nature to him," said Mrs Flanagan.

"Patrick delayed paying in the cheque. I'm sure we'll find it in here somewhere. He hid the magazine under the carpet so that your father shouldn't find out, but the old chap managed to get hold of a copy."

"He sent me out to buy it."

"And when he saw the competition page, he was outraged. The main object of his life was to win that competition. He'd been robbed of his moment of glory by a shabby trick from his son-in-law. So last night he went to the study and collected the gun and lay in wait. The rest you know."

The inspector let out a breath so deep and so long it seemed to empty his lungs. "You're clever, Father."

"A man's soul was at stake, Inspector."

"Not a good man."

"It's not for us to judge."

Mrs Flanagan said, "What was the winning entry?"

"Well, the phrase was 'A Policeman's Lot'."

"'A Lawfully Big Adventure'," said the murderer with pride, entering the room.

RAZOR BILL

Constable Thackeray gripped his skirt and managed a few more steps towards the next lamp. Then he tried glancing over his shoulder, as women of that profession do. Difficult. He was wearing a leather collar that was meant to protect his throat. This was the most worrying assignment of his long career.

"It's simple," Sergeant Cribb had told him. "You're a decoy. We dress you up as a streetwalker, fit you with a padded leather choker and invite Razor Bill to slash your throat." Regardless that Thackeray looked nothing like a streetwalker and anything but inviting. "In a bonnet and skirt on a foggy night, you'll do famously. Our man isn't too particular."

In that harsh winter of 1882, Razor Bill was the Yard's top priority. Four prostitutes had perished on the streets of Pimlico, throats severed from ear to ear. Not much detective work was needed to tell that the murder weapon was a razor; not much editorial work from the press to give the perpetrator his nickname. Newspaper sales shot up.

Thackeray sniffed meat-pie as he passed an eating-house. No use thinking of supper. He was under constant surveillance by Cribb and a handful of B Division detectives disguised as revellers across the street. The minute the attack came, they would pounce, so they said. All he had to do was grab some part of Bill's anatomy and hang on.

Hang on with what? He could barely feel his fingers. He was hungry, cold and miserable. Cribb had insisted his beard came off

– five years' magnificent growth. "What are you griping for? It'll grow again."

Worse, they'd got to work on his pale face with paint and powder. In the end he'd submitted to the whole boiling: petticoats, skirt, blouse, boots, feather boa, wig and a large plush hat. His first concern wasn't Razor Bill. It was being recognised by someone he knew.

Around two p.m. Chelsea Bridge Road started to empty. All the activity of the last hour dwindled to an occasional cab. This was when Bill was most likely to strike. One unfortunate creature in Lupus Street. One in Turpentine Lane, behind the railway depot. Another where Denbigh Street crossed Belgrave Road. The fourth in Buckingham Palace Road. No witnesses. Someone said they'd heard a scream in Lupus Street. Nothing exceptional in that.

"One moment, young lady."

As yet, Thackeray hadn't fully identified with his role, so this enquiry from behind passed him by.

"Young lady." The voice was closer this time, and insistent.

He turned. Too quickly. His shaven chin rasped against the collar.

The speaker was male, average in height, wearing a top hat and long grey overcoat. His black beard was almost as handsome as the one Thackeray had sacrificed. "Are you looking for company?"

Oh, glory, Thackeray thought. A genuine client.

"Don't be shy of me, my dear." The accent was educated, the tone kindly.

Thackeray shook his head and pointed into his mouth as if to show his throat was sore.

"Have I made a mistake?" the man asked. "I assumed – seeing you out on the street so late – that you are here for a purpose. That – not to put too fine a point upon it – you are a lady of the town."

Thackeray shook his head and tried to move away, but the man stepped closer.

"There's no need to be afraid, my dear." With a ceremonious air he slid his hand under the beard and revealed that he, too, was wearing a high collar, except that his was clerical. "You see? I am a minister of the gospel, the Reverend Eli Mountjoy, on a mission of salvation to rescue poor, deluded creatures like yourself from the toils of sin. I urge you now to forsake the path of wickedness and accompany me to the Terminus Wash-house in Lupus Street, where my devoted wife Lettice is waiting to plunge you into clean, warm water and wrap you in a blanket."

"No thank you," Thackeray said, appalled at the thought.

"And after that we shall share a bowl of reviving eel-broth and speak of how you may be saved."

"I'm not what you take me for."

"How often have I heard the same denial from unfortunate women like you," the Reverend Mountjoy said. "The key to the Kingdom has to be earned, you know. You must first admit what you are."

"I'm a policeman in disguise."

The minister felt in his pocket and put on a pair of spectacles. "Did I hear correctly? A policeman?"

"Keep your voice down, for pity's sake," Thackeray said.

The tone altered abruptly. "I thought there was something peculiar about you. What's the matter with you, dressing up as a tart?"

"I'm on the trail of Razor Bill."

"Oh, yes?"

"The killer. You must have heard of him. It's supposed to be a trap."

After a pause, the minister said, "The best of luck to you, then. I'll be about my business." He was soon out of sight.

Thackeray glanced across the street to where Cribb was supposed to be. If Eli Mountjoy had been the killer – and he could have been for all Cribb knew – the speed of the response had not been encouraging. Some people were over there for sure, but they hailed a cab and got in. It all seemed worryingly quiet now. A mist was coming off the river. The dampness increased Thackeray's discomfort. He decided to walk on a bit, swinging his hips in the spirit of the *Police Code*. '*It is highly undesirable for detectives to proclaim their official character to strangers by walking in a drilled style, or by wearing regulation boots, or by openly recognising constables in uniform, or saluting superior officers.*' No one would accuse him of walking in a drilled style. He'd already fooled the Reverend Mountjoy.

The hip-swinging became a touch less energetic when Chelsea Barracks came up on his right. It wouldn't be wise to over-excite the army. In fact, he didn't care to pass the barracks at all, so he turned up Commercial Road. Almost immediately he heard footsteps behind him.

They were steady and heavy. Male, for sure. His skin prickled. He resisted the urge to look round. With the collar strapped so tight, it would have required a complete about turn. He walked faster, trying to make the next lamp-post so as to be more visible to the rescue squad. How he wished he'd stuffed a truncheon up his bodice. "You'll have surprise on your side," Cribb had said. Thanks a lot, Sarge, Thackeray thought. And which would you rather have on your side – surprise, or an open razor?

The steps quickened.

They were closer.

He felt a tug on his waist, but it wasn't from his pursuer. He'd stepped on the hem of the skirt and the whole thing tightened. Thrown off balance, he lurched forward. Trying to recover, he planted the other boot on the skirt. He sank to his knees like a shot stag.

The sensation of helplessness was horrible. Hampered already by the steel collar, he was dragged further down by the clothes. He struggled against them, hoping the material would give a little, but the weave was too strong and he pitched over and rolled on his back.

Before he had time to sit up, the attacker was on him, a hand thrust against his shoulder, pinning him to the pavement, strong, vicious, bent on the kill. He couldn't see who it was. There was just the gleam of the blade as it slashed downwards.

He had the sense to grab the arm with both hands just as the razor sliced open his collar. Thank heaven for the wad of stuffing inside. He held onto that arm, tugged it across his body and crashed the hand against the pavement. There was a yell. The razor slid away and out of reach.

Now Thackeray used surprise to more effect, rolling sideways onto the arm that had held the razor. The move caught Razor Bill off guard and toppled him sideways. Thackeray raised a knee and heard a grunt of pain as it made contact with the man's most vulnerable area. Legs flailed and the body arched, but Thackeray wasn't distracted. He'd done some wrestling in his time. That was what this was about now: all-in wrestling. He hung onto that arm, pressing down on it with his body weight.

Razor Bill struggled like an alligator, but Thackeray gritted his teeth and held on.

Thoughts tumbled into his brain. Where was Cribb?

He shouted, "Sarge!"

The only response was from Razor Bill: a vicious kick in the kidneys, followed by another. Thackeray groaned. He shifted his hip, backing hard against Bill's chest and stomach.

Bill's free hand groped at Thackeray's face and clawed his cheek, missing his eye by a fraction. This couldn't go on.

Thackeray yelled, "Police!"

They're never around when you need them. Bill cracked his fist into Thackeray's ribs. This was a strong man.

"Sarge!"

"The minute he strikes, we'll pounce."

That vicious left hand came exploring his face again. This time he bit into the fleshy part and heard a screech.

Encouraged, Thackeray said, "Better give up, mate. You're nicked."

For that, he took a knee in the small of his back.

Then he was grabbed and rolled aside. There was shouting. Hands grasped his arms and lifted him. Finally the reinforce-ments had arrived.

Razor Bill was formally arrested and cuffed. He said nothing.

"You all right?" Cribb asked Thackeray.

"A bit sore."

"Could be so much worse, though. Smart of me to think of the collar, wasn't it?"

When they tried to interview the prisoner at Chelsea police station, there was a snag. He refused to speak. Wouldn't even give his name.

Big and swarthy, with the coldest eyes Cribb had seen, he sat staring back like a caged bear.

"It won't help you, saying nothing," Cribb told the man. "You were caught red-handed. We picked up the open razor. You attacked one of my men, mistakenly taking him for a streetwalker. You might as well sing now, and save us all a long night."

They'd searched him thoroughly. He carried no papers, no pocketbook, nothing. His clothes were those of a working man. His hands had done manual work.

"You'll be hungry by now," Cribb said. "Speak up and we'll feed you a hot meal."

Not a glimmer of interest..

"I'm beginning to think he's stone deaf."

"Or a foreigner," Thackeray said.

"You could be right. He was yelling a bit when you were on the ground with him. What was he saying?"

"Nothing I remember, Sarge."

"Weren't you paying attention? What were you doing?"

"Fighting for my bloody life."

"There's no need for coarseness. Fetch Inspector Jowett. He speaks some French. He'll enjoy showing off to us."

But Jowett, when he tried, made no impression, despite employing all the animated gestures of a Frenchman. "Are you certain this is Razor Bill?" he said to Cribb.

"I'd put my last shilling on it, sir. He attacked Thackeray with a razor – Thackeray being artfully disguised as a woman of the street. He does a very good impersonation of a woman, does Thackeray."

"Indeed." Jowett glanced at Thackeray, seeing him in a whole new light, and took a step away. "Well, your prisoner is no Frenchman. Of that I'm sure. You'd better bring in an interpreter."

"No gratitude," Cribb said after Jowett had left the room. "All of London was living in fear of this monster and what thanks do I get for nabbing him? Not a squeak."

"I know exactly how you feel, Sarge," Thackeray said.

The papers were full of the arrest next morning. "*An unidentified detective posed as a woman of the unfortunate class*," the *Morning Chronicle* stated, "*and was set upon by the murderer with an open razor. Thanks to the foresight of Inspector Jowett of the Criminal Investigation Department, the officer concerned was wearing a protective leather collar and succeeded in detaining his assailant and calling for assistance from his colleagues nearby. The arrest was effected immediately.*"

" '... the foresight of Inspector Jowett?'" Cribb said, flinging the paper aside. "He didn't even know about this plan of mine."

"Ah, but he knows how to tell a good story to the newspapers," Thackeray said.

"Most of it untrue."

"Well, yes. It didn't seem to me like an immediate arrest."

Cribb ignored this dig. He had too much else to deal with. "The interpreter is coming in at noon. Claims to speak nine languages."

"That ought to be enough," Thackeray said. "How many languages are there?"

"More than that."

"London's full of Poles and Russians. He looks like a Russian to me."

Towards the end of the morning a gentleman in a top hat arrived and asked to speak to the officer who had arrested Razor Bill.

"Right, sir. You'll be the interpreter, I dare say," the desk sergeant said.

"No, sir, I am not. I am the Reverend Eli Mountjoy."

"Might I inquire what you're here for?"

"*That* officer." The Reverend Mountjoy pointed a finger at Thackeray, who was on his way to an early lunch. "He's the one I came to see."

"Right, your reverence." The desk sergeant beckoned to Thackeray with a curled finger.

There was no escape. Thackeray ushered Eli Mountjoy into a room where they wouldn't be overheard.

"You look almost normal without your face painted," the minister said. "I saw in *The Times* that you arrested a man last night."

"That's right, sir."

"Are you sure he's the murderer?"

"Well, he did his best to cut my throat," Thackeray said.

"Who is he?"

"That's something I can't reveal, sir."

"Can't, or won't?"

"Both, sir. He's not speaking to us."

"Perhaps I can be of assistance. Through my missionary work on the streets I come across many of the local ne'er-do-wells. Would you like me to take a look at him?"

Thackeray pondered for a moment, scratching his chin. "I suppose it would do no harm."

The interpreter hadn't yet arrived, so he took Eli Mountjoy downstairs and slid open the Judas hole of Razor Bill's cell door.

"That's Vladimir," Mountjoy said at once. "He's a Russian."

Thackeray smiled to himself. "I thought so. You know him, then?"

"By sight. He doesn't talk. Can't understand us, I suppose. Well, there's a thing. I'd never have thought of Vladimir as a murderer."

"We've got an interpreter coming in. We'll find out what he's got to say for himself if he isn't completely mad."

"Let's hope he isn't," Mountjoy said. "It would be so encouraging if he asks his Maker for forgiveness before you hang him. How many women did he kill?"

"We know of four." Thackeray slid the cover over the slot in the door. "Would you happen to know his second name?"

Mountjoy shook his head. "People call him Vladimir, or Vlad. That's all I can tell you. Four, you say. Is that certain?"

"Four corpses, all with their throats cut."

"That's beyond dispute." He stroked his beard thought-fully. "I expect you'll make sure."

Thackeray frowned. "Make sure of what, sir?"

"That he killed all four."

"Is there any doubt?"

"I suppose not. I was reflecting that if – for the sake of argument – he was responsible for only three of the murders, and he refused to speak, or is mad, you might never find out who carried out the fourth."

Thackeray thought about that for some time. "It's pretty far-fetched, isn't it? There isn't much chance of two evil people cutting women's throats in Pimlico at the same time of year."

"I have to concede that it is. Pretty far-fetched." On the way upstairs, Mountjoy said, "They'll all flood back onto the streets now, all those women who were too frightened to parade themselves while Razor Bill was about. He did more to clean up the streets of Pimlico than you or I."

"That's another way of looking at it," Thackeray said. He was pleased when the Reverend Eli Mountjoy raised his hat and left. The man made him feel uncomfortable.

Cribb was decent enough to congratulate Thackeray on finding out that Razor Bill was a Russian called Vladimir. He said the interpreter had made no headway at all. "He tried all of his nine languages. The only response he got was when Bill spat on his shoes."

"But we have got the right man, sarge?"

"I'm sure we've got the right man."

"Is he mad?"

"No, I've come to the conclusion that he's clever. He was caught in the act, so he's got no way of talking himself out of it. By saying nothing, he opens a chink of doubt. But we know something he doesn't."

"What's that?"

"He doesn't know we know he's a Russian called Vladimir."

"Speaking of a chink of doubt, sarge, there was something the reverend said that made me uneasy." Thackeray explained about Eli Mountjoy's suggestion that someone else might have carried out one of the murders.

Cribb was intrigued. "Did he have a reason for this theory?"

"No."

"It's a strange thing to suggest."

"He did say something about the women being too scared to walk the streets while Bill was at large. He said they'd all come back to Pimlico now."

"He's right about that. I think I'd better meet your clergyman. What's his address?"

Thackeray had to admit he hadn't enquired.

"No matter," Cribb said. "He's a local. We'll find him."

The same evening they called at the Terminus Wash-house in Lupus Street and met Mrs Lettice Mountjoy. She was sitting inside the entrance with a pile of folded towels on a table beside her. There was also a large urn of soup simmering over a paraffin burner.

She was about forty-five, slim, with a lined face. She was wearing a white pinafore over a black dress.

"Is this where the sins are washed clean?" Cribb asked.

"Ladies only, I'm afraid," Mrs Mountjoy said.

"Gentlemen sinners need not apply?"

"It's the rules," she said without a smile. "The mission hires the bath from ten o'clock until two. We aren't permitted mixed use."

"I understand," Cribb said. "You *are* Mrs Lettice Mountjoy? We're police, wanting a word with your husband."

"Oh, dear."

He held up his hand. "It's all right. He's been helping us over these murders. He's a public-spirited man, your husband."

"He's more than that," she said with animation. "He's a saviour."

"And are they saved for good, or do they go back on the streets after the bath and the soup?"

She looked upset by the suggestion. "It's permanent in almost every case. He's very persuasive."

"And let's not underestimate your part in the process. Has he brought any in tonight?"

"Not yet, but he will."

"We'll wait, then. He's on the streets every night, is he?"

"Except Sundays."

"So in the past three weeks, when these horrible murders were happening, he's carried on as usual, out every night saving souls?"

"There were three days last week, Monday to Wednesday, when he was unable to do it. He was suffering from a bad cough."

"So he spent those nights at home inhaling friar's balsam?"

"He was at home, yes."

Tuesday was the night the fourth victim, Mary Smith, had been killed in Buckingham Palace Road.

There was not long to wait. Out of the mist came a hansom cab, and from it stepped the Reverend Mountjoy looking so worthy of his calling that a halo wouldn't have been out of place. He helped down a young woman heavily rouged and in a fur jacket. His wife greeted her charitably and handed her a bar of carbolic soap and a clean towel and took her into the bath-house.

Cribb introduced himself. "I want to clarify something you said to Constable Thackeray here."

"By all means."

"You suggested someone other than Razor Bill might have carried out the fourth murder."

"I floated the possibility, no more," Mountjoy said. "It seemed to me that if some person were disposed to kill one of these unfortunate women, they might adopt the same *modus operandi* as the murderer in the expectation that Razor Bill would be blamed for the crime."

"It's an ingenious idea," Cribb said. "Do you have any reason for believing it happened?"

He hesitated. "Nothing tangible."

"As a religious man, you'd owe it to the One Above to tell me everything, wouldn't you?"

Now the Reverend Mountjoy coloured deeply. "It's no more than a theory, sergeant. I'm a pastor, not a policeman."

"Did you know any of these unfortunate women who were killed?"

"Only one. The latest."

Thackeray said, "Strike a light!"

"Don't misunderstand me. I didn't know her as, em –"

"In the Old Testament sense?" Cribb said.

"Gracious, no. I knew her at arm's length, as a sinner I tried to save. Some, unhappily, will not be persuaded whatever I say. Some, a few, give promise of redemption and then back-slide."

"They take the bath and the clean towel without meaning to reform?"

"Who can say what they truly intend?"

"Was the fourth victim, Mary Smith, a back-slider?"

"Regrettably, yes."

"That must be a savage blow."

"A kick in the teeth," Thackeray added.

"But I wouldn't have wished her to suffer, if that's what you're thinking."

"Far from it, sir. To change the subject, I was wondering if my constable and I might be permitted a look inside the bath-house."

"Absolutely not," Mountjoy said in a shocked tone. "That young woman will be in a state of nature by now."

"I wouldn't trouble yourself about that," Cribb said. "In her profession she's used to being seen by all and sundry."

"It would be improper."

Cribb smiled. "It's *our* immortal souls you're concerned about, isn't it?"

He spread his hands. "You are God's creatures, too. If you *must* see inside – and I can't understand why it's necessary – you can come back at two after midnight, when we leave the premises."

"As you wish."

They watched Eli Mountjoy climb into the waiting cab for another rescue mission.

"We can just walk in," Thackeray said.

"No, we'll play his game," Cribb said. "Let's find somewhere to eat. I don't like the smell of this soup."

They returned at two, when the streets were more quiet. The Reverend Mountjoy was waiting while his wife washed the soup bowls.

"How many did you save tonight?" Cribb asked.

"Three, if the Lord pleases."

"Good going. Can we look inside now?"

"Certainly. There's no one in there."

Cribb insisted that the couple came in with them, so Mountjoy led the way and turned up the gas for a proper view of the interior. The air was still steamy, and wasn't the sweetest to inhale. To the left was a row of wash basins, each with a simple mirror over it. Opposite were the bathrooms. Cribb glanced inside the one that had been used for the mission and immediately turned away. The wash basins interested him more.

"It brings it all back," he said. "When I started out in the police, I lived in a section-house without running water. Used a wash-house like this as a daily practice. Penny a wash and shave, twopence for a second-class bath, which was a once-a-week treat."

"Have you seen enough?" Mountjoy asked, impatient with the reminiscing.

"Not quite. I'm picturing this place in the morning, full of working men standing at the basins shaving. Do you own a razor, sir? No, you wouldn't, with such a fine beaver as yours. For a clean-shaven man like me, a razor is an everyday object. I keep mine beside the kitchen sink at home. But in those days I'd leave it in the wash-house after my shave, tucking it out of sight above the basin. There were ventilation windows over the mirrors just like these." He reached up and ran his hand along the ledge under the window. "Dusty."

"It would be."

"What do you know?" Cribb said. "Someone else has the same idea." He took down a razor from the ledge."

"There's nothing remarkable in that," Mountjoy said. "You'd find others up there, I'm sure."

"Yes, I'm not saying this is the murder weapon. I'm just satisfying myself that a razor could be acquired by anyone using this wash-house on a regular basis."

"Razor Bill, you mean?"

"No, I was thinking of the killer of Mary Smith. That murder has been troubling your conscience, hasn't it?"

"I didn't do it."

"No, sir, I'm not suggesting you did, but you have a suspicion who did, which is why you came to see us. You've noticed things at home, heard things said, perhaps. You don't know for sure, but you have a horrible suspicion Mary Smith was killed by your own wife Lettice. Hold her, Thackeray."

Lettice Mountjoy had already made a move for the door. Thackeray grabbed her by the wrist and hauled her back. Cribb switched his words to her. "You're the one who works inside the wash-house. You're the one with access to the razors." Thackeray, a strong man, had to struggle to hold her. This devoted woman, the gentle soul who welcomed fallen women to the mission, was abruptly transformed into a virago. "Yes," she said with chilling ferocity, "I killed Mary. The night he was at home I collected a razor from here and went looking for her. He told me he feared she'd gone back on the streets, and she had. She didn't deserve to live after the chance of redemption he gave her, after the solemn promise she gave him. He's a saintly man. These feckless sluts hold his happiness in their hands, and this one betrayed him. I'm not sorry."

Mountjoy had covered his face and was sobbing.

"You did the right thing, reverend, passing on your suspicions," Cribb said, as Thackeray handcuffed Lettice Mountjoy and led her outside. "It could have happened a second time."

"But I blame myself. She acted out of loyalty to me."

Towards dawn, when statements had been made, and a long spell of duty was coming to an end, Thackeray said to Cribb, "Was the Reverend right, Sarge, about the motive? Was it loyalty that drove her to kill that woman?"

"Loyalty, my foot. She was jealous. Didn't you hear what she called them – 'feckless sluts'? There her own husband was, saving all these woman's souls and taking her for granted. All right if they reformed, but heaven help them if they didn't. Makes you grateful for the job we're in."

"Why is that, Sarge?"

"Our wives never know what we get up to."

Thackeray observed a philosophic silence. Cribb didn't need to know what Mrs Thackeray had said about the clean-shaven chin and the rouge on the pillow.

NEEDLE MATCH

Murder was done on Court Eleven on the third day of Wimbledon, 1981. Fortunately for the All England Club, it wasn't anything obvious like a strangling or a shooting, but the result was the same for the victim, except that he suffered longer. It took three days for him to die. I can tell you exactly how it happened, because I was one of the ball boys for the match.

When I was thirteen I was taught to be invisible. But before you decide this isn't your kind of story let me promise you it isn't about magic. There's nothing spooky about me. And there was nothing spooky about my instructor, Brigadier Romilly. He was flesh and blood all right and so were the terrified kids who sat at his feet.

"You'll be invisible, every one of you before I've finished with you," he said in his parade-ground voice, and we believed him, we third-years from Merton Comprehensive.

A purple scar like a sabre-cut stretched downwards from the edge of the Brigadier's left eye, over his mouth to the point of his chin. He'd grown a bristly ginger moustache over part of it, but we could easily see where the two ends joined. Rumour had it that his face had been slashed by a Mau Mau warrior's machete in the Kenyan terrorist war of the fifties. We didn't know anything about the Mau Mau, except that the terrorist must have been crazy to tangle with the Brigadier – who grabbed him by the throat and strangled him.

Don't ever get the idea that you're doing this to be seen. You'll be there, on court with Mr McEnroe and Mr Borg – if I think you're good enough – and no one will notice you, no one. When the game is in play you'll be as still as the net-post, and as uninteresting. For Rule Two of the Laws of Tennis states that the court has certain permanent fixtures like the net and the net posts and the umpire's chair. And the list of permanent fixtures includes you, the ball boys, in your respective places. So you can tell your mothers and fathers and your favourite aunties not to bother to watch. If you're doing your job they won't even notice you."

To think we'd volunteered for this. By a happy accident of geography ours was one of the schools chosen to provide the ball boys and ball girls for the Championships. "It's a huge honour," our headmaster had told us. "You do it for the prestige of the school. You're on television. You meet the stars, hand them their towels, supply them with the balls, pour their drinks. You can be proud."

The Brigadier disabused us of all that. "If any of you are looking for glory, leave at once. Go back to your stuffy class-rooms. I don't want your sort in my squad. The people I want are functionaries, not glory-seekers. Do you understand? You will do your job, brilliantly, the way I show you. It's all about timing, self-control and, above all, being invisible."

The victim was poisoned. Once the poison was in his system there was no antidote. Death was inevitable, and lingering.

So in the next three months we learned to be invisible. And it was damned hard work, I can tell you. I had no idea what it would lead to. You're thinking we murdered the Brigadier? No, he's a survivor. So far as I know, he's still alive and terrifying the staff in a retirement home.

I'm going to tell it as it happened, and we start on the November afternoon in nineteen-eighty when my best friend Eddie Pringle and I were on an hour's detention for writing something obscene on Blind Pugh's blackboard. Mr Pugh, poor soul, was our chemistry master. He wasn't really blind, but his sight wasn't the best. He wore thick glasses with prism lenses, and we little monsters took full advantage. Sometimes Nemesis arrived, in the shape of our headmaster, Mr Neames, breezing into the lab, supposedly for a word with Blind Pugh, but in reality to catch us red-handed playing poker behind bits of apparatus or rolling mercury along the bench-tops. Those who escaped with a detention were the lucky ones.

"I've had enough of this crap," Eddie told me in the detention room. "I'm up for a job as ball boy."

"What do you mean – Wimbledon?" I said. "That's not till next June."

"They train you. It's every afternoon off school for six months – and legal. No more detentions. All you do is trot around the court picking up balls and chucking them to the players and you get to meet McEnroe and Connors and all those guys. Want to join me?"

It seemed the ideal escape plan, but of course we had to get permission from Nemesis to do it. Eddie and I turned ourselves into model pupils for the rest of term. No messing about. No detentions. Every homework task completed.

"In view of this improvement," Nemesis informed us, "I have decided to let you go on the training course."

But when we met the Brigadier we found we'd tunneled out of one prison into another. He terrified us. The regime was pitiless, the orders unrelenting.

"First you must learn how to be a permanent fixture. Stand straight, chest out, shoulders back, thumbs linked behind your back. Now hold it for five minutes. If anyone moves, I put the stopwatch back to zero again."

Suddenly he threw a ball hard at Eddie and of course he ducked.

"Right," the Brigadier announced, "Pringle moved. The hand goes back to zero. You have to learn to be still, Pringle. Last year one of my boys was hit on the ear by a serve from Roscoe Tanner, over a hundred miles per hour, and he didn't flinch."

We had a full week learning to be permanent fixtures, first standing at the rear of the court and then crouching like petrified sprinters at the sideline, easy targets for the Brigadier to shy at. A couple of the kids dropped out. We all had bruises.

"This is worse than school," I told Eddie. "We've got no freedom at all."

"Right, he's a tyrant. Don't let him grind you down," Eddie said.

In the second and third weeks we practised retrieving the balls, scampering back to the sidelines and rolling them along the ground to our colleagues or throwing them with one bounce to the Brigadier.

This was to be one of the great years of Wimbledon, with Borg, Connors and McEnroe at the peaks of their careers, challenging for the title. The rivalry would produce one match, a semi-final, that will be remembered for as long as tennis is played. And on an outside court, another, fiercer rivalry would be played out, with a fatal result. The players were not well known, but their backgrounds ensured a clash of ideologies. Jozsef Stanski, from Poland, was to meet Igor Voronin, a Soviet Russian, on Court Eleven, on the third day of the Championships.

Being an ignorant schoolboy at the time, I didn't appreciate how volatile it was, this match between two players from Eastern Europe. In the previous summer, 1980, the strike in the Gdansk shipyard, followed by widespread strikes throughout Poland, had forced the Communist government to allow independent trade unions. Solidarity – the trade union movement led by Lech Walesa – became a powerful, vocal organisation getting massive international attention. The Polish tennis star, Jozsef Stanski, was an outspoken supporter of Solidarity who criticised the state regime whenever he was interviewed.

The luck of the draw, as they say, had matched Stanski with Voronin, a diehard Soviet Communist, almost certainly a KGB agent. Later, it was alleged that Voronin was a state assassin.

Before all this, the training of the ball boys went on, a totalitarian regime of its own, always efficient, performed to numbers and timed on the stopwatch. There was usually a slogan to sum up whichever phase of ball boy lore we were mastering. "Show before you throw, Richards, show before you throw, lad."

No one dared to defy the Brigadier.

The early weeks were on indoor courts. In April, we got outside. We learned everything a ball boy could possibly need to know, how to hold three balls at once, collect a towel, offer a cold drink and dispose of the cup afterwards, stand in front of a player between games without making eye contact. The training didn't miss a trick.

At the end of the month we "stood" for a club tournament at Queen's. It went well, I thought, until the Brigadier debriefed us. Debriefed? He tore strips off us for over an hour. We'd learnt nothing, he said. The Championships would be a disaster if we got within a mile of them. We were slow, we fumbled, stumbled and forgot to show before the throw. Worse, he saw a couple of us (Eddie and me, to be honest) exchange some words as we crouched either side of the net.

"If any ball boy under my direction so much as moves his lips ever again in the course of a match, I will come onto the court and seal his revolting mouth with packing tape."

We believed him.

And we persevered. Miraculously the months went by and June arrived, and with it the Championships.

The Brigadier addressed us on the eve of the first day's play and to my amazement, he didn't put the fear of God into me. By his standards, it was a vote of confidence. "You boys and girls have given me problems enough this year, but you're as ready as you ever will be, and I want you to know I have total confidence in you. When this great tournament is over and the best of you line up on the Centre Court to be presented to Her Royal Highness before she meets the Champion, my pulses will beat faster and my heart will swell with pride, as will each of yours. And one of you, of course, will get a special award as best ball boy – or girl. That's the Championship that counts, you know. Never mind Mr Borg and Miss Navratilova. The real winner will be one of you. The decision will be mine, and you all start tomorrow as equals. In the second week I will draw up a short list. The pick of you, my elite squad, will stand in the finals. I will nominate the winner only when the tournament is over."

I suppose it had been the severity of the build-up; to me those words were as thrilling and inspiring as King Henry's before the Battle of Agincourt. I wanted to be on Centre Court on that final day. I wanted to be best ball boy. I could see that all the others felt like me, and had the same gleam in their eyes.

I've never felt so nervous as I did at noon that first day, approaching the tall, creeper-covered walls of the All England Club, and passing inside and finding it was already busy with people on the terraces and promenades chatting loudly in accents that would have got you past any security guard in the world. Wimbledon twenty years ago was part of the social season, a blazer and tie occasion, entirely alien to a kid like me from a working class family.

My first match was on an outside court, thanks be to the Brigadier. Men's singles, between a tall Californian and a wiry Frenchman. I marched on court with the other five ball boys and mysteriously my nerves ended the moment the umpire called "Play." We were so well-drilled that the training took over. My concentration was absolute. I knew precisely what I had to do. I was a small, invisible part of a well-oiled, perfectly tuned machine, the Rolls Royce of tennis tournaments. Six-three, six-three, six-three to the Californian, and we lined up and marched off again.

I stood in two more matches that first day, and they were equally straightforward in spite of some racquet abuse by one unhappy player whose service wouldn't go in. A ball boy is above all that. At home, exhausted, I slept better than I had for a week.

Day Two was Ladies' Day, when most of the women's first round matches were played. At the end of my second match I lined up for an ice-cream and heard a familiar voice, "Got overheated in that last one, Richards?"

I turned to face the Brigadier, expecting a rollicking. I wasn't sure if ball boys in uniform were allowed to consume ice cream.

But the scar twitched into a grin. "I watched you at work. You're doing a decent job, lad. Not invisible yet, but getting there. Keep it up and you might make Centre Court."

I can tell you exactly what happened in the Stanski-Voronin match because I was one of the ball boys and my buddy Eddie Pringle was another, and has recently reminded me of it. Neither player was seeded. Stanski had won a five-setter in the first round against a little-known Englishman, and Voronin had been lucky enough to get a bye.

Court Eleven is hardly one of the show courts, and these two weren't well known players, but we still had plenty of swivelling heads following the action.

I'm sure some of the crowd understood that the players were at opposite extremes politically, but I doubt if anyone foresaw the terrible outcome of this clash. They may have noticed the coolness between the players, but that's one of the conventions of sport, particularly in a Grand Slam tournament. You shake hands at the end, but you psych yourself up to beat hell out of your rival first. Back to the tennis. The first set went narrowly to Voronin, seven-five. I was so absorbed in my ball boy duties that the score almost passed me by. I retrieved the balls and passed them to the players when they needed them. Between games, I helped them to drinks and waited on them, just as we were programmed to do. I rather liked Stanski. His English wasn't up to much, but he made up for it with the occasional nod and even a hint of a smile.

Stanski won the next two sets, six-four, six-three.

Half the time I was at Voronin's end. Being strictly neutral, I treated him with the same courtesy I gave his opponent, but I can't say he was as appreciative. You can tell a lot about players from the way they grab the towel from you or discard a ball they don't fancy serving. The Russian was a hard man, with vicious thoughts in his head.

He secured the next set in a tie-break and took the match to a fifth. The crowd was growing. People from other courts had heard something special was happening. Several long, exciting rallies drew gasps and shrieks.

Voronin had extraordinary eyes like wet pebbles, the irises as black as the pupils. I was drilled to look at him each time I offered him a ball, and his expression never changed. Once or twice when Stanski had some luck with a ball that bounced on the net, Voronin eyeballed him. Terrifying.

The final set exceeded everyone's expectations. Voronin broke Stanski's service in the first game with some amazing passing shots and then held his own in game two. In the third, Stanski served three double faults and missed a simple volley.

"Game to Voronin. Voronin leads by three games to love. Final set."

When I offered Stanski the water he poured it over his head and covered his face with the towel.

Voronin started game four with an ace. Stanski blocked the next serve and it nicked the cord and just dropped over. He was treated to another eyeballing for that piece of impertinence. Voronin walked slowly back to the line, turned, glared and fired a big serve that was called out. The second was softer and Stanski risked a blinder, a mighty forehand, and succeeded – the first winner he'd made in the set. Fifteen-thirty. Voronin nodded towards my friend Eddie for balls, scowled at one and chucked it aside. Eddie gave him another. He served long. Then foot-faulted. This time the line judge received the eyeballing. Fifteen-forty.

Stanski jigged on his toes. He would never have a better opportunity of breaking back.

The serve from Voronin was cautious. The spin deceived Stanski and the ball flew high. Voronin stood under, waiting to pick it out of the sun and kill it. He connected, but heroically Stanski got the racquet in place at the far end and almost fell into the crowd doing it. The return looked a sitter for the Russian and he steered it cross-court with nonchalance. Somehow Stanski dashed to the right place again. The crowd roared its appreciation.

Voronin chipped the return with a dinky shot that barely cleared the net and brought Stanski sprinting from the back to launch himself into a dive. The ball had bounced and risen through another arc and was inches from the turf when Stanski's racquet slid under it. Miraculously he found enough lift to sneak it over at a near-impossible angle. Voronin netted. Game to Stanski.

Now there was an anxious moment. Stanski's dive had taken him sliding out of court and heavily into the net-post, just a yard from where I was crouching in my set position. He was rubbing his right forearm, green from the skid across the grass, and everyone feared he'd broken a bone. After a delay of a few seconds the umpire asked if he needed medical attention. He shook his head.

Play resumed at three games to one, and it felt as if they'd played a full set already. The fascination of the game of tennis is that a single shot can turn a match. That diving winner of Stanski's was a prime example. He won the next game to love, serving brilliantly, though clearly anxious about his sore arm, which he massaged at every opportunity. Between games the umpire again asked if he needed assistance, but he shook his head.

Voronin was still a break up, and when play resumed after the change of ends he was first on court. He beckoned to me aggressively with his right hand, white with resin. I let him see he wouldn't intimidate me. I was a credit to the Brigadier, showing and throwing with the single bounce, straight to the player.

Stanski marched to the receiving end, twirling his racquet. Voronin hit the first serve too deep. The second spun in, shaved the line and was allowed. Fifteen-love. Stanski took the next two points with fine, looping returns. Then Voronin met a return of serve with a volley that failed to clear the net. Fifteen-forty. The mind-game was being won by Stanski. A feeble serve from the Russian allowed him to close the game.

Three all.

The critical moment was past. Stanski's confidence was high. He wiped his forehead with his wristband, tossed the ball up and served an ace that Bjorn Borg himself would have been incapable of reaching. From that moment, Voronin was doomed. Stanski was nerveless, accurate, domineering. He took the game to love. He dropped only one point in winning the next two. It was over. The crowd was in ecstasy. Voronin walked to the side without shaking hands, slung his racquets into his bag and left the court without waiting for his opponent – which is always regarded as bad form at Wimbledon. Some of the crowd booed him.

Stanski seemed to be taking longer than usual in packing up. He lingered by the net-post looking down, repeatedly dragging his foot across the worn patch of turf and raising dust. Then he bent and picked something up that to me looked liked like one of the needles my mother used on her sewing-machine. After staring at it for some time he showed it to the umpire, who had descended from his chair. At the same time he pointed to a scratch on his forearm. The umpire nodded indulgently and I heard him promise to speak to the groundsman.

I learned next day that Stanski was ill and had withdrawn from the tournament. It was a disappointment to everyone, because he had seemed to be on a roll and might have put out one of the seeds in a later round.

Two days after, the world of tennis was shocked to learn that Jozsef Stanski had died. He'd been admitted to St Thomas's complaining of weakness, vomiting and a high temperature. His pulse-rate was abnormally high and his lymph glands were swollen. There was an area of hardening under the scratch on his right forearm. In the night, his pulse rose to almost two hundred a minute and his temperature fell sharply. He was taken into intensive care and treated for septicaemia. Tests showed an exceptionally high count of white blood cells. Blood was appearing in his vomit and he was having difficulty in passing water, suggesting damage to the kidneys.

The next day an electrocardiogram indicated further critical problems, this time with the heart. Attempts were made to fit a pacemaker, but he died whilst under the anaesthetic. It was announced that a post mortem would be held the following day.

I'm bound to admit that these medical details only came to my attention years later, through my interest in the case. At the time it happened, I was wholly taken up with my duties at Wimbledon, programmed by the Brigadier to let nothing distract me. We were soon into the second week and the crowds grew steadily, with most interest on the show courts.

Eddie and I were picked for the men's semi-finals and I had my first experience of the Centre Court in the greatest match ever played at Wimbledon, between Bjorn Borg, the champion for the previous five years, and Jimmy Connors. Borg came back from two sets down, love-six and four-six, to win with a display of skill and guts that finally wore down the seemingly unstoppable Connors. I will go to my grave proud that I had a minor role in that epic.

I'm proud, also, that I was one of the ball boys in the final, though the match lacked passion and didn't quite live up to its promise. John McEnroe deserved his Championship, but we all felt Borg had fired his best shots in the semi.

Like Borg, I was forced to choke back some disappointment that afternoon. I'd secretly hoped to be named best ball boy, but a kid from another school was picked by the Brigadier. My pal Eddie (who wasn't on court for the final) put an arm around my shoulder when it was over. We told each other that the kid had to be a brown-noser and the Brigadier's nephew as well.

I may have heard something later on radio or television about the post mortem on poor Jozsef Stanski. They concluded he died from blood-poisoning. Samples were sent for further analysis, but the lab couldn't trace the source. At the inquest, a pathologist mentioned the scratch on the arm and said some sharp point had dug quite deep into the flesh. The match umpire gave evidence and spoke of the needle Stanski had picked up. He described the small eye close to the point. Unfortunately the needle had not been seen since the day of the match. In summing up, the coroner said it would not be helpful to speculate about the needle. The match had been played in full view of a large crowd and there was no evidence of anyone attempting to cause Stanski's death.

Huge controversy surrounded the verdict. The international press made a lot of the incident, pointing out that as recently as 1978 a Bulgarian writer, Georgi Markov, a rebel against his Communist government, had been executed in a London street by a tiny poison pellet forced into his thigh, apparently by the tip of an umbrella. The poison used was ricin, a protein derived from the castor oil seed, deadly and in those days almost undetectable in the human bloodstream. He took four days to die, protesting that he was the victim of political assassination. Nobody except his wife took him seriously until after he died. The presence of the poison was only discovered because the pellet was still embedded in a piece of Markov's flesh sent for analysis. If ricin could be injected in a public street using an umbrella, was it so fanciful to suggest Jozsef Stansky was targeted by the KGB and poisoned at Wimbledon two years later?

In Poland, the first months of 1981 had been extremely tense. A new Prime Minister, General Jaruzelski, had taken over and a permanent committee was set up to liaise with Solidarity. Moscow was incensed by this outbreak of liberalism and summoned Jaruzelski and his team to the Kremlin. The Politburo made its anger known. Repression followed. Many trade union activists were beaten up.

The papers noted that Stanski's opponent Voronin had quit Britain by an Aeroflot plane the same evening he had lost. He was unavailable for comment, in spite of strenuous efforts by reporters. The Soviet crackdown on Solidarity was mentioned. It was widely suspected that the KGB had been monitoring Stanski for over a year. He was believed to be acting as a conduit to the free world for Walesa and his organisation. At the end of the year, martial law was imposed in Poland and the leaders of Solidarity were detained and union activity suspended.

Although nothing was announced officially, the press claimed Scotland Yard investigated the assassination theory and kept the file open.

Since the Cold War ended and the Soviet bloc disintegrated, it is hard to think oneself back into the oppression of those days, harder still to believe orders may have been given for one tennis player to execute another at the world's top tournament.

In the years since, I kept an open mind about the incident, troubled to think murder may have happened so close to me. In my mind's eye I can still see Stanski rubbing his arm and reaching for the water I poured.

Then, last April, I had a phone call from Eddie Pringle. I hadn't seen him in almost twenty years. He was coming my way on a trip and wondered if we might meet for a drink.

To be truthful, I wasn't all that keen. I couldn't imagine we had much in common these days. Eddie seemed to sense my reluctance, because he went on to say, "I wouldn't take up your time if it wasn't important – well, important to me, if not to you. I'm not on the cadge, by the way. I'm asking no favours except for one half-hour of your time."

How could I refuse?

We arranged to meet in the bar of a local hotel. I told him I have a beard these days and what I would wear, just in case we didn't recognise each other.

I certainly wouldn't have known Eddie if he hadn't come up to me and spoken my name. He was gaunt, hairless and on two sticks.

"Sorry," he said. "Chemo. Didn't like to tell you on the phone in case I put you off."

"I'm the one who should be sorry," I said. "Is the treatment doing any good?"

"Not really. I'll be lucky to see the year out. But I'm allowed to drink in moderation. What's yours?"

We found a table. He asked what line of work I'd gone into and I told him I was a journalist.

"Sport?"

"No. Showbiz. I know why you asked," I said. "That stint we did as ball boys would have been a useful grounding. No one ever believes I was on court with McEnroe and Borg, so I rarely mention it."

"I made a big effort to forget," Eddie said. "The treatment we got from that Brigadier fellow was shameful."

"No worse than any military training."

"Yes, but we were young kids barely into our teens. At that age it amounted to brain-washing."

"That's a bit strong, Eddie."

"Think about it," he said. "He had us totally under his control. Destroyed any individuality we had. We thought about nothing else but chasing after tennis balls and handing them over in the approved style. It was the peak of everyone's ambition to be the best ball boy. You were as fixated as I was. Don't deny it."

"True. It became my main ambition."

"Obsession."

"OK. Have it your way. Obsession." I smiled, wanting to lighten the mood a bit.

"You were the hotshot ball boy," he said. "You deserved to win."

"I doubt it. Anyway, I was too absorbed in it all to see how the other kids shaped up."

"Believe me, you were the best. I couldn't match you for speed or stillness. The need to be invisible he was always on about."

"I remember that."

"I believed I was as good as anyone, except you." Eddie took a long sip of beer and was silent for some time.

I waited. It was obvious some boyhood memory was troubling him.

He cleared his throat nervously. "Something has been on my mind all these years. It's a burden I can't take with me when I go. I don't have long, and I want to clear my conscience. You remember the match between the Russian and the Pole?"

"Voronin and, er . . . ?"

"Stanski – the one who died. It should never have happened. You're the one who should have died."

Staring at him, I played the last statement over in my head.

He said, "You've got to remember the mental state we were in, totally committed to being best boy. It was crazy, but nothing else in the world mattered. I could tell you were better than I was, and you told me yourself that the Brigadier spoke to you after one of your matches on Ladies' Day."

"Did I?" I said, amazed he still had such a clear recollection.

"He didn't say anything to me. It was obvious you were booked for the final. While you were on the squad, I stood no chance. It sounds like lunacy now, but I was so fired up I had to stop you."

"How?"

"With poison."

"Now come on, Eddie. You're not serious."

But his tone insisted he was. "If you remember, when we were in the first year, there was a sensational story in the papers about a man, a Bulgarian, who was murdered in London by a pellet the size of a pinhead that contained an almost unknown poison called ricin."

"Georgi Markov."

"Yes. We talked about it in chemistry with Blind Pugh. Remember?"

"Vaguely."

"He said a gram of the stuff was enough to kill thirty-six thousand people and it attacked the red blood cells. It was obtained from the seeds or beans of the castor-oil plant, *ricinus communis*. They had to be ground up in a pestle and mortar because otherwise the hard seed-coat prevented absorption. Just a few seeds would be enough. Old Pugh told us all this in the belief that castor oil plants are tropical, but he was wrong. They've been grown in this country as border plants ever since Tudor times."

"You're saying you got hold of some?"

"From a local seedsman, and no health warning. I'm sorry if all this sounds callous. I felt driven at the time. I plotted how to do it, using this."

Eddie spread his palm and a small piece of metal lay across it. "I picked it out of a litter bin after Stanski threw it away. This is the sewing machine needle he found. My murder weapon."

I said with distaste, "You were responsible for that?"

"It came from my mother's machine. I ground the needle to a really fine point and made a gelatine capsule containing the poison and filled the eye of the needle with it."

"What were you going to do with it – stick it into my arm?"

"No. Remember how we were drilled to return to the same spot just behind the tramlines beside the umpire's chair? If you watch tennis, that place gets as worn as the serving area at the back of the court. The ballboys always return to the same spot. My plan was simple. Stick the needle into the turf with the sharp point upwards and you would kneel on it and inject the ricin into your bloodstream. I'm telling you this because I want the truth to come out before I die. I meant to kill you and it went wrong. Stanski dived at a difficult ball and his arm went straight down on the needle."

"But he went on to win the match."

"The effects take days to kick in, but there's no antidote. Even if I'd confessed at the time, they couldn't have saved him. It was unforgivable. I was obsessed and it's preyed on my mind ever since."

"So all that stuff in the papers about Voronin being an assassin . . ."

"Was rubbish. It was me. If you want to go to the police," he said, "I don't mind confessing everything I've told you. I just want the truth to be known before I go. I'm told I have six months at most."

I was silent, reflecting on what I'd heard, the conflicting motives that had driven a young boy to kill and a dying man to confess twenty years later.

"Or you could wait until after I've gone. You say you're a journalist. You could write it up and tell it in your own way."

He left me to make up my own mind.

Eddie died in November.

And you are the first after me to get the full story.

A BLOW ON THE HEAD

Almost there. Donna Culpepper looked ahead to her destination and her destiny, the top of Beachy Head, the great chalk headland that is the summit of the South Downs coast. She'd walked from where the taxi driver had left her. The stiff climb wasn't easy on this gusty August afternoon, but her mind was made up. She was thirty-nine, with no intention of being forty. She'd made a disastrous marriage to a man who had deserted her after six weeks, robbed her of her money, her confidence, her dreams. Trying to put it all behind her, as friends kept urging, had not worked. Two years on, she was unwilling to try any longer.

Other ways of ending it, like an overdose or cutting her wrists, were not right for Donna. Beachy Head was the place. As a child she'd stayed in Eastbourne with her Gran and they came here often, 'for a blow on the Head', as Gran put it, crunching the tiny grey shells of the path, her grey hair tugged by the wind, while jackdaws and herring-gulls swooped and soared, screaming in the clear air. From the top, five hundred feet up when you first saw the sea, you had a sudden sensation of height that made your spine tingle. There was just the rim of eroding turf and the hideous drop.

On a good day you could see the Isle of Wight, Gran had said. Donna couldn't see anything and stepped closer to the edge and Gran grabbed her and said it was dangerous. People came here to kill themselves.

This interested Donna. Gran gave reluctant answers to her questions.

"They jump off"

71

"Why?"

"I don't know, dear."

"Yes, you do. Tell me, Gran."

"Some people are unhappy."

"What makes them unhappy?"

"Lots of things."

"What things?"

"Never mind, dear."

"But I do mind. Tell me what made those people unhappy."

"Grown-up things."

"Like making babies?"

"No, no, no. Whoever put such ideas in your head?"

"What, then?"

"Sometimes they get unhappy because they lose the person they love."

"What's love?"

"Oh, dear. You've such a lot to learn. When you grow up you fall in love with someone and if you're lucky you marry them."

"Is that why they jump off the cliff?'"

Gran laughed. "No, you daft ha'porth, it's the opposite, or I think it is. Let's change the subject."

The trouble with grown-ups is that they always change the subject before they get to the point. For some years after this Donna thought falling in love was a physical act involving gravity. She could see that falling off Beachy Head was dangerous and would only be attempted by desperate people. She expected it was possible to get in love by falling from more sensible heights. She tried jumping off her bed a few times, but nothing happened. The kitchen table, which she tried only once, was no use either.

She started getting sensuous dreams, though. She would leap off the cliff edge and float in the air like the skydivers she'd seen on television. If that was falling in love she could understand why there was so much talk about it.

Disillusion set in when she started school. Love turned out to be something else involving those gross, ungainly creatures, boys.

After a few skirmishes with over-curious boys she decided love was not worth pursuing any longer. It didn't come up to her dreams. This was a pity because other girls of her age expected less and got a more gradual initiation into the mysteries of sex.

At seventeen the hormones would not be suppressed and Donna drank five vodkas and went to bed with a man of twenty-three. He said he was in love with her, but if that was love it was unsatisfactory. And in the several relationships she had in her twenties she never experienced anything to match those dreams of falling and flying. Most of her girlfriends found partners and moved in with them. Donna held off.

In her mid-to-late thirties she began to feel deprived. One day she saw the Meeting Place page in a national paper. Somewhere out there was her ideal partner. She decided to take active steps to find him. She had money. Her Gran had died and left her everything, ninety thousand pounds. In the ad she described herself as independent, sensitive and cultured.

And that was how she met Lionel Culpepper.

He was charming, good-looking and better at sex than anyone she'd met. She told him about her Gran and her walks on Beachy Head and her dreams of flying. He said he had a pilot's licence and offered to take her up in a small plane. She asked if he owned a plane and he said he would hire one. Thinking of her legacy she asked how much they cost and he thought he could buy a good one secondhand for ninety thousand pounds. They got married and opened a joint account. He went off one morning to look at a plane offered for sale in a magazine. That was the last she saw of her husband. When she checked the bank account it was empty. She had been married thirty-eight days.

For a long time she worried about Lionel, thinking he'd had an accident. She reported him missing. Then a letter arrived from a solicitor. Cruelly formal in its wording, it stated that her husband, Lionel Culpepper, wanted a divorce. She was devastated. She hated him then and knew him for what he was. He would not get his divorce that easily.

That was two years ago. Here she was, taking the route of so many who have sought to end their troubles by suicide. Some odd sense of completion, she supposed, was making her take those last steps to the highest point. Any part of the cliff edge would do.

She saw a phone box ahead. Oddly situated, you would think, on a cliff top. The Samaritans had arranged for the phone to be here just in case any tormented soul decided to call them and talk. Donna walked past. A short way beyond was a well-placed wooden bench and she was grateful for that. She needed a moment to compose herself.

She sat. It was just the usual seat you found in parks and along river banks all over the country. Not comfortable for long with its slatted seat and upright back, but welcome at the end of the stiff climb. And it did face the sea.

In a moment she would launch herself. She wasn't too scared. A small part of her still wanted the thrill of falling. For a few precious seconds she would be like those sky-divers appearing to fly. This was the way to go.

Revived and resolute, Donna stood and checked to make sure no one was about. Perfect. She had the whole headland to herself . . .

Well, then.

What it was that drew her attention back to the bench she couldn't say. At the edge of her vision she became aware of a small brass plaque screwed to the top rail. She read the inscription.

> In memory of my beloved wife Donna Maria Culpepper, 1967-2004, who loved to walk here and enjoy this view.

A surreal moment. Donna swayed and had to reach out and clutch the bench. She sat again, rubbed her eyes, took a deep breath and looked a second time because she half wondered if her heightened state of mind had made her hallucinate.

The words were just as she'd first read them. Her name in full. She'd never met anyone with the same name. It would be extraordinary if some other Donna Maria Culpepper had walked here and loved this view. The year of birth was right as well.

Two things were definitely not Donna. She hadn't died in 2004 and the way her rat of a husband had treated her made the word 'beloved' a sick joke.

Was it possible, she asked herself now, still staring at the weird plaque, that Lionel had paid for the bench and put it here? Could he have heard from some mistaken source that she had died? Had he done this in a fit of conscience?

No chance. Freed of that foolish infatuation she'd experienced when she met the man and married him, she knew him for what he was. Conscience didn't trouble Lionel. He'd had the gall to ask for a divorce – through a solicitor and after weeks of silence. He was cowardly and callous.

How could this bench be anything to do with Lionel, or with her?

It was a mystery.

Cold logic suggested there had been another Donna Maria Culpepper born in the same year who had died in 2004 and had this touching memorial placed here by her widowed husband, who was obviously more devoted and considerate than Lionel. And yet it required a series of coincidences for this to have happened: the same first names, surname, date of birth.

She took another look. In the bottom right corner of the plaque was a detail she hadn't noticed – the letters 'L.C.' – Lionel's initials. This, surely, clinched it. The odds against were huge.

She no longer felt suicidal. Anger had taken over. She was outraged by Lionel's conduct. He shouldn't have done this. She had come here in a wholly negative frame of mind. Now a new challenge galvanized her. She would get to the truth. She was recharged, determined to find an explanation.

First she had to find him. After their break-up she'd had minimal contact, and that was through solicitors' letters. She had no idea where he lived now.

She walked down the path towards the town.

The Parks and Recreations Department at Eastbourne Council said that about forty seats had been donated as memorials by members of the public. A helpful young woman showed her the records. The bench had been presented last spring. A man had come in with the plaque already inscribed. He'd particularly asked for a teak seat to be positioned at the top of Beachy Head. He'd paid in cash and left no name, though it was obvious he had to be a Mr Culpepper.

Donna asked if he'd left his address or phone number and was told he had not. She took a sharp, impatient breath and explained about the shock she'd had. The clerical assistant was sympathetic and said it could only be an unfortunate duplication of names.

While Donna was explaining why she thought it couldn't be coincidence, an assistant at the next desk asked if they were talking about the seat at the top of Beachy Head. She said a few months ago she'd had someone else in, a woman, asking about the same seat and the man who presented it.

"A woman? Did she say why?" Donna asked.

"No, but she left her business card. I put it in the folder, just in case we found out any more."

The card had slipped to the bottom of the folder. Donna was given a pencil and paper to make a note of the name and phone number. *Maggie Boswell-Jones, Starpart Film, TV and Theatrical Agency, Cecil Court, Off Charing Cross Road, London.* There were phone, fax and e-mail numbers.

Donna didn't have her mobile with her. She hadn't intended using it on this last day of her life. She used a public phone downstairs.

The conversation was all very bizarre.

"You're Lionel's wife? But you're dead," Maggie Boswell-Jones said. "You were killed in a flying accident."

"I promise you I wasn't," Donna said. "'I'm who I say I am.'"

"How can you be? There's a seat on Beachy Head with your name on it. Lionel put it there in your memory."

"He ran out on me in the second month of our marriage. May I ask why you were looking for him?"

"Because he's my boyfriend, darling, and he's missing."

Donna felt as if she'd been kicked in the stomach. She knew Lionel was a rat. Now she knew he was a two-timing rat. He'd walked out on her and started up with this woman. She made an effort to save her fury for Lionel.

"How did you know about the seat?"

"He took me up there specially. He wanted me to know that you were dead. I made it very clear to him that I don't get involved with married guys. He spoke nicely of you."

"Look, can I come and see you?"

"Is that necessary?"

"I'm determined to find him. With your help I'm sure I can do it."

At the agency Donna recognised a man who stepped out of the lift. He was an actor she often saw in *Coronation Street*. In the waiting room upstairs there were framed movie posters. In a glass showcase were various awards, including what looked like an Oscar.

Maggie appeared high-powered with her black fringe, tinted glasses and purple suit, but she turned out to be charming. Coffee and biscuits were ready on a low table in her office. They sat together on a black leather sofa. "I've been trying to understand what's going on with Lionel ever since you phoned and I'm still at a loss," Maggie said. "He's such a bright guy. I can't think how he got to believe you'd passed away."

"He made it up," Donna said.

"Oh, I don't think so. He said the kindest things about you. I mean, why would he go to the trouble and expense of buying a seat for you?"

"To fool you into believing I was dead and he was free to have an affair. Can't you see that?"

Maggie took a lot of convincing. Clearly she was still under Lionel's spell. Just as Donna had believed him incapable of leaving her, so Maggie insisted he must have lost his memory in the flying accident.

"There was no flying accident," Donna said. "He talked about taking me in a plane, but it never happened. He took ninety thousand pounds from our account."

"Really? This shocks me." The colour had drained from Maggie's face. "I certainly need to find him because I lent him sixty grand to renovate a house he'd bought for us in the south of France."

"You'll never see that money again," Donna said. "He's a conman. He befriends women like you and me and fleeces them. If you don't mind me asking, how did you meet him? Was it through a newspaper?"

"What a skunk!" Maggie said, and Donna knew she'd got through to her at last.

That evening Maggie took Donna for a meal at a restaurant near the agency. "I'm not short of a bob or two," she said, "but let's admit it, I'm unattached and on the lookout. I meet plenty of hunky blokes in my job, but it doesn't do to mix work and pleasure, so I put my ad in the *Guardian*. Lionel was the best of the bunch who responded – or seemed to be."

"I wonder how many other women he's conned," Donna said. "It really upsets me that he went to all that trouble to make out I was dead and he was a free man. There must be some way of stopping him."

"We can't stop him if we can't find him."

"Couldn't we trace him through the newspaper?"

"I don't think so. They're very strict about box numbers. And they cover themselves by saying you indemnify the newspaper against all claims." Maggie thought for a while, and took a long sip of wine. "Righty," she said finally. "What we do is this."

> GORGEOUS Georgie, 38, own house, car, country cottage,
> WLTM Mr Charming 35-45 for days out and evenings in and
> possible LTR. Loves fast cars, first nights and five star
> restaurants.

"What's LTR?"

"Long term relationship. That should do it," Maggie said.

"It's a lot more pushy than mine," Donna said

"How did you describe yourself?"

She blushed a little. "'Independent, sensitive and cultured."

"Independent is good. He's thinking of your bank balance. But we can't use it a second time. This will pull in quite a few gold-diggers, I expect. We just have to listen carefully to the voice messages and make sure it's Lionel."

"I'll know his voice."

"So will I, sweetie."

"And who, exactly, is Gorgeous Georgie?"

"One of the best stuntmen in Britain."

"A *man*?"

"Ex-boxer and European weightlifting champion. He's been on my agency books for years. He'll deliver Lionel to us, and the money he stole from us. When Georgie has finished with the bastard he'll beg for mercy."

Maggie called ten days later. "He's fallen for it. A really unctuous voice message. Made me want to throw up. He says he's unattached –"

"That's a lie."

"Professional, caring and with a good sense of humour. He'll need that."

"So what's the plan?" Donna asked.

"It's already under way. I got my film rights director to call him back. She has the Roedean accent and very sexy it sounds. I told her to play the caution card. Said she needed to be certain Lionel isn't married. He jumped right in and said he's a widower and would welcome the opportunity to prove it. They're meeting for a walk on the Downs at Beachy Head followed by a meal at the pub."

"Your rights director?"

"No, silly. She was just the voice on the phone. He'll meet Georgie and get the shock of his life. All you and I have to do is be there to take care of the remains."

Donna caught her breath. "I can't be a party to murder."

"My sense of humour, darling. Georgie won't do anything permanent. He'll rough him up a bit and put the fear of God in him. Then we step up and get our money back."

Maggie drove them to Eastbourne on the day of the rendezvous. She took the zigzag from Holywell and parked in a lay-by with a good view of the grass rise. From here you wouldn't know there was a sheer drop. But if you ventured up the slope you'd see the Seven Sisters, the chalk cliffs reaching right away to Cuckmere Haven. It was late on a fine, gusty afternoon. George and the hapless Lionel were expected to reach here about five-thirty.

"Coffee or champagne?"

"You *are* well provided," Donna said. "Coffee, I think. I want a clear head when we meet up with him."

Maggie poured some from a flask. "We'll save the champers for later."

Donna smiled. "I just hope it stops him in his tracks. I don't want other women getting caught like we did. I felt so angry with myself for being taken in. I got very depressed. When I came up here I was on the point of suicide."

"That's no attitude. Don't ever let them grind you down."

"I'm not very experienced with men."

"Well, at least you persuaded the bastard to marry you, darling. You can't be a total amateur. Me, I was conned every which way. Slept with him, handed him my money, accepted his proposal."

"Proposal? He proposed to you? Actually promised to marry you?"

"The whole shebang. Down on one knee. We were engaged. He bought the ring, I'll say that for him. A large diamond and two sapphires. He knew he had to chip in something to get what he wanted. What did it cost him? – a couple of grand at most, compared to the sixty he got off me."

"I had no idea it got that far."

"He'd have married me if I hadn't caught him out. Bigamy wouldn't have troubled our Lionel."

Donna was increasingly concerned about what she was hearing. "But you *didn't* catch him out. When I first phoned, you called him your boyfriend. I had to persuade you that he was a conman."

"Don't kid yourself, ducky," Maggie said with a harder edge to her voice. "I knew all about Lionel before you showed up. I had him checked out. It's easy enough to get hold of a marriage certificate, and when he gave me the guff about the flying accident I checked for a death certificate as well, and there wasn't one, so I knew he was lying. He was stupid enough to tell me about the memorial bench before I even saw it. I went to the council and made sure it was bloody Lionel who paid to have it put there. He handed them the plaque and a wad of cash. What a con. He could go on using that seat as his calling card every time he started up with a new woman."

"If you knew all that, why didn't you act before? Why are you doing this with me?" Donna said.

"'Do you really want to know?" Maggie said. She reached for the champagne bottle and turned it in her hands as if to demonstrate good faith. "It's because you would have found out. Some day his body is going to be washed up. The sea always gives up its dead. Then the police are going to come asking questions and you'll lead them straight to me."

"I don't know what you're talking about."

"Get with it, Donna dear. Lionel is history."

She felt the hairs rise on her neck. "You killed him?"

"The evening he brought me up here to look at the stupid bench. I waited till we got here and then told him what an arsehole he was. Do you know, he still tried to con me? He walked to the cliff edge and said he would throw himself off if I didn't believe him. I couldn't stand his hypocrisy, so I gave him a push. Simple as that."

Donna covered her mouth.

"The tide was in," Maggie said in a matter-of-fact way, "so I suppose the body was carried out to sea."

"This is dreadful," Donna said. She herself had felt hatred for Lionel and wanted revenge, but she had never dreamed of killing him. "What I can't understand is why we're here now – why you went through this charade of advertising for him, trying to find him – when you knew he was dead."

"If you were listening, sweetie, I just told you. You knew too much even before I gave you the full story. You're certain to shop me when the police come along."

It was getting dark in the car, but Donna noticed a movement of Maggie's right hand. She had gripped the champagne bottle by the neck.

Donna felt for the door handle and shoved it open. She half fell, trying to get out. Maggie got out the other side and dashed round. Donna tried to run, but Maggie grabbed her coat. The last thing Donna saw was the bottle being swung at her head.

The impact was massive.

She fell against the car and slid to the ground. She'd lost all sensation. She couldn't even raise her arms to protect herself.

She acted dead, eyes closed, body limp. It wasn't difficult.

One of her eyes was jerked open by Maggie's finger. She had the presence to stare ahead.

Then she felt Maggie's hands under her back, lifting. She was hauled back into the car seat. The door slammed shut. She was too dazed to do anything.

Maggie was back at the wheel, closing the other door. The engine started up. The car bumped in ways it shouldn't have done. It was being driven across the turf, and she guessed what was happening. Maggie was driving her right up to the cliff edge to push her over.

The car stopped.

I can't let this happen, she told herself. I wanted to die once, but not any more.

She heard Maggie get out again. She opened her eyes. The key was in the ignition, but she hadn't the strength to move across and take the controls. She had to shut her eyes again and surrender to Maggie dragging her off the seat.

First her back thumped on the chalk at the cliff edge, then her head.

Flashes streaked across her retina. She took a deep breath of cold air, trying to hold on to consciousness.

She felt Maggie's hands take a grip under her armpits to force her over the edge.

With an effort born of desperation she turned and grabbed one of Maggie's ankles with both hands and held on. If she was going, then her killer would go with her.

Maggie shouted, "Bitch!" and kicked her repeatedly with the free leg. Donna knew she had to hold on.

Each kick was like a dagger-thrust in her kidneys.

I can't take this, she told herself.

The agony became unbearable. She let go.

The sudden removal of the clamp on Maggie's leg must have affected her balance. Donna felt the full force of Maggie's weight across her body followed by a scream, a long, despairing and diminishing scream.

Donna dragged herself away from the crumbling edge and then flopped on the turf again. Almost another half-hour passed before she was able to stagger to the phone box and ask for help.

When she told her story to the police, she kept it simple. She wasn't capable of telling it all. She'd been brought here on the pretext of meeting someone and then attacked with a bottle and almost forced over the edge. Her attacker had tripped and gone over.

Even the next day, when she made a full statement for their records, she omitted some of the details. She decided not to tell them she'd been at the point of suicide when she discovered that bench. She let them believe she'd come on a sentimental journey to remember her childhood. It didn't affect their investigation.

Maggie's body was recovered the same day. Lionel, elusive to the end, was washed up at Hastings by a storm the following October.

He left only debts. Donna had expected nothing and was not discouraged. Since her escape she valued her life and looked forward.

And the bench? You won't find it at Beachy Head.

THE MUNICH POSTURE

Adolf Hitler stared across the restaurant.

Camilla, blonde, eighteen and English, succeeded in saying without moving her lips, "He's looking, he's looking, he's looking!"

"For a waiter, not you, dear," Dorothy Rigby remarked. Rigby was, at this formative stage in her life, less flagrantly sexy than her friend Camilla. Rigby's appeal was subversive and ultimately more devastating. Here in Munich, in September, 1938, the girls were at the Countess Schnabel's Finishing School. Rigby's lightly permed brown hair was cut in a modest style approved by the Countess, so that a small expanse of neck showed above the collar of one's white lawn blouse.

It was Camilla who had dragged her into the Osteria Bavaria. Their table was chosen for the unimpeded view it afforded of the Führer and his party, or rather, the view it afforded the Führer of Camilla. Flamboyant Camilla with her blue Nordic eyes, her cupid's-bow pout and her bosom plumped up with all the silk stockings she owned. She was resolved to enslave the most powerful man in Europe. It wasn't impossible. It had been done by Unity Mitford, the Oxfordshire girl turned Rhine-maiden, who had staunchly occupied this same chair in Hitler's favourite restaurant through the winter of 1935 until she had been called to his table. From that time Unity had been included on the guest lists for Hitler's mountain retreat at Obersalzberg, and for the Nuremburg rallies, the Bayreuth Festival and the Olympic Games.

Until this moment, Camilla had unaccountably failed to emulate Miss Mitford, though she was just as dedicated, just as blonde and, by her own assessment, prettier.

Until this moment.

"Oh, my hat! He's talking to his Adjutant. He's pointing to this table. To *me*!"

"Calm down, Cami."

Camilla gripped the edge of the tablecloth. "God, this is it! The adjutant is coming over."

Undeniably he was. Young, clean-shaven, cool as a brimming *Bierglas*, he saluted and announced, "Ladies, the Führer has commanded me to present his compliments ..."

"So gracious!" piped up Camilla in her best German.

"... and states that he would prefer to finish his lunch without being stared at." Another click of the heels, an about-turn, and that was that.

"I'm dead," said Camilla after a stunned silence. "How absolutely ghastly! Let's leave at once."

"Certainly not," said Rigby. "He wants to be ignored, so we'll ignore him. More coffee?"

"Is that wise?"

They remained at their table until Hitler rose to leave. For a moment he glared in their direction, his blue eyes glittering. Then he slapped his glove against the sleeve of his raincoat and marched out.

"Odious little fart," said Rigby.

"I hope Mr Chamberlain spits in his eye," said Camilla.

"He'll have Mr Chamberlain on toast."

Outside, in Schellingstrasse, heels clicked and the young adjutant saluted again. "Excuse me, ladies. I have another message to convey from the Führer."

"We don't wish to hear it," said Rigby. "Come on, Camilla. We're not standing here to be insulted."

Camilla was rooted to the pavement. "A message from him?"

"This is difficult. The message is for the dark-haired young lady."

"*Me?*" said Rigby.

Camilla gave a sudden sob and covered her eyes.

"The Führer will dine at Boettner's this evening. He has arranged for you to join his party. Fräulein, er ..."

"I am not one of your Fräuleins. I am *Miss* Rigby."

"From England?" The adjutant frowned and reddened.

Rigby said off-handedly. "Actually I was born in Madras. India, you know. I expect he thought I was a starry-eyed little Nazi wench. Will you be there?"

He stared back. "I beg your pardon?"

"I said, will you be there?"

"As it happens, no."

"A night off?"

"Well, yes."

"How convenient. You can tell Herr Hitler that when you found out the young lady's dusky origins you did what any quick-witted officer of the Reich would have done – arranged to take her to dinner yourself, thus saving your Führer from sullying his snow-white principles."

His eyes widened. First they registered shock, then curiosity, then capitulation.

His name was Manfred, he told her in the candlelight at Walterspiel that evening. "It's strange," he said. "I took you for an English girl."

"Oh, I am by blood. Daddy served in India with the Army."

He frowned. "Then why did you decline the Führer's invitation – such an honour?"

"I didn't care for the way it was communicated, as if I was biddable, to put it mildly."

"But I think your friend was biddable."

She laughed. "Still is. She's stopped talking to me. She can't understand why she was overlooked. Frankly, neither can I. Camilla has the fair hair and blue eyes, and much more."

He leaned forward confidentially. "With respect, Miss Rigby, I think you misunderstood the Führer's motives. He is not in want of female companionship. There is a lady at Obersalzberg."

"Eva Braun?"

"Ah. You are well informed."

"Then why did he ask me to dinner?"

Manfred took a sip of wine. "Some years ago there was a girl, his stepniece actually, who died. He was very devoted to her, more than an uncle should be. No, I mean nothing improper. Like a father. She was eighteen when she came to Munich. He took her about, to picnics, the opera, paid for singing lessons, rented a room for her."

"What was her name?"

"Angela Raubal, known to him as Geli. She looked remarkably like you. The dark hair, the cheekbones, the whole shape of your face, your beautiful hazel eyes. This, I think, is why he wanted to meet you."

"I see. And you say she died?"

"Shot herself with the Führer's own gun." He paused. "No one knows why. I think perhaps it was best that he did not meet you. But please understand that it was not because you are English. The Führer and Mr Chamberlain are much in agreement, wanting to keep the peace in Europe."

"Neville Chamberlain does, without a doubt," said Rigby with a quick, ironic smile.

"So does the Führer."

"Yes – if the other powers allow him to march into Czechoslovakia."

He frowned. "You speak of international politics – a young girl?"

Rigby decided to take the remark as a compliment. She was a great reader of newspapers. She'd often been told that comments on international affairs came oddly from a girl of her age, but she wasn't perturbed. Crisply she analysed the crisis over Germany's claims to the Sudeten regions of Czechoslovakia and the dangerous effects of Hitler's *Lebensraum* policy. Manfred used the stock German argument that something had to be done about the crushing restrictions imposed at Versailles after the Great War.

"It won't wash," commented Rigby. "It's transparently clear that Czechoslovakia is next on your Führer's list. God help us all."

He gave the grin of someone with inside information. "But it will not lead to war."

She said, "You're very close to him, aren't you?"

He nodded.

"He thinks he has the measure of our Prime Minister, doesn't he?"

He gave a shrug that didn't deny it.

Patriotically casting about for something in the Prime Minister's favour, she said, "You tell him that Neville Chamberlain may be almost seventy, but he forgets nothing. His memory is phenomenal."

"Is that important?"

She said, "Hitler relies on people having short memories, doesn't he?"

He said, "I think it is time we talked of something else. Shall we walk in the Englischer Garten?"

There they followed the twists of the stream among the willows until almost midnight. They sat on a bench, listening to the trickle of the water, and she allowed him to kiss her.

She murmured, "What would the Führer say about this?"

He laughed softly. "What happens tonight is nobody's business but yours and mine."

Resting her face against his shoulder, she said, "Manfred, if I were very bold and made a suggestion, would you do something to please me – something really daring?"

"What is it?"

"It's a practical joke. I need your help to make it work. It will be enormous fun."

He said, "If you wish." Then, bleakly, "I thought for a moment you were going to suggest something else."

She smiled and nestled closer. "That's not for me to suggest."

It was a measure of the priorities at the Countess Schnabel's Finishing School that the Countess herself took the deportment class. "Upright in body is upright in mind," she repeatedly informed the seventeen young ladies in her care. "Perfect posture is perfectly obtainable. Cross the room once more, Camilla, if you please. *Ooh! Grotesk!* Don't rotate the hips so."

The lesson ended at noon. The Countess clapped her hands. "Before you leave, I give you a thrilling announcement. Tomorrow the school is to be honoured by a visitor, a visitor so important that I am not yet at liberty to mention his name. No finishing school in Munich has ever been so favoured. Suffice to say that you will all be perfectly groomed, immaculately dressed and silent unless spoken to."

Camilla told Rigby sourly that it was obvious who the V.I.P. was. "And I can't bear to face him when it's perfectly clear that he's coming to ogle you. I shall report sick."

So when the Countess swept into the gym at ten next morning and triumphantly announced the Führer, only sixteen girls were present to say, "*Heil* Hitler," and salute.

Rigby had no eyes for the strutting figure in the black mackintosh with his Chaplin moustache. She gazed steadily at Manfred, standing a pace to the rear, feet astride and arms folded, wearing his brown uniform with the swastika arm-band. He appeared twice as handsome this morning. He had more than proved his daring. This stunt was incredibly reckless and he had engineered it himself, simply because she had asked him.

She rather thought she had fallen in love.

"Dorothy, I hope you are paying attention," said the Countess. The timetable had been adjusted. Deportment again. A chance for the Countess to make an impression. For twenty minutes the class went through its paces, breathing, balancing and walking gracefully, all without a noticeable hitch. Then the Countess turned, curtsied, and asked if the Führer would gracefully consent to present the posture medal to the girl with best deportment, and certificates to the others.

It was a pleasing little ceremony. Of course, the Countess nominated her favourite for the medal, an obnoxious girl called Dagmar who was one of the Hitler Youth, but everyone else stepped forward in turn for a certificate.

His handshake was damp and flabby, Rigby noted as she collected hers.

At Manfred's suggestion, the certificates had been typed that morning in the school office. They read simply: *Presented by the Führer for Good Posture.*

And now the Countess was asked whether every girl in the school had received a certificate. She had to explain that one of the girls was unfortunately in the sick-bay. The Führer insisted on going upstairs to meet Camilla.

Rigby almost purred, things were going so well.

The official party moved out.

Frustratingly she couldn't contrive to witness the scene upstairs. But she imagined it vividly: Camilla saucer-eyed as the Führer entered and approached the bedside; speechless when he asked if she was the young lady he had seen in the Osteria Bavaria; and flabbergasted when he grasped her hand, leaned close and whispered that he wouldn't mind climbing into bed with her.

Rigby shook with silent laughter.

Then her daydream was shattered by gunfire.

Panic.

Girls screamed.

Rigby dashed to the staircase. On the landing she met Portland, the fellow in the black mackintosh who had posed as Hitler. He was a limpet-like admirer she had dragooned into this performance after he'd followed her to Munich. His Hitler impersonation had been a highlight of the Chelsea Arts Ball.

"What happened?"

Portland was ashen. He peeled off the moustache. "She must be barmy, that friend of yours. She drew a gun before I said a damned thing. She tried to blow my brains out."

"Oh, God! Are you all right?"

"I shoved the gun aside, but she put a bullet into your German friend."

"Manfred! No!"

All caution abandoned, Rigby rushed up the remaining stairs and into the sick-bay, into mayhem. Camilla, sobbing hysterically, her nightdress spattered with blood, knelt by the motionless body of Manfred. The Countess was at the medical chest, grabbing boxes and bottles and throwing them down as if they'd been put there to thwart her.

Rigby went to Manfred and turned his face. It was deathly white.

"She shot him!" wailed the Countess. "She meant to shoot the Führer, wicked girl, but the Adjutant got in the way. I don't know what will happen to us all."

"Is he dead?"

"Passed out. The bullet went through his foot. Did you pass the Führer on the stairs?"

"No," said Rigby truthfully.

The Countess handed her a bottle. "Smelling salts. Do your best. I'm going to find the Führer."

"That isn't possible, ma'am."

In the next five minutes, everyone became wiser. Rigby confessed to the practical joke that had misfired – literally. The Countess made a great show of being scandalised but couldn't suppress her relief that there had not, after all, been an assassination attempt on the Führer in her school. It wasn't for want of trying, Camilla rashly told them. Far from hero-worshipping Hitler, she had planned cold-bloodedly to rid the world of him. The vigil in the Osteria Bavaria had been her attempt to entrap him.

"Enemy of the Reich!" cried the countess. "She-devil! You are expelled from my school!"

"Then I shall go to the newspapers."

"On second thoughts, I see it as my duty to reform you."

Then Manfred opened his eyes and groaned. "Help me to stand, please. I must leave at once."

"Out of the question," the Countess told him. "I'm going to put you to bed."

He said with desperation, "I report to the Führer at noon. It is the four-power conference with Chamberlain, Mussolini and Daladier. I'm on duty."

"With a shot foot? Don't be idiotic!"

He propped himself on an elbow, moved the leg, grimaced with pain and immediately passed out again, giving the countess the opportunity to make good her promise. With Rigby's and Camilla's help she lifted him on to the bed, then instructed them to look the other way while she stripped him of his uniform. The doctor who usually attended the school arrived to dress the wound. He injected Manfred with morphine. Nobody told the doctor who Manfred was: by a process of nods and shrugs he formed the impression that Manfred was on the staff of the school and had shot himself by accident while investigating a noise in the cellar.

"Rats," said the doctor, with a knowing look.

The rest of the morning was torment for Rigby as she speculated what would happen to Manfred. Soon enough his absence would be noticed – absence without leave. What explanation could he give?

He was going to be on crutches for weeks. Hitler, a man utterly devoid of humour, would take it as treason. Manfred would be lucky to escape with his life.

Her own fate, as the instigator of the stunt, paled into insignificance. So, it must be admitted, did Camilla's, as the would-be assassin of the Führer.

That afternoon Rigby missed the German lesson, saying she had a toothache, and slipped upstairs to the sick-bay. She found Manfred semiconscious, too drugged to move, but capable of recognising her. He smiled. She stroked his forehead. How much made sense to him was difficult to judge.

"I've thought about this for hours and something drastic has to be done, my darling. I'm going to speak to your Führer. He expressed a wish to meet me, and now he will. I shall make a personal appeal to him. He's got to be told that this was just a practical joke got up by some high-spirited girls who tricked you into taking part. You were injured heroically trying to put a stop to it. All I want from you is the pass you carry, or something to get me into Hitler's flat. I must see him alone. It's no use with all those aides around him. How will I gain entry? Is there a password?"

Manfred gazed at her blankly.

She went to the wardrobe and searched his uniform. In an inside pocket was a wallet containing various identification documents.

Munich buzzed with stories about the Conference. Hitler had pushed Europe to the brink of war over the Sudeten question. Germany was set to occupy the disputed territories on October 1st and it was now September 29th. Chamberlain had flown in that morning from London for his third meeting with Hitler in a fortnight. Daladier, the French premier, was already installed at the Four Seasons Hotel. And Hitler had gone by train to the German-Italian border to escort his ally, Mussolini, to Munich. The talks at the Führerbau had started soon after lunch and were likely to last until late.

About six-twenty p.m., a taxi drew up at the building in Prinz Regenten Platz where Hitler had his private apartment. Rigby, dressed in a black pillbox hat with a veil, a bottle-green jacket with velvet revers and a black skirt, got out and approached the guard. She gave the Nazi salute.

"I am here on the personal instructions of the Führer. I am to go up and wait for him."

"Your identification, Fräulein?"

"Examine this. It is the pass of his Adjutant, Oberleutnant Reger."

"Do you have some identification of your own?"

"This is sufficient. My presence here is highly confidential. Mention it to nobody. Nobody. Do you understand?"

Her voice carried authority. He saluted, stepped aside and swung back the iron gate of the lift.

At the door of number sixteen, she repeated the performance for the benefit of Hitler's housekeeper. She got a long look before she was admitted to a modestly proportioned flat furnished with ornate dark wood furniture and insipid oil paintings. She sat in a chintz-covered armchair and listened to the clock for a time.

About seven p.m., the housekeeper returned and said she was going out to her sister's. "Are you sure the Führer wished you to wait?"

"Absolutely."

"Then it is better, I think, if you sit in my apartment. There is a connecting door."

So Rigby transferred. The adjoining flat was more agreeable; for one thing, it had a kitchen where she was able to make coffee for herself. After two hours she made a second cup and there came a time when she had made four. She had resolved not to leave without speaking to Hitler, but the possibility now arose that he had gone elsewhere to sleep, because it was past two a.m. Apparently the housekeeper wasn't coming back either. In the next hour or so

Rigby twice dozed until her head lolled uncomfortably. She got up to look for somewhere to stretch out.

She didn't care to be found in the housekeeper's bedroom. If there was a guest room she would use that. She tried a door opposite the bathroom and found it locked, but the key was in place. She turned it and reached for the light switch. How charming, she thought, and what a surprise! Pastel colours. White, modern furniture. All very feminine. A single bed with the sheets turned back as if for airing. A pale yellow night-dress tossed across the pillows. A pierrette's carnival costume with black pompoms hanging from the white wardrobe. Dance programmes and invitation cards ranged along the mantelpiece. Rigby picked one up. The date of the dance was September, 1931.

1931?

She looked at the other cards. All were dated 1931 – *seven years ago.*

She crossed to the bed and picked up the nightdress. It smelt musty. Horrible. She'd heard of this morbid custom before. When some loved one died, their room was preserved exactly as they left it. On Queen Victoria's orders, Prince Albert's room at Windsor had been left intact for forty years after his death. Rigby had just walked into a shrine.

Feeling the gooseflesh rise, she turned to leave. Something else caught her eye, a photograph in a silver frame on the dressing-table. Out of some intuition she picked it up. A young girl was pictured beside Hitler. He had his hand on her shoulder. Rigby stared at the picture. The girl could have been herself. The face was her own. The photo-frame slipped from her fingers and hit the floor, shattering the glass.

She gave a cry, not merely from shock. Footsteps were coming fast along the corridor, the heavy tread of a man. She spun around to face the open door. Hitler stood there in his braces, an older, more strained Hitler than the photograph had shown.

For once he looked unguarded, vulnerable, not in command. He said in a whisper, "Geli?"

Rigby shook her head.

He stepped towards her, hands outstretched as if to discover whether she was flesh and blood. His eyes glistened moistly.

She shrank from him.

Suddenly words gushed from her. "I'm not your Geli. I shouldn't be here, I admit. I'm English. My name is Dorothy Rigby and I came to see you to explain about your Adjutant –"

Terrifyingly, he became the Führer again, shouting her down with his tirade. "You have no right in here! Nobody is allowed in here. You've smashed her picture, defiled her memory, mocked me, the Führer. What are you, a spy, a witch, a streetwalker? You'll be punished. How did you get here? Who let you in?"

She said, "You asked to meet me. You spotted me in the Osteria Bavaria." And it sounded appallingly lame.

He grabbed her arm. "Out of this room! Out! I spend fifteen hours settling the future of Germany, of Europe, dealing with old men and popinjays, and I come home to this. I shall call the Gestapo."

Rigby shouted back, "If you do, my friend from the finishing-school – remember her with the blonde hair? – will go to the British Ambassador and tell him you importuned me. You – the Reich Chancellor – importuned a foreign schoolgirl in a restaurant. Pick up that telephone, Herr Hitler, and your reputation is scarred for ever."

He let go of her and flapped his hand. "Ach – this is nonsense. Be off with you. I'm too tired to take this up."

It was a crucial moment. Manfred's fate was still paramount in Rigby's plans. "I refuse to leave until you've listened to what I have to say."

Hitler marched away towards his own apartment, but she followed him, talking fast, making sure that he heard her much-rehearsed, much doctored version of the practical joke she had played on Camilla, in which Manfred was blameless because he had answered a summons supposedly from his Führer, and been shot in the foot, heroically trying to prevent an assassination.

Hitler spun around and faced her. "How can you prove one word of this horse-shit?"

She felt the blood drain from her head. How *could* she prove the story. He was calling it horse-shit, but he wouldn't have asked the question unless he gave it some credence.

With a flair that would serve her well in years to come, Rigby picked her handbag off the chintz armchair she had first sat in, took out her posture certificate and handed it to Hitler.

He stared at it for longer than he needed to read it. Finally he handed it back and said in a hard, tight voice, "Go back to my housekeeper's quarters. Tonight you will remain there."

Rigby obeyed. She heard the key turn in the lock behind her. She didn't need telling that every exit would be locked. She pushed two armchairs together, climbed into them and curled up, praying she had done the right thing for Manfred.

"Last night you said you were English."

She opened her eyes to Hitler, in uniform, leaning over the back of the armchair. It was daylight. In the background were the voices of others in the flat.

"Yes."

"You speak good German also."

"I like languages."

"This morning I am to receive your Prime Minister on a private visit before he returns to England. You will assist my regular translator, Dr Schmidt. Tidy yourself."

Rigby collected her wits. "I see. You want to pass me off as your interpreter."

"Do as I say."

She saw presently that the two apartments throbbed with activity. Aides, secretaries and domestic staff had been hastily summoned after word had come through from Neville Chamberlain that he wanted one more session with Hitler. Clearly, Rigby's presence in the place wanted some explaining, so a job had been found for her.

When the British delegation arrived, Rigby was in the room, at Schmidt's elbow. She knew nothing of the agreement signed the previous night, so it shocked her to glean from what Chamberlain was saying that Hitler had run rings around the English and the French. Czechoslovakia now had ten days to hand over the Sudetenland to Germany. In the cold light of morning Chamberlain was looking for something to save his face when he got back to England.

That face, which Rigby had never seen except in photographs, looked strained and anxious. The Prime Minister expressed the wish that the Czechs would not be "mad enough" to reject the agreement. He said he hoped it would not be necessary for Germany to bomb Prague; in fact, he had hopes of an international agreement to ban bomber aircraft.

Hitler listened impassively to the translation. Finally, when it was clear that no more progress was possible, Chamberlain took two sheets of paper from his pocket and asked if Hitler would be willing to sign a statement on the future of Anglo-German relations.

"What is it?" asked Hitler. He passed it to Rigby. "You can translate."

She asked if she could have a moment to draft an accurate version in German. She took it to the writing-table, the famous "piece of paper" that Chamberlain was to proclaim as the evidence of "peace for our time".

When Rigby's translation was ready, Hitler gave it a glance. "Yes, I'll sign."

Chamberlain stepped forward to add his signature below Hitler's. Rigby blotted each copy of the document. She handed Hitler his, and then turned her back on him. This was her opportunity. Dexterously she made a substitution and handed

Chamberlain a note she had jotted on the reverse of her posture certificate: *SOS. Essential I return with you to England with a man who has vital information.*

To his credit, Chamberlain gave it a glance and placed it smoothly in his pocket. He shook hands with Hitler. Then he turned to Rigby and said, "And how charming to meet you once more, my dear. Perhaps the Führer will allow me to drive you home if your duties are over."

"They are," said Rigby.

The British had come in two cars, and Rigby travelled in the second. It made a detour to the finishing school. On the advice of one of the diplomatic staff she didn't go in. It was possible that the Gestapo were inside. But her heart pounded when a figure presently emerged on crutches and limped towards the waiting car.

Only it wasn't Manfred.

It was Camilla, disguised as a man. She sank beside Rigby, slammed the door and said to the driver, "Start up, for God's sake! The Gestapo are on their way." To Rigby she said, "Manfred's safe."

"What happened? Where is he?"

"Rigby – I'm sorry to tell you this. His wife collected him."

"His *wife*? *Manfred is married*?" The world caved in on Rigby.

"I know. It was a complete shock. There were two young children. Absolute sweeties. He doesn't deserve them. She arrived in a car twenty minutes ago. One of Manfred's colleagues had tipped her off that Hitler had ordered a raid on the school. I think they'll make it to the border. I dressed up like this in case the place is being watched. To put them off, you see."

Rigby was numb.

Even when the plane took off she felt no sense of relief at escaping. She would never trust a man again.

Fifty years on, that flight home is still a void in her memory. She does have some recollection of the landing at Croydon, when Chamberlain stepped off the plane to make his famous announcement to the press. In some of the photographs Rigby can be seen in the background, standing beside Camilla, who is wearing a trilby. She remembers the moment of horror when Chamberlain produced his famous piece of paper and waved it triumphantly. She recalls opening her handbag and checking that it still contained the agreement Hitler had signed.

Chamberlain was holding up a piece of paper with the words *Presented by the Führer for Good Posture.*

How was it, then, that shortly after, he appeared to read out the text of the agreement? As Rigby had observed, you could say one thing for Neville Chamberlain – his memory was phenomenal.

THE BEST SUIT

She was a talkative redhead and he couldn't hear a thing she was saying. Night clubs aren't places for conversation. Her mouth moved, sometimes making words, sometimes smiling. But it didn't matter. She'd moved in so close as she danced that her breasts kept touching him. Herbie tried to look cooler than he felt. He wasn't used to women coming onto him. He was forty-three, paunchy and five foot four. He wasn't even a regular clubber. He was there with about sixty other friends of Paddy, one of the regulars at his local. Paddy had decided to celebrate his fortieth in style.

After twenty minutes the strain got too much, and Herbie gestured that it might be time for a drink. The woman nodded and reached for his hand and they threaded a route to the bar. Even there it was difficult to talk without shouting, so he suggested finding a pub outside. But when they were in the street she said, "You're coming to my place. It's only a short walk."

Herbie didn't argue.

Her place was a two-storey house on Richmond Hill with a spectacular view of the lights reflected in the river. This was one classy lady. She handed him a bottle and told him to open it while she changed into something more relaxing. "I hope you're not a connoisseur," she said.

"What do you mean?" he said. "This is vintage bubbly."

"It isn't chilled."

"No problem." He popped the cork and filled two tall glasses.

"Tell me about yourself," she said when she came back in a red silk kimono. "What do you do for a living?"

"This and that." He didn't want to say he was unemployed. He'd been made redundant in April. "How about you?"

"I'm an entrepreneur."

Herbie wished he'd said he was an entrepreneur. It sounded better than this and that. "Cheers."

They touched glasses and drank.

"You're not married?" she asked.

"Divorced."

"Want to come to bed with me?"

"Try and stop me," Herbie said, and it seemed a smart answer. But she said, "Yes, I will."

He wasn't sure if he'd heard right. "What – stop me?"

"I'm not ready yet."

"So why did you mention it?"

"I wanted to make sure you fancy me. Relax. It's not a total no-no."

"Why invite me back and open a bottle if you're not in the mood?"

"I said relax." She reached for a remote and switched on Billie Holliday. "I don't even know your name yet."

He told her.

She said, "I'm Chloe. What's your taste in music?"

They talked jazz for a while, but Herbie's mind was about ten per cent involved. He was trying to understand why she'd invited him back and gone cold on him.

Then he had his answer. The door behind him opened and a man in a dark suit strolled in, as calm as the manager in a shoe shop except that he looked like a state executioner. Chloe wasn't fazed. She said, "What do you think?" And it was obvious she was speaking to the man, not Herbie.

The man took a long look at Herbie and said, "Turn your head."

This was so unexpected that Herbie did as he was told.

The man said, "He'll do."

Chloe said, "I knew you'd agree." Turning back to Herbie, she said, "I told him you were amazing."

Herbie had been called many things in his time. Amazing wasn't
one of them. "What's going on?" he asked, not liking this at all.

The man said to Chloe, "You tell him. I'm off." He crossed the
room to the main door and let himself out.

"Did I dream that?" Herbie asked.

"Brady's all right. He was giving me a second opinion."

"What for?"

"Don't worry. You passed. Want to make five grand and get an
Armani suit for nothing?"

"I don't get you."

"You might . . . if you play your cards right." She widened her
eyes a fraction.

"I don't follow any of this."

"That's the beauty, Herbie. You don't need to. If you're bright
– and I know you are – you take what's on offer and ask no
questions."

"Is it legal?"

"There you go – another question."

"I need to know what I'm getting into."

"No one's asking you to hold up a bank."

"What am I supposed to do?"

"Nothing, except be yourself."

"For five grand?"

"And a designer suit. And a date with me."

"Tonight, you mean?"

"You don't give up, do you? Tomorrow, you go for a fitting at
the Armani shop in Knightsbridge. It's important you look right.
Did I say you also get a shirt and tie and shoes? A dark shirt and a
white tie."

"Who's paying for all this?"

"Not you. I'll meet you in Sloane Street. You get the first
payment of a thousand pounds just for turning up. Would two-
thirty do?"

"I suppose."

"Do you want me to call a taxi?"

"Now?"

She nodded. He'd already concluded he wouldn't get lucky tonight. No bad thing. He'd lost most of his confidence when the man called Brady appeared from nowhere.

"I'll walk."

On the way home, he went over everything in his mind. Five grand *and* all the clothes. There had to be a catch. She'd said he wouldn't be asked to rob a bank, but what other scam could she be planning? In the club he'd got the impression she fancied him. What had happened later suggested another scenario. It seemed as if he'd been earmarked for a job. Chloe had brought him to the house to be vetted by Brady. Maybe she, or others, had been watching him before he ever set foot in the club.

She hadn't asked him to do anything illegal. What could he lose by going along to Knightsbridge tomorrow?

She stepped out of a silver Porsche the minute he arrived in Sloane Street. He couldn't see who was driving before it moved off.

"Let's get you suited," she said, taking his arm. She was in a white leather coat and red shoes with amazing high heels.

He wasn't used to shopping in Knightsbridge. The assistant showed them to a sofa and brought coffee and biscuits before any business was done. Then they were handed a book of designs. Herbie was measured and they looked at cloths.

Chloe made all the choices. She had a clear idea of what would look best. She also picked the shirt, the tie, the shoes and the socks. The suit would be ready on Friday.

"That will do," she said to the salesman, "and this is my treat, so I'll settle for everything now." While the bill was being prepared she took a wad of fifty-pound notes from her bag and handed it to Herbie. "The first thou, as promised. You don't need to count it. Put it in your pocket and don't get mugged on the way home."

"What happens next?" he asked.

"You come back for a fitting in about a week and then you collect the suit when they tell you."

"Will you be here?"

She laughed. "You're a big boy. You can manage without me."

"So what happens after?"

"You have a mobile?"

He told her the number and she stored it in her phone.

"I'll be in touch," she said. "Don't lose any sleep. When it comes, it'll be your benefit night." She was texting as she spoke. "To my driver," she explained.

As they left the shop, the Porsche pulled up outside. She kissed Herbie lightly on the lips before getting in. "See you soon, Herbie."

He hailed a taxi. He wasn't returning in the tube. He was in a bigger league now with his boxes of new clothes and a grand in his pocket.

In under two weeks the suit was ready. Superb. No one would have known he had a paunch. He was tempted to wear it to the pub, just to get a reaction from Paddy and the others, but he decided against it. They'd demand an explanation and he didn't want to tell them the truth of it. Those yobs wouldn't understand why he hadn't spent the night with Chloe. He'd be a laughing-stock. And if he told them about the money they'd insist on drinks all round for the rest of the evening. Anyway, this adventure wasn't over yet. Chloe had promised him a benefit night.

He heard nothing else for ten days. The suit waited in his wardrobe in its zipped cover. He'd unpacked the shirt and it was on a hanger next to the suit. He was beginning to arrive at an understanding of that strange evening at the night club – how a classy lady like Chloe must have been attracted by his chunky physique and rhythmic movement in the strobe lighting and then a touch disappointed by his Chelsea FC shirt and blue jeans when she got him home. Clearly she liked formality in her men.

He'd pushed to the back of his mind the sinister Brady who'd looked him over and said he would do. In Herbie's eyes the night club episode had been all about Chloe and her taste in men.

The call came early on a Thursday morning when Herbie was walking back from collecting his paper and milk at the corner shop. Chloe's sexy voice was unmistakable. "Hi, Herbie. Are you up for it today?"

"Try me."

"Do you know the Black Bess in Hounslow?"

"I've heard of it." But not in a good connection, a little voice said inside his head.

"Be there at nine-thirty sharp tonight."

"In the gear?"

"Of course. Take a taxi. I'll be inside with some friends. Walk in and kiss me on the lips and take a seat beside me. Someone will bring you a Diet Coke. That's what you drink, right?"

"Actually I drink bitter."

"Tonight you're on Diet Coke. Everyone will treat you with respect, but you have to conduct yourself with dignity. At the end of the evening you get your reward."

"I'm not much good in company."

"Stay quiet then. Let the others do the talking."

The suit made him feel like a movie star. He looked in the mirror and winked. Benefit night. He dabbed on some of his favourite aftershave.

He took the taxi as instructed. The Black Bess was a large pub in Hounslow High Street with an ornate Victorian exterior and a sign with a masked Dick Turpin galloping his famous horse. Maybe the idea of highway robbery had been the reason Herbie had been troubled when the pub was mentioned. He paid the driver, checked his watch, took a deep breath and went in. There was loud music and the yeasty smell of beer. He looked for Chloe and spotted her with some people at a table to his right. She had her back to him. He strolled over, rested a hand on her shoulder, leaned down and kissed her on the lips.

She said just for his ears, "What are you wearing?"

He said, "The things we bought."

"The aftershave. It's cheap. Wash it off at the first opportunity."

The group had suspended whatever had been under discussion. They eyed Herbie with what seemed to be respect, even awe. One of them, he was disturbed to see, was Brady. Those cold eyes locked briefly with Herbie's. Chloe said, "We left a chair for you."

Herbie noticed it was a better chair than anyone else's. He sat and drummed his fingers on the arms. One of the men (there were four altogether, all in good suits, and two women in black spaghetti-strap dresses) said, "What's your poison?"

Herbie twitched. His nerves were getting to him.

"What are you drinking?"

"A pint of – " Herbie had to correct himself. "No, a Diet Coke."

Brady snapped his fingers. The barmaid was watching, poised for the summons, and came over to the group. A fresh round of drinks was ordered. The others were drinking beer and vodka martinis. Herbie was envious but said nothing.

Chloe said to the others, "Well – what do you think of my discovery?"

Herbie came under full scrutiny again.

One of the men said, "You could have fooled me."

The second woman said, "It's uncanny."

The man nearest to him said, "He'd good. He's very good. But something isn't right."

Thinking of the aftershave, Herbie said, "Which way is the gents?"

The woman said, "Even the voice is spot on."

Brady said, "I'll show you."

Two of them accompanied him. He felt as if he had minders, especially when neither of them used the facilities. He rinsed his face and used the dryer. On the way back to the table, Brady said, "Relax. We know who you are."

But relaxing was difficult. The next two hours went slowly. The others talked among themselves about football and television, told a few jokes, ordered more drinks and did a lot of laughing. Brady took a few pictures with a digital camera. Herbie followed instructions and stayed quiet and sipped his Diet Coke, but it was a strain. He knew some better jokes than they did. He glanced a few times at Chloe to see if she'd forgiven him for the aftershave. He couldn't be certain.

Finally Chloe said, "It's eleven thirty, everyone."

They got up to leave.

Then a camera flashed. Someone who had been drinking at the bar had moved in and sneaked a picture. Immediately Brady grabbed the man and pinned him to the wall. Chloe said to Herbie, "Keep walking. He'll deal with it."

The group reassembled outside the pub. Herbie wondered if he was going home with Chloe, but that didn't seem to be in the plan. She said, "I've arranged for you to be driven home in the Porsche. You'll find your pay on the back seat. If we need you again I'll be in touch."

"Is that it?"

"For tonight, yes. You did a good job."

"I'd like to see you again."

She said in a low voice, "Don't push it, Herbie."

The Porsche drew up and Herbie got in. As promised, an envelope stuffed with fifty pound notes was on the back seat. He tried to be philosophical and let the money cushion his frustration.

Back in his comfortable jeans and Chelsea shirt next day, he could hardly believe his strange experience. But the four grand in his top drawer was real and so was the suit hanging in his wardrobe. He decided to treat himself to an early beer at his local. The barman held the fifty pound note to the light to look for the watermark, just as Herbie had done when he took it from the packet. It was kosher.

The pub was quiet. Just a couple of pensioners playing crib and one of the regulars picking horses from a paper. He'd discarded the inside pages, so Herbie picked them up to see what was happening in the world.

Not much. Another drug scandal involving a pop star. A feature on violence in the classroom.

Then he turned a page and saw a large picture of himself wearing his Armani suit. The caption, in large letters, was OUT. With heart pounding, he read the story underneath.

> Spotted last night in his favourite haunt, the Black Bess in Hounslow, Jimmy "The Suit" Calhoun. The feared king of West London's underworld was released this week after a three year stretch in Pentonville for the injuries inflicted on "Weasel" Mercer, leader of a rival gang in Chelsea. One of Mercer's ears was slashed off with a cut-throat razor said to have been wielded by Calhoun himself in the fracas behind Stamford Bridge in 2005. Our crime correspondent, Phil Kingston, writes that Calhoun's reappearance will be viewed in some quarters as a declaration of intent considering that Mercer has taken over much of his territory in the three years since. Nicknamed The Suit for his taste in

expensive clothes, Calhoun was alleged to be making millions in protection, "putting the arm" on pubs, betting shops and restaurants south of the river, but his funds were never traced. A police source said Scotland Yard will deal vigorously with any revival of the out and out gang warfare of the recent past.

Herbie dropped the paper. No question: the picture was of him. It hadn't been Jimmy Calhoun in the Black Bess last night. It had been Herbie Collins. How could they get it so wrong?

He was shaking. He turned the paper over so that no one else would see the picture, thinking as he did so that he couldn't stop a million other readers from seeing it. He picked up his glass and had to grip it with both hands. People were going to think he was an underworld king, a vicious hoodlum who'd slashed off another man's ear and been locked away for three years. He could ask the paper to print a correction, he supposed, but really the damage to his reputation was done.

With a sense of doom he pieced together the clues that made sense of this. The people in the Black Bess had looked at him in his suit and made comments like "uncanny" and "you could have fooled me". They'd stared at him in a way he'd never experienced before, and the explanation could only be that he resembled the real Jimmy Calhoun. Everyone is supposed to have a double somewhere in the world. His unfortunately happened to be the most vicious man in London.

His thoughts moved on to Chloe. It was hard to credit that such a stunningly attractive woman should have got into bad company – the worst, in fact. Clearly she felt some loyalty to Calhoun or she wouldn't be working for him. Herbie could only suppose money had been the turn-on. Money and power are said to be irresistible to women. She'd gone to all the trouble of seeking out a double, someone to take the risk of sitting in that pub with the rest of Calhoun's henchmen, symbolically reclaiming his manor, an act of provocation that could have resulted in death.

Herbie shuddered. Good thing he hadn't been aware how dangerous it was.

Still, he'd carried it off, and carried off five grand and the Armani suit. Pity he hadn't carried off Chloe as well, but that would have been pushing it, as she had pointed out.

Three weeks passed and he heard no more from Chloe. He supposed he'd served his purpose and been taken off the payroll. The trouble was that he couldn't get Chloe out of his mind. She was a lovely, misguided woman seduced by money and power, he'd convinced himself. How could she respect Calhoun after he'd behaved in such a cowardly fashion, letting someone else double for him and risk being killed?

He'd thrown away the aftershave she'd called cheap. What a fool he'd been to use it. He ought to have expected such a classy woman to know it was third-rate.

Thinking about her constantly, he went to Harrods and purchased an aftershave that cost sixty pounds. It was called *Je t'adore*. He also bought a new tie, pure silk, by Galliano.

That evening, in what he now thought of as his slob clothes, the jeans and the Chelsea shirt, he was in his local with Paddy and the others watching football on the big screen TV and trying to forget Chloe. At half-time there was a short news bulletin. None of them paid much attention. Herbie only caught the item when it was almost through:

"... are treating it as a gangland killing. Mercer, known as the Weasel, had become increasingly powerful in recent years and taken over much of the so-called empire formerly run by Jimmy the Suit Calhoun, who was released from prison last month after serving three years for grievous bodily harm. Calhoun's present whereabouts are unknown."

Herbie didn't stay for the second half. He told the others he was meeting a friend.

At home he turned on the 10.30 news and got the full story. Someone had pumped two bullets into Mercer's head in a barber's shop in Fulham. The killer had made his escape in a silver Porsche.

Herbie's first reaction was immense relief. He'd not felt safe since his picture had been in the paper. It had been no fun walking the streets of West London wondering if one of the Weasel's mob would mistake him for Calhoun. The killing of the Weasel had to be good news.

But it wasn't.

The more Herbie pondered the changed situation, the more alarming it became. The Weasel was dead, but his people weren't going to disband. Gang warfare had broken out. Anyone with a resemblance to Calhoun was in mortal danger.

Moreover, as the TV news had strongly hinted, Calhoun was the obvious suspect for the murder of the Weasel. Every copper in London would be on the lookout.

His situation was perilous.

He decided he needed protection. He was entitled to it. After all, he hadn't asked to become involved with Calhoun's mob. They'd pressganged him. To put it better, he'd been snared in a honey trap.

OK, they'd paid him good money, but they hadn't told him his life was on the line. They had to understand the consequences of their actions. He didn't have much confidence in approaching them, but he reckoned if he could appeal to Chloe's conscience she might have some influence. After all, she'd hinted at more than just monetary rewards. He still believed she fancied him.

He waited till after dark the next evening, when he felt safer out on the streets. He would have taken a taxi, but he didn't know

Chloe's address except that it had been somewhere on Richmond
Hill. He'd decided to walk, wearing the suit and the new tie and the
Je t'adore.

The house was higher up the steep hill than he remembered.
He'd been on cloud nine when he'd come here before. Tonight the
place seemed to be in darkness. He hoped she was home. As he
opened the gate and walked up the small path towards the porch a
pair of coachlamps came on and a security light dazzled him.

A voice at his side said, "What do you want?"

He turned to find himself almost nose to nose with the scary
Brady.

Should have realised Chloe's house would be under guard, he
thought. "I, em – "

Brady cut in, his tone and manner transformed. "It's you, boss.
Sorry. Didn't expect you so early."

The new tie, the artificial light or the unscheduled appearance.
Whatever it was, Brady himself had fallen for it.

Herbie shrugged and smoothly got into character. "Make
yourself useful and let me in. Is she home?"

"Yes, boss." Brady produced a key and opened the door.

Herbie stepped inside. "See we're not disturbed."

"You bet." The door closed.

Chloe's voice called out, "Who's there?"

"It's OK," Herbie called back. "It's me."

"Hey, what a wonderful surprise!" She came into the hall and
hugged him. Then she stood back and smoothed her hand under his
tie. "This is new. Cool. And you smell so nice. Someone knows
how to turn a girl on."

He'd been rehearsing a little speech about the dangers he was in
now that the Weasel had been murdered, but it would have to wait.
Chloe was still holding his tie, loosening it. She said, "Shall we go
upstairs?"

Herbie said, "Why not?"

And that was how he finally got his benefit night. Deceitful? Yes. Unforgivable? No. Not in the light of what happened. Two or three times she said, "You're amazing. They should lock you up more often. I swear you're bigger than ever."

He said, "It's because of you. So amazing. I've waited so long for this." He was coming to his third climax when there was a bang like a car backfiring.

Chloe said, "Was that in my head, or did you hear it too?"

"It was out in the street."

"Yes. Hold me closer, Jimmy. Don't stop."

He didn't, but he felt compelled to say, "Actually, I'm Herbie." She was crying out in ecstasy.

Finally the moment passed and she said, "You were kidding, of course."

"No." He paused. "I did say I'd like to see you again."

He was prepared for the backlash and he deserved it. But she said nothing to him. Instead she reached for the phone at her bedside and pressed one of the buttons. "Brady, was that a gun going off just now?"

Herbie was so close that he heard every word of Brady's answer.

"It's OK, Chloe. I dealt with it."

"What was it?"

"Only that little runt we used as a double. He tried to get past me, making out he was the boss, so I totalled him."

"Oh my God! Killed him?"

"Put one through his head. No problem. He was a nobody. I'll take care of the body."

She put down the phone. She had her hand to her mouth. "The dumbfuck shot Jimmy. We're all finished."

"I'm not finished," Herbie said. "But I could have been. Seems to me I've had a lucky escape."

"We were all on his payroll."

"Do you know where he kept the money?"

"Various accounts under other names."

"You have the details?"

"I know where to look for them. But Jimmy always collected the cash in person."

Herbie folded his arms and grinned. "Then it looks as if you're going to need my help."

There was a long pause. Chloe's eyes widened. "Would you?"

"No one else needs to know he's gone," Herbie said. "Not even Brady. Let him carry on thinking he murdered me. I'll feel safer that way."

"You'll have to practise the signatures he used."

"I can do that."

"And if you're going to carry this off, you'll have to take over his life."

"And all that goes with it," Herbie said, stretching his limbs.

The police never succeeded in solving the murder of The Weasel, or the disappearance of Herbie Collins. But they earned some praise when the crime rate in West London dipped dramatically. The Calhoun gang seemed to have lost interest in armed robberies and protection rackets. The probation service said it spoke volumes for prison as a instrument of reform.

Herbie moved in with Chloe and found no difficulty adapting to the lifestyle of a millionaire ex-crook. On a Saturday he was often seen in the directors' box at Chelsea and he'd pass the evenings in the Black Bess with his friends. The nights were always spent with Chloe and the last thing she would whisper to him before falling asleep was always, "You're the best Suit."

THE MAN WHO JUMPED FOR ENGLAND

I laughed when I was told. I took it for a party joke. There was nothing athletic about him. People put on weight when they get older and they shrink a bit, but not a lot. Willy Plumridge was five-two in his shoes and the shape of a barrel. His waistline matched his height. If Sally, my hostess, had told me Willy sang at Covent Garden or swam the Channel, I'd have taken her word for it. *Jumped for England*? I couldn't see it.

"High jump?" I asked Sally with mock seriousness.

She shrugged and spread her hands. She didn't follow me at all.

"They're really big men," I said. "You must have watched them. If you're seven feet tall, there are two sports open to you – high-jumping and basketball."

"Maybe it was the long jump."

"Then you're dealing in speed as well as size. They're sprinters with long legs. Look at the length of his. And don't mention triple jumping or the pole vault."

"Why don't you ask him which it was?"

"I can't do that."

"Why?"

"He'd think I was taking the piss."

"Well," she said. "All the time I've known him – and that's ten years at least – people have been telling me he once jumped for England."

"In the Olympics?"

"I wouldn't know."

"Bunjee-jumping, I could believe."

117

"Is that an international sport?"

"Oh, come on!"

Sally said, "Why don't I introduce you? Then maybe he'll tell you himself."

So I met Willy Plumridge, shook the hand of the man who jumped for England. I can't say his grip impressed me. It was like handling chipolatas. He was friendly, though, and willing to talk. I didn't ask him straight out. I came at it obliquely.

"Have we met before? I seem to know your face."

"Don't know yours, sport," he said, "and my memory is good."

"Could be from way back, like school, or college."

"I doubt it, unless you were in Melbourne."

"Melbourne, Australia?" My hopes soared. If he was an Aussie, I'd nailed the lie already.

"Yep. That's where I did my schooling. My Dad worked for an Australian bank. The family moved there when I was nine years old."

"You're English?"

"Through and through."

Not to be daunted, I tried another tack. "They like their sport in Australia."

"And how," he said.

"It's all right if you're athletic, but it wouldn't do for me," I said. "I was always last in the school cross-country."

"If you were anything like me," Willy said, "you stopped halfway round for a smoke. Speaking of which, do you have one on you? I left my pack in the car."

I produced one for him.

"You're a pal."

"If I am," I said, "I'm honoured."

That first dialogue ended there because someone else needed to be introduced and we were separated. Willy waved goodbye with the fag between his fingers.

"Any clues?" Sally asked me.

"Nothing much. He grew up in Australia, but he's English all right."

She laughed. "That's half of it, then. Next time, ask about the jumping."

Willy Plumridge and his jumping interrupted my sleep that night. I woke after about an hour and couldn't get him out of my mind. There had to be some sport that suited a stunted, barrel-like physique. I thought of ski-jumping, an event the English have never excelled at. Years ago there was all that fuss about Eddie the Eagle, that likeable character who tried the jump in Calgary and scored less than half the points of any other competitor. A man of Willy's stature would surely have attracted some attention if he'd put on skis. The thought of Willy in skintight Lycra wasn't nice. It was another hour before I got any sleep.

I knew I wouldn't relax until I'd got the answer. I called Sally next morning. "Is it possible he did winter sports?"

"Who?"

"Willy Plumridge."

"Are you still on about him? Why don't you look him up if you're so bothered about this?"

"Hey, that's an idea."

I went to the reference library and started on the sports section, checking the names of international athletes. No Willy Plumridge. I looked at winter sports. Nothing. I tried the internet without result.

"He's a fraud. He's got to be," I told Sally when I phoned her that night. "I've checked every source."

She said, "I thought you were going to look him up."

"I did, in the library."

"You great dummy. I meant look him up in person. He's always in the Nag's Head lunchtimes."

"That figures," I said with sarcasm. "The international athlete, knocking them back in the Nag's Head every lunch-time."

But I still turned up at the bar next day. Sally was right. Willy Plumridge was perched on a bar stool. I suppose it made him feel taller.

"Hi, Willy," I said with as much good humour as I could raise. "We met at Sally's party."

"Sure," he said, "and I bummed a fag off you. Have one of mine."

"What are you drinking, then?"

The stool next to him was vacant. I stood him a vodka and tonic.

"Do you work locally?" I asked.

"Work?" he said with a wide grin. "I chucked that in a long while ago."

He was under forty. Of course, professional sportsmen make their money early in life, but they usually go into coaching later, or management. He'd made a packet if he could spend the rest of his life on a bar stool.

I had an inspiration. I pictured him slimmed down and dressed in silks and a jockey cap. "Let me guess," I said. "You were at the top of your profession. Private jet to get you around the country. Cheltenham, Newbury, Aintree."

He laughed.

"Am I right?" I said. "Champion of the jumps?"

"Sorry to disappoint," he said. "You couldn't be more wrong. I wouldn't go near a horse."

Another theory went down the pan.

"Wouldn't put money on one either," he said. "I invest in certainties. That's how I got to retire."

"I wish I knew your secret," I said, meaning so much more than he knew.

"It's simple," he said. "I got it from my Dad. Did I tell you he was in banking? He knew the way it works. He told me how to make my fortune, and I did. From time to time I top it up, and that's enough to keep me comfortable."

Believe it or not, I'd become so obsessed with his jumping that I wasn't interested in how he'd made his fortune through banking. Maybe that was why he persisted with me. I was a challenge.

"If you were to ask me how I did it, I couldn't tell you straight off," he said. "It wasn't dodgy. It was perfectly legit, well, almost. I'm an honest man, Michael. Thanks for the drink, but I have to be going. Next time it's on me."

I ran into Sally a couple of days later. She asked if I was any the wiser. I told her I was losing patience with Willy Plumridge. I didn't believe he'd jumped for England. Ever.

"But are you getting to know him?" she asked.

"A bit. He strikes me as a bullshitter. He was on about making a fortune out of banks. No one does that without a sawn-off shotgun."

"He's not kidding," she said. "He's fabulously rich. Drives a Porsche and updates it every year. If he offers to let you in on his secret, let me know."

"Sally, the only thing I want to know –"

"Ask him, then."

One more possibility came to me during another disturbed night. I broached it next lunchtime in the pub. "You must have done plenty of flying in your life, Willy."

"Enough."

"I was wondering if you ever went in for parachuting."

"Me? No way. What makes you think that?"

"Someone told me you were a very good jumper."

"*That*?" he said with a laugh. "That wasn't parachuting."

"They said you jumped for England."

"And it's true." He took a sip of his drink.

I waited for more and it didn't come.

"What do you do to earn a crust, Mike?" he said.

"I'm a freelance illustrator. Kids' books, mostly."

"Satisfying work – but not too well-paid, I reckon."

"That's about right."

"Suppose there was a way to set yourself up with a good amount of cash. Would you take it?"

"Depends," I said. "It would have to be honest."

"I like you," he said, "so I'll tell you how I made my first million. You've heard about Swiss bank accounts?"

"Where people salt away money with no questions asked?"

"That's the myth. Actually a lot of questions are asked. It's no simple matter to open a Swiss bank account with a suitcase full of banknotes. The gnomes of Zurich have strict banking laws these days. Customers have to be identified. You have to convince the bank that what you are depositing isn't the proceeds of a crime. Various money-laundering scandals have led to stringent legislation being introduced. These days you can't open a numbered account, as you once could, without identifying yourself. The beneficial owners of accounts have to be declared. As they should."

"Agreed," I said, uncertain where this was leading.

"They've also tightened up on withdrawals. The whole point of using Switzerland is that every account is rigidly protected. Great Uncle Edward dies and leaves you everything and there's a rumour that he was stashing away money in a Swiss account. Can you find out from the bank? No. All you get is a petrifying glare and a reminder that they are bound by their banking codes. In another twenty years, the bank can claim the money. There are said to be tens of billions locked away in dormant accounts in Switzerland. The gnomes bide their time and then collect."

"What a racket," I said.

"Yes, and as soon as any of the big names gets in trouble and questions are asked about the funds they salted away, the banks freeze the accounts. Noriega, Markos, Ceausescu, Sukarno. But I don't care about monsters like that. It's Great Uncle Edward I feel sore about. I won't say the little people because we're talking serious money here. Let's say family money, Mike. It should stay in the family, right?"

"Right."

"Well, I'm uniquely placed to help out people like the family of Great Uncle Edward. My Dad – the banker – had a contact in one of the great Swiss banks. Someone he trusted, a man of honour who had a conscience about these unfortunate families trying to get information. His hands were tied. There was nothing he could do within the Swiss banking system. But he knew the magic numbers the families needed, you see. He passed the numbers to Dad, who passed them to me. Then it was just a matter of matching the right families to the money that rightly belonged to them. It involved some basic research. Anyone can look at a will in most countries of the world. You find the beneficiaries and you offer to help."

"For a fee?"

"A small commission."

"A small percentage of a big sum?"

He smiled. "You're getting the idea, Mike."

"So you pass on the information about the account numbers?"

"And the sums involved. Dad's friend listed the balances with the numbers. So I'm the bearer of good news. I've made a big difference to some people's lives."

Including your own, I thought. Not bad.

I said, "I guess some of this money is ill-gotten gains."

"I never enquire," he said. "If Great Uncle Edward was a train robber, or painted fake Van Goghs, it's no concern of mine. The way I see it, the family has more right to it than the bank. Are you with me?"

"I think so," I said.

"I'm only mentioning this because I think you can help me."

I hesitated. "How?"

"Well, I still have details of a few accounts I haven't been able to follow up, and time is running out. The twenty-year rule means that the banks will scoop the pool if something isn't done. I begrudge them that. I feel I owe it to the memories of my old Dad and his friend – who also died about the same time – to recover that money.

These are families I haven't traced yet. I've found the wills, but the beneficiaries are more elusive."

"You want someone to do the research, track them down?"

He shook his head. "There isn't the time. What I need is someone I can trust to approach the bank and show them the documentation and claim the money for the estate."

"What – go to Switzerland?"

"That isn't necessary. They have a City of London branch. I'd do it myself, but they know my face from a previous claim."

"You want me to pretend I'm acting for the family?"

"Pretend? You *will* be acting for them, Mike. I've opened an executors' account. You show them the copy of the will and the death certificate and they verify that the names match. You give them the account details, which they confirm with Zurich. They write you a cheque, and bingo!"

"Why should they deal with *me*?"

"To keep them happy, you say you're one of the executors."

"I don't like the sound of that."

"Don't worry, Mike. I'll give you proof of identity."

"No, this isn't right."

"Would five per cent make it right?"

I didn't speak.

"Think it over," he said. "Let me know tomorrow, or the next day. No sweat."

Plenty of sweat. Another night of disturbed sleep. This time I was wrestling with my conscience. It was a scam and a clever scam. But the only loser would be a bank that was about to get a fortune that didn't belong to it.

Much neater than pointing a gun at a cashier. This was beating them at their own game, with account numbers and cheques.

Could I trust Willy Plumridge? He had the lifestyle that backed his story. Good suits, a Porsche, usually parked outside the pub. I hadn't seen his house, but Sally had told me he had two, and they were both big places.

In the morning my credit card statement arrived. I owed them three grand and some more.

"If I did this," I said to Willy, "how much would I make out of it?"

He took out a calculator and pressed some buttons. "Give or take a few pence, fifty-five grand."

I tried to sound unimpressed. "So it's a sizeable inheritance?"

"You can work it out."

"And there won't be any problem with the family?"

He grinned. "The beauty of it is that we don't know where they are. And when we trace them – if we do – they're going to be so delighted by this windfall that they won't begrudge us our commission. Believe me, Mike, this isn't the first such deal I've negotiated."

I had my doubts whether Willy's efforts to trace the family would yield a quick result. Maybe, like the bank, he reckoned the money should come to him after a passage of time.

Fifty-five grand would set me up for a couple of years at least. I could do some real painting for a change, get off the treadmill of cute teddy-bears and badgers dressed as postmen.

"Would this be a one-off?"

"Has to be," Willy said. "I couldn't use you again. I have to find some other guy I can trust."

"So we can draw a line under it?"

"You'll never hear from me again. It'll be as if we never met."

"I'd prefer the money in cash, if that's possible."

"No problem."

He was efficient. He'd done this before. A packet arrived at my house two days later. Inside were the details of the Swiss bank account of the late James Alexander Connelly, standing at £1,106,008, his death certificate and his last will and testament, including the names of two executors, Harry and Albert Smith. I was to be Albert. There was a letter from Harry giving me authority to act on his behalf, and another from an English bank confirming that an executors' account had been opened. A birth certificate in Albert Smith's name was included as proof of identity.

Willy had told me to make an appointment. Banks don't like people coming in off the street and making big withdrawals. I was to say I was an executor for James Connelly's estate enquiring about the possibility of a bank account in his name. No more than that.

I called the bank and spoke to someone who listened without much show of interest and invited me in the next morning at eleven-thirty.

After another uneasy night I put on the only suit I owned, dropped my documents into a briefcase and took the train to London. Sitting there shoulder to shoulder with the business-men who commuted daily, I felt isolated, one of another species about to venture into their territory.

The bank was right in the City of London, a massive building with grey pillars. Unlike my own suburban bank, this one had a security guard and a receptionist. I mentioned my appointment and was shown to a seat. The décor was intended to intimidate: marble, mahogany and murals. Don't let them get you down, I told myself. They're the crooks.

They kept me waiting ten minutes, and it felt like an hour.

"Mr Smith."

I almost forgot to respond.

"This way, please."

The young woman showed me upstairs, where it was Persian carpets and embossed wallpaper. She opened a door. "Please go in and sit down. Mr Schmidt will be with you shortly."

Schmidt. One of the family? I said to myself, trying to stay loose. I sat back in a large leather chair and patted my thighs. I wasn't going to cross my legs in case I looked nervous.

Schmidt entered through another door. He looked younger than I expected, dark, with tinted glasses. "How can I help?"

I gave him the spiel, stressing that Uncle James had repeatedly spoken about his special account with the bank. After his death there had been a delay of some years before we – the executors – found his notes with the account details. "His filing system was non-existent," I said. "We came across the note in a book of handwritten recipes. We almost threw it out. As a cook, he was a dead loss."

"May I see?"

"I didn't bring the recipe book," I said. "I copied the figures."

"And do you have other evidence with you?"

I removed everything from the briefcase and passed it across.

Schmidt spent some minutes studying the documents. "It seems to be in order," he said. "Would you mind if I showed the papers to a colleague? We have to verify anything so major as this."

"I understand."

When he left the room I found I'd crossed my legs after all. I took deep breaths.

The wait tested me to the limit. Just in case there was a hidden camera, I tried to give an impression of calm, but pulses were beating all over my body.

When Schmidt returned, there was a cheque in his hand. "This is what you were waiting for, Mr Smith, a cheque for a million and just over two hundred thousand pounds. The account accrued some interest. All I require is your signature on the receipt."

Resisting the urge to embrace the man, I scribbled a signature.

"Your documents." He handed them across. "And now I'll show you out." He opened the door.

Slipping the cheque into an inner pocket, I stuffed the rest of the paperwork into the briefcase and went through that door walking on air.

Some people were in the corridor outside. I wouldn't have given them a second glance had not one of them said, "Mr Michael Hawkins."

My own name? I froze.

"I'm DI Cavanagh, of the Serious Fraud Squad."

I didn't hear the rest. I believe I fainted.

Three months into my sentence, I was transferred to an open prison in Norfolk. There, in the library one afternoon, I met Arthur, and we talked a little. He seemed more my sort than some of the prisoners. As you do, I asked him what he was in for.

"Obtaining money by deception."

"Snap," I said.

"Only I was caught with the cheque in my pocket," he said.

"Me, too. I was caught in a Swiss bank, of all places."

"How odd," he said. "So was I."

It didn't take long to discover we had both been talked into the same scam by Willy Plumridge.

"What a bastard!" I said. "And he's still at liberty."

"Waiting to find another mug to tease some money out of the bank," Arthur said. "I bet I wasn't the first."

"Well, he got rich by doing it himself, I gather," I said.

"True, but with less risk. In the early days of this racket, he traced the families and advised them. They made the approach to the bank, and it worked. They paid him well for the information. Later, he was left with the account numbers he couldn't link to a family, so he thought up this idea of finding people to pose as executors. Maybe it worked a few times, but banks aren't stupid."

"So I discovered. What I can't understand is why they haven't pulled him in. He's Mr Big. You and I are small fry."

"They won't touch him," Arthur said.

"Why?"

"He's the man who jumped for England."

That again. "Give me a break!" I said. "How does that make a difference?"

"Don't you know?" Arthur said. He glanced to right and left to make sure no one could overhear him. "One of those account numbers he got from his father belonged to someone pretty important. A former prime minister, in fact."

"No! Which one?"

"I never found out, except they're dead. Supposed to have been a model of honesty when in fact they were salting away millions in bribes. Willy got onto the family and offered to liberate the money without anyone finding out. The next generation had some heavy expenses to meet, so they hired him. The bank, of course, was utterly discreet and totally duped. Willy pulled it off and was handed the cheque. Then I don't know if his concentration went, or he was light-headed with his success, but he slipped on the stairs at Bank tube station, fell to the bottom and suffered severe bruising and concussion. He was rushed to hospital and no one knew who he was."

"Except that he was carrying the cheque?"

"Right. And various documents linking him to the family. The police called them. They panicked and said they knew nothing about Willy. He had to be an impostor and all the documents must be faked. After a night in the cells, he was charged with obtaining money by deception and brought before the magistrate at Bow Street. They put him on bail, pending further investigation. Only it never came to trial."

"Why?"

"The secret service intervened to avert the scandal. If it had ever got to court it would have destroyed a prime minister's reputation. They decided the best way to deal with it was for Willy to jump bail and go into hiding. No attempt was made to find him and the matter was dropped. The family cashed the cheque, Willy got his commission, and the good name of a great prime minister was saved from disgrace. That's why you and I are locked in here and Willy Plumridge is sitting in the Nag's Head enjoying his vodka and tonic. He did the decent thing and jumped for England."

SECOND STRINGS

M r Small was Mr Big, and that was no joke. It isn't wise to make fun of an underworld king.

"This is in confidence, right?"

"Goes without saying, Mr Small," Bernie said. Bernie wasn't the sharpest knife in the drawer, but he'd survived by being respectful of men of violence. He didn't much care for blood and guts. Crime didn't have to be messy. By nature he was a gatherer, rather than a hunter.

"I've got a job for you."

"Thanks," Bernie said, hoping it didn't involve murder.

"You've still got that Transit Van, I hope."

"Er, yes." Maybe a bullion job, Bernie thought, looking steadily into Sly Small's lizard eyes.

"I want you to collect something for me."

"No problem, Mr Small."

"You haven't heard the rest. This is a sizeable item. I'd say it weighs as much as you or me and is about your height. What are you – six feet?"

"Just over six." Oh, no, it's a corpse, Bernie thought. He wants me to collect a stiff.

"It's an instrument."

Bernie's mind switched to torture and his mouth went dry.

"A Horngacher."

It sounded excruciating.

"A musical instrument."

Now Bernie doubted if he was hearing right. What on earth would Sly Small – a man of brutal tastes – want with a musical instrument?

"You're a man who likes music, aren't you? I mean serious music. Beethoven and stuff."

Bernie listened to Classic FM on the car radio sometimes. It was scary how much Sly Small knew. "I suppose."

"This is in confidence," Sly said for the second time. "I'm only telling you because of your high taste in music. I sent my boy Rocky to one of them posh schools thinking it would help him when he steps into my shoes. Cost me an arm and a leg and after ten years of it, he's still pig ignorant. The only thing he can do is music. They sent him for an interview at the Royal College and he's in."

"Top result," Bernie said.

"Are you being sarky?"

"No, Mr Small. No way."

"If I thought you was being sarky I'd nail you to the wall."

"And you'd be right to do it," Bernie said.

Sly Small gave Bernie a long look. "I don't want this to get around. Rocky is getting a Horngacher. From me."

Bernie nodded.

"Don't look as if you know what a Horngacher is, you thick berk. I didn't know myself until a couple of days ago. It's a harp, a bloody great harp. Have a good laugh. My son and heir plays the harp. That's his instrument, okay?"

A *harp*. Bernie understood Sly Small's problem now. The criminal world would fall about laughing if it learned that Sly's son had turned into a harpist.

"He's flesh and blood," Sly said. "What can you do? If the boy had asked me for a Harley-Davidson I'd have given him one. He doesn't want a Harley, he wants a Horngacher. There's one called the Meisterharfe Horngacher. It's the Harley-Davidson of harps he says, worth fifty grand, easy. Your job is to pick one up for me."

"From a harp shop?" Bernie said.

"I didn't say *buy* one. What do you think I am? I've made inquiries, and there are only two Meisterharfe Horngachers known to be in Britain. One is in the Museum of Music in Winchester, and that's as secure as Fort Knox. But the other is out there being played. It's coming in tomorrow."

"Coming in where?"

"The Albert Hall, for some concert. It was being played last weekend in Prague, with the Royal Philharmonic. They use a big furniture van to drive the instruments across the continent. Should be arriving around mid-day. That's when you pick up the harp."

"It's all arranged?" Bernie said, much relieved.

"Plonker," Sly said. "What do you think you are – American Express? No one's going to ask you for the paper work. You're knocking it off, right?"

"It's a hold-up?"

"Depends how you want to play it. If I was you I'd wear a brown coat and say I was staff. Shove it in the van – carefully, mind – and drive off fast. Make sure you're not being followed and bring it here."

He made it sound simple. Bernie wasn't so confident. "If you don't mind me mentioning this, Mr Small, is this harp easy to recognise?"

"You know what they look like," Sly said. "Ever see a Marx brothers film?"

"No, what I'm saying is that when Rocky turns up at the Royal College with a harp that's hot – a hot Horngacher – he's likely to be in trouble, isn't he?"

"It's for home use, dickhead, for Rocky to enjoy in private. When he goes to college he can play one of theirs."

"Right."

It had to be faced. There was no persuading Sly Small that this was an ill-fated enterprise.

"It'll be in a case," Sly said. "But you handle it like it was a newborn baby, right? They're easily damaged. The carving, the gold leaf gilding. Over two thousand parts go into a harp, Rocky told me. I don't want a single one of them missing when you bring it here tomorrow night."

The next morning found Bernie parked on a meter opposite the Albert Hall. He was wearing a brown coat over his t-shirt and jeans. In the rear of his Ford Transit were straps, ropes and foam rubber mats. The Horngacher would be well protected. And so would he, with a Smith and Wesson Combat Magnum under his arm. He didn't plan to use the shooter. The sight ought to be enough.

He had got here early and found the only possible goods entrance. While he watched, a caterer's van arrived with food supplies. A couple of men in brown coats came from inside the building and started unloading. Maybe the coats were a shade darker than Bernie's, but he couldn't see that anyone would make an issue of it. Half the battle was behaving as if you belonged.

The driver finished the delivery and drove away. Bernie switched on the radio. Classic FM would help get him in the mood. A bit of Chopin would do wonders for his nerves.

Just after mid-day, his heartbeat increased noticeably as a large brown furniture van came up the street. On the side was written *Gentle and Good, Specialists in Musical Removals*. At the same time, four Albert Hall porters in their brown coats appeared.

Bernie waited for the van to back up to the arched entrance and then got out and crossed the street and walked around the back to join the porters. They would assume he was a Gentle and Good man; and the Gentle and Good men would assume he was on the Albert Hall roster. That was the theory, anyway.

"What have you got for us?" one of the porters asked.

"Royal Phil," Bernie said, trying to sound as if he'd been doing the job for years.

"The Bechstein grand," the porter said, pulling a face.

Bernie pulled a face as well. The Bechstein grand was evidently bad news.

The van driver and one other man came to the back and nodded to the others and said something about the traffic. They seemed to know each other, which was not good news for Bernie. He sidled to the back and waited with arms folded while they unlocked and opened up. What a relief it was to see a large case the shape of a harp lashed to the side of the van.

First he made a show of assisting with the grand piano, a heavy brute. It had to be wheeled with great care onto the lift mechanism. When it was at ground level, the Albert Hall team took over.

Bernie was left with the Gentle and Good men. "I'll take the harp," he said with authority. He'd noticed a set of wheels on the case. It would be just a matter of trundling it across the street to his own van. He stepped up and started unbuckling the straps.

"You want help?" the driver said.

"No, mate. I can handle this."

"We don't want an accident. You know who it belongs to?"

"Tell me then," Bernie said, giving his main attention to the straps.

"Igor Gurney."

"Ah." Bernie hadn't thought of the harp as belonging to anyone. He'd assumed it was owned by the Royal Philharmonic. On reflection, it was obvious that musicians liked to use their own instruments. He said, "He needn't worry. It's in good hands." He tilted it away from the side of the van and let the wheels take the weight. It was mobile. He manoeuvred it onto the lift, took a firm grip and said, "Bombs away."

The platform descended. Bernie wheeled the harp off. Now all he had to do was cross the street with it. "Want me to sign for this?"

The driver had his clipboard in his hand. "What?"

"The harp. I'm supposed to be taking it to the Festival Hall."

"I was told it was wanted here."

"Yes, but tonight he's giving a recital at the South Bank."

"You'd better sign for it, then."

Bernie signed the name of his ex-wife's current partner. Then, trying not to show undue haste, he steered the precious Horngacher across the street and opened the back of his Transit. It took quite an effort to hoist the thing inside. He attached the straps and bunched the foam rubber against the sides. When the job was done he stepped out and glanced across the street. The first of the porters was just coming through the archway. Bernie got in and started up. Mission almost accomplished.

He didn't put his foot down as he made his getaway along Kensington Gore Road. He drove with a care for the instrument. And he didn't want to get stopped for exceeding the limit.

On the radio they were doing commercials. Then the news. It crossed Bernie's mind that his daring heist might make the news bulletins later in the day.

The voice on the radio said, "And now a piece we should play more often, because I think you'll agree it touches the heart – the Mozart Concerto for Flute and Harp. This is a live recording made at the proms last year and featuring Jane Stine as the solo flautist and Igor Gurney, the blind harpist, with the Hall Orchestra."

Igor Gurney, the blind harpist.

Bernie's hands gripped the wheel. God help us, he thought, I've stolen a blind man's harp. What kind of monster am I?

He'd felt a twinge of conscience earlier, when he was told the harp belonged to a musician, and not the orchestra. To learn that the man was blind made him groan out loud. He pictured Igor Gurney with his white stick shuffling to the place where the Horngacher was supposed to be and finding nothing, his hands plucking at air.

He could also picture Sly Small sitting in his Surrey mansion waiting for the harp to be delivered, idly turning the cylinder of his revolver.

The soul-stirring notes of the concerto filled the van. Mozart and Igor Gurney were making a joint appeal. Get this, Bernie. Robbing a blind man of his harp is as low as you can get.

Bernie had done bad things in his life, like break-ins and hijacks. He'd stolen cars, shoplifted, cheated at cards and conned a few mugs out of a few grand. Until this point in his life he'd never wilfully hurt a handicapped person. There were limits, things even a hardened criminal hesitated to do.

I won't be able to live with myself, he thought.

Sucks to Sly Small. At the next turn he veered left, down Palace Gate. Shaking, sick with fear, he turned left again and worked his way though the streets towards Prince Consort Road and the Albert Hall.

The men were still unloading. His parking spot had gone, so he drew in beside the Gentle and Good van.

"You're back, then?" the driver said without any suggestion of blame. "Is something up?"

"Someone got their dates wrong," Bernie said. "Good thing I phoned ahead." He did this kind of deception well. People always believed him. "It's to go inside with the other instruments." He got out and unstrapped and lifted the Horngacher from the rear of the Transit. There was an immediate sense of relief. For once in his life he had done the decent thing. "Listen, I'd better find somewhere to park," he told the driver.

"No problem," the driver said. "I'll get one of your mates to wheel it in."

Bernie got in and drove away. The glow of virtue lasted about five seconds, until Sly Small reared up in his thoughts. What on earth could he do now? Go into hiding? Seek another identity? Verdi's Requiem was playing on the radio. He switched it off.

The solution came to him as he was waiting at a red light in Kensington High Street. Sly Small had spoken of a second Horngacher in some museum in Winchester. He glanced at the time. Winchester was a couple of hours' drive from here, straight down the M3. He could be there by four. He'd have no qualms about lifting a Horngacher belonging to a pesky museum. A harp shouldn't be gathering dust. It should be out there being played by some up-and-coming musician like Rocky Small. This would be an act of liberation.

Bernie put his foot down and headed for Winchester.

The signs for the Museum of Music came up on the outskirts of the city. The building, in its own grounds off Worthy Road, was a modern glass and concrete structure that looked pretty secure to Bernie's expert eye. Hadn't Sly likened it to Fort Knox? No matter. Bernie had devised a plan on the way down.

"We're closing at five," the young woman at the turnstile said. "Are you sure you wouldn't like to leave it for another day? There's so much to see."

"I'll have a quick trot round and get a sense of what's here," Bernie told her. "Is there a guidebook?"

She gave him a plan and he made a beeline for the harp section on the second floor. It was well stocked. They were Irish, Welsh, Grecian, Gothic and early American. He studied the labels of the larger harps. There was a Wurlitzer, an Erard and a Venus Paragon. They all looked pretty similar to Bernie's untutored eye. Where was the flaming Horngacher?

No need to panic, he told himself. Maybe they kept it in some other part of the museum. He looked at his watch. Four-thirty already. He studied the plan again. Somewhere on the ground floor was a display described as *The Layout of a Symphony Orchestra*. They had harps in symphony orchestras, didn't they? Bernie hurried downstairs.

At the far end of the building he found a large semi-circular area set out with music stands and the various instruments beside them. The harp was on a raised part at the rear left. He moved closer. A beautiful thing six feet high with gold leaf gilding. But was it the Horngacher?

He studied the label and groaned out loud. "*Obermeyer harp, made in Starnberg, Austria, about 1977.*"

Over the public address system came the voice of the woman at the admissions desk. "The museum will close in twenty minutes."

Beside him a different voice spoke up. She was wearing an official badge that said she was staff. "You look as if you're trying to find something. Can I help?"

With so little time left, he had no choice. He told her he'd come hoping to see a Horngacher.

"You're standing beside it," she said.

"But it says Obermeyer."

"Read the small print, and I think you'll find it was made by Horngacher. He took over the business from Obermeyer. If anything, he improved on them. He's known as the Stradivari of harp makers. Isn't the carving exquisite?"

Bernie wasn't looking at the carving. If anything was exquisite, it was the label that confirmed what he'd just been told. He'd found the Horngacher. All he had to do now was remove it from the building.

He glanced around at the security arrangements, the video surveillance and the metal shutters on the windows. This would not be simple.

The attendant glanced at her watch. "We're closing soon, I'm afraid."

On an inspiration, Bernie said, "Organs?"

She didn't understand.

"Where can I find the organs?"

"They're near the entrance. You must have passed them on the way in."

"Didn't notice. I was looking for this."

He thanked her and headed for the organ section. Organs were the biggest instruments Bernie could think of. Some fine examples were ranged along the main walkway to the entrance. After checking the video cameras he picked his organ, a Victorian church instrument with a fine set of pipes. It wasn't the largest in the display, but it suited him well. Making sure no one was about, he squeezed out of sight between the pipes and the wall.

A bell went off and he thought he'd triggered an alarm, but it was the five-minute warning that the museum was closing.

Now it was a matter of holding his nerve. The staff may have noticed he hadn't left yet. With luck, their minds were on other things like getting home as soon as possible. He listened to the footsteps as other visitors departed.

It went so quiet he could hear the woman on admissions say to someone, presumably a security officer, "All clear, then?"

"I'll do my check with the dog. Leave it to me."

With the dog? The hairs rose on the back of Bernie's neck.

What could he do? Wait here, to be savaged by a guard-dog? The woman said goodnight, followed by a door slamming. Then the rumble of something mechanical. The elevator. The security man was starting his check upstairs.

Bernie heard the sliding door open and close, and knew this was his opportunity. Two floors upstairs had to be checked. He must grab that harp and be away before the man and his dog reached the ground floor.

Speed mattered more than stealth. He emerged from his hiding place and ran to the far end, where the orchestra was displayed. Took a grip on the Horngacher and tried to shift it. Difficult. Not only was it heavy, but awkward, too. The harp at the Albert Hall, cased and on wheels, had lulled him into thinking this would be simple. It would take far too long to drag this thing the length of the building and out through the front door.

He looked around for inspiration. No convenient trolley, of course. But desperation breeds inventiveness. Bernie looked at the wood-block floor. And the conductor's dais, covered with a square of red carpet. He could use that carpet. With strength born of panic, he ripped it free of the tacks and placed it where he could persuade the Horngacher onto it. One big effort and the harp was in position. Now he could move it, tugging the rug with one hand and supporting the harp with the other.

The method worked. Once the rug was in motion, he was able to get up a reasonable speed. Of course it was a risk supporting fifty grands-worth of harp with one hand as he ran backwards, but Bernie had gone past the point of risk assessment.

He reached the entrance with its turnstile system. No way could he get the harp through or over the turnstile. There had to be another entrance for large items, and there was: a metal gate at the side. Locked.

There was no obvious way to shift it. After rattling the gate several times like a gorilla, he climbed over and looked at the other side. The bolt seemed to work by some electronic mechanism. Cursing, he went into the kiosk where the woman issued tickets. He found a switch and flicked it.

An alarm bell sounded.

In the din, he started flicking every switch, every key he could find. He tried the gate again. No result. And the security man and his dog would be down any second.

Instinctively he reached under his arm and drew the gun. Should have thought of it before. He fired at the bolt securing the gate. Magic. It swung free. He hauled the rug and harp through and across the stone floor of the foyer. Several finger bolts secured the front door. He loosed them and opened up. Outside, some porter, bless him, had left a hand trolley. Bernie grasped the harp and lifted it on and steered the precious load across the car park to where his van stood.

There wasn't time to strap the Horngacher in place. It would have to take its chance on the rubber mats. He opened the doors, heaved it in and slammed them shut.

Behind him he heard a shout. The security guard was at the museum door. The dog, a German shepherd, was racing across the car park. Bernie almost reached the front of the van when the dog sank its teeth into his leg below the knee. The pain was wicked. He fisted the dog, but it hung on, snarling. He dragged open the van door. More by luck than judgement the door struck the dog and threw it off him. Bernie heaved himself inside, closed the door, started up and drove off.

In the long history of thefts, this one didn't rate among the most efficient and ingenious, but so what, it had come off. Leg throbbing, breath rasping, heart racing, Bernie headed towards Surrey.

A couple of Mercs and a limo were on Sly Small's drive when Bernie drove up. Inside the limo, the driver was reading a paperback. He didn't give Bernie a glance.

"What kept you, birdbrain?" Sly said when he opened the door.

Bernie had his story ready. "There were too many police about. I took some back roads and got a bit lost."

"Did you fetch the harp?"

"No problem, Mr Small."

"Why are you limping if there was no problem?"

"My dodgy knee. I'm not used to humping heavy things around."

Sly didn't have much sympathy. "Hump it inside, then. We want to see this goddam thing."

Bernie noted the use of the plural and assumed Rocky was inside the house. It wouldn't have hurt Rocky to help lift his father's gift inside – an idea Bernie decided against mentioning. It wouldn't have hurt that driver, either, but he was still reading. Bernie braced himself for one final effort, grasped the Horngacher and staggered inside with it.

"In here," Sly's voice announced from the front room.

He just succeeded in getting in there before his arms gave way. The harp's base struck the floor with a thump. "Sorry." He stopped it from keeling over. Nothing seemed to be broken.

He took a couple of deep breaths before noticing who was in the room. Not Rocky, but a silver-haired man wearing shades. The man had started to rise from his chair when the harp hit the floor, but he sank down again.

"Do you want to check it, maestro?" Sly said to the man. "Good idea. Here, take hold of my arm."

This struck Bernie as odd. Sly wasn't the sort who offered his arm to anyone.

But the man seemed to take it as normal. He stood and waited for Sly to cross the room. Then he rested his hand lightly on Sly's arm and Bernie understood. The man was blind.

Sly was leading him towards the harp. He'd called him maestro. It didn't make any sense, but this had to be Igor Gurney, the harpist. Was it possible that Sly Small, for all his evil reputation, had experienced a crisis of conscience, just as Bernie had? Was he about to reunite the harp with its owner?

If so, they were in for a surprise.

The blind man reached the harp and felt for it. "Why isn't it in its case?" he asked. "It should have travelled in its case."

"I, em . . . the wheels came off," Bernie improvised. "It got too heavy, so I lifted it out."

The hands were all over the harp, feeling the carved columns and pedestals. "This isn't mine."

Bernie felt a surge of panic. He'd hoped one Horngacher was very like another. This one from Winchester would have fooled Sly for sure. And Rocky. He hadn't bargained on Igor Gurney checking it over.

"What do you mean?" Sly said. "It's got to be yours." He turned to Bernie. "You picked it up from the Albert Hall like I said, didn't you?"

"Well, yes . . ." Bernie started to say.

"It's a very fine instrument, but it isn't mine," Gurney insisted. He plucked at the strings. "It wants tuning. What have you done with my harp?"

"He's shafted us, the bastard," Sly said. "What kind of fools do you take us for?" Without warning, he pulled out a gun and shoved it into Bernie's ribcage. "I'll show you what I do to two-timing finks like you."

"No violence, please," Gurney said. Then the familiar bars of the *William Tell Overture* sounded from somewhere in his pocket. He pulled out a mobile phone and listened. His face registered extreme shock. "It's my chauffeur. The police are at the door."

"Flaming hell." Sly dropped his gun and kicked it out of sight under an armchair.

Bernie removed his and did the same. Just in time, because three armed officers stormed into the room and ordered them to lie face down on the floor.

"What's this about?" Sly said. "This is a private house."

"Having a musical evening were you?" one of the police said. "We decided to join you. I'm Sergeant Brinkley from the drugs squad and I have reason to believe you've just taken possession of a consignment of cocaine."

"Untrue," Sly said.

"Shut up. We have a search warrant. We've tracked this operation every mile of the way from Prague. You may be hot stuff on the harp, Mr Gurney, but you're no angel. We know how you bring the stuff in. Mike, open the top of the harp – known as the crown, isn't it, Mr Gurney? – and let's see how much is in there."

"I don't know what you're talking about," Gurney said.

"You're going to blame the driver, are you? We watched him at the Albert Hall loading the harp into his van. Got it on video. After that all we had to do was get down here and wait for him to make the delivery. Hurry up, Mike."

"It's hard to shift," the officer called Mike said.

Bernie's confidence began to grow again. If they'd really tracked every mile of the operation they'd know he'd returned Gurney's harp to the Albert Hall. Clearly they didn't.

"All right, the lid's off," Mike said. "Hang about – there's nothing in it."

Bernie, still with his face to the floor, smiled.

They asked Gurney if this was his harp and he said with total sincerity that it was. Blind men can't always be trusted.

They brought in the sniffer dog next. The only thing that interested it was Bernie's torn trouser leg. The tail wagged when it got a whiff of that.

After the police had quit in disarray, Sly cracked open a bottle of champagne. "I think some debriefing is in order now," he said. "If this isn't the maestro's harp, what is it?"

"I, em, borrowed it," Bernie said, digging deep for a plausible story. "I spotted the police surveillance at the Albert Hall soon after I'd lifted Mr Gurney's harp, so I returned that one pretty damn quick."

"My harp is safe?" Gurney said with relief.

"Safe in the Albert Hall."

Bernie told them how he'd removed the other Horngacher from the museum.

"Nice work," Sly said.

"Nice work? The man's saved our skins. You promised me he was totally reliable and he is," Gurney said. "I've learned my lesson. You and I can never do business again, Mr Small."

"That's bleeding obvious," Sly said. "It wasn't my end of the operation that the police were onto."

"So all that stuff about young Rocky and the Royal College wasn't true?" Bernie said.

"Hogwash," Sly said. "Rocky's in a young offender's institution."

"Why didn't you tell me I was smuggling heroin?"

"You didn't need to know. It isn't that I didn't trust you with a parcel of the finest Peruvian flake, just that I trusted you more with a fifty grand harp. As a music lover, you'd be sure to treat it with respect."

BERTIE AND THE CHRISTMAS TREE

I t's almost too much for one man, being the Prince of Wales AND the son of Father Christmas. In case this confuses you, I'd better explain. My Papa, the late Prince Albert of blessed memory, is credited with inventing Christmas as we know it. He is supposed to have introduced the Christmas tree (a German tradition) to Britain, started the practice of sending cards and – for all I know – served up the first plum pudding. Never mind that this is absolute bunkum. People believe it and who am I to stand in the way of public opinion?

The true facts, if you want them, are that a Christmas tree was first put up at Windsor by my great-grandmother, Queen Charlotte (of Mecklenburg-Strelitz), as early as 1800, and my Mama's childhood Christmases were never without a decorated tree. It was only thanks to a popular periodical, the *Illustrated London News*, that our family custom was made public in 1848 and my parents were depicted standing beside a fine tree decked with glass ornaments. My father was no fool. The year in question had been an absolute stinker for royalty, with republicanism rearing its odious head all over Europe, so it did no harm to show ourselves in a good light. Decent British sentiment was wooed by Papa and it became *de rigeur* to dig up a spruce, bring it into the home and cover it with tinsel and trinkets. Truth to tell, Papa was tickled pink at being the man who invented Christmas. He started presenting trees to all and sundry, including the regiments. If you're a royal and revolution is in the wind it's no bad thing to keep the army on your side.

From that time, the festive season fizzed like a sherbert drink. "A most dear, happy time," Mama called it. We royals were well used to exchanging gifts and rewarding the servants, and it now extended to the nation at large. Suddenly carol-singing was all the rage. And thanks to the penny post, the practice of sending greetings cards became a universal custom, if not a duty.

I was a mere child when all this happened and a callow youth when the unthinkable burst upon us and Papa caught a dreadful chill and joined the angels. As fate would have it, his passing occurred just before Christmas, on December 14th, 1861. I shan't dwell on this tragedy except to remark that Christmases from that year on were tinged with sadness. As a family, we couldn't think about saluting the happy morn until the calendar had passed what Mama always spoke of as "the dreadful fourteenth". So you see, dear reader, we would wake up on the fifteenth and discover we had ten days in which to prepare. I mention this as a prelude to my account of the great crime of Christmas, 1890.

It all started most innocently.

"Bertie," my dear wife Alexandra said in her most governessy tone, "you'd better not lie there all morning. Ten days from now it will be Christmas and we've done nothing about it."

I don't think I answered. I had much else on my mind at the end of 1890, not least the Queen's displeasure at my involvement in what was termed the Baccarat Scandal.

"Bertie, you're awake. I can see. It's no use closing your eyes and wheezing like a grampus. That won't make it go away. What are we going to do about presents for the courtiers and servants?"

I sighed and opened my eyes. "The usual. Lockets and chains for the ladies and pearl studs for the gentlemen. Books for the governesses. A framed picture of you and me for everyone else."

"Yes, but not one of these items is ordered yet."

"Francis Knollys can attend to it."

"But you must tell him today. And we can't ask Francis to write the Christmas cards. That's a job for you and me, as well as presents for the children and decorations for the tree." Her voice slipped up an octave, her vocal cords quavering with distress. "The tree, Bertie! We haven't even got a tree."

"My dear Alix," I said, reaching for an extra pillow and sitting up in bed, "Sandringham is eight thousand acres with about a million trees. If the estate manager can't find a decent spruce among them he'll get his pearl stud from me in the place where he least wants it."

"There's no need for vulgarity, Bertie. It's got to be a tall tree."

"And it shall be. What happened to last year's?"

A question I should never have asked.

Her eyes filled with tears. "It died, poor thing. It scattered needles all over the ballroom. I have my suspicion that it had no root, that some unthinking person sawed the trunk at the base and thrust it into the tub."

"Iniquitous."

"Poor tree. They're living things, Bertie. Make sure such an act of cruelty is not repeated this year. Tell them they must dig up the roots as well and find a really large tub to plant it in and keep the soil moist. When Christmas is over we'll plant the living tree outside again."

"What a splendid idea," I said, and added a slight evasion. "I can't think who sanctioned the murder of last year's tree."

She gave me a look and said, "I'll choose the menu for the Christmas dinner."

"Whitstable oysters," I said.

"Bertie, oysters aren't traditional."

"What do you mean? There's an R in the month."

"But the rest of us want roast goose."

"So do I. Roast goose and oysters."

"Very well. That's your treat settled. And you must think up some treats for the children. A magic lantern show."

"They're children no more," I said. "The youngest is sixteen and Eddy is twenty-six."

"Well, I want the magic lantern," she said, practically stamping her little foot. Christmas was definitely coming.

The magic lantern was my annual entertainment for the family and they knew the slides by heart. We would drape a large bedsheet between two sets of antlers and project the pictures onto it. They were mostly scenes of Scotland, about seventy in all, except for the last, which was the climax of the show, a star that altered shape several times as I cranked a little handle. This required me to stoop over the machine and one year my beard caught fire, causing more gaiety than any of the Scottish scenes.

After a hearty breakfast I summoned my long-serving secretary, Sir Francis Knollys, and arranged for the keepsakes to be ordered by telegraph from my usual jeweller, Mr Garrard, of the Haymarket. He's a fortunate fellow, for we are obliged to keep a large retinue at Sandringham. As well as the pins and lockets, I thoughtfully ordered a gift for Alix of a large silver inkstand, which I knew she would adore. I believe the bill for everything was in excess of six hundred pounds. I've always lived beyond my means, but if the nation wants an heir presumptive, then it must allow him to be bounteous, I say. Garrard wired back promising to deliver the articles in presentation boxes by December 23rd, just time to wrap them and write labels on each one.

Next, I spoke to Hammond, my estate manager. The main tree, I said, should be at least twenty feet high and healthy.

"I'll pick it myself, your Royal Highness," he said. "I know exactly where to go. In fact, I'll fell it myself as well."

"No, no, no, no, no," I said. "Felling won't do at all."

"But last year you said – "

"That was last year. The Princess has a sentimental regard for trees and she insists that we – that is to say you – dig the whole thing from the ground, roots and all, and plant it in a tub so that it will survive the experience."

"With respect, sir, the ground's awfully hard from the frosts."

"With respect, Hammond, you'll have to dig awfully hard."

"As you wish, sir."

"No. As I command."

I ordered a search for the magic lantern. It always goes missing. In a house as large as Sandringham there are hundreds of cupboards. The show wouldn't be until Christmas afternoon, but I like to have a rehearsal and make sure the slides are the right way up. You wouldn't believe the catcalls when I get one wrong. Some of my family think they can get away with bad behaviour in the dark. I don't know where they get it from.

That evening Alix and I started the chore of signing Christmas cards. My festive spirit is well tested in the days before Christmas and I must admit to unparliamentary language when Alix produces yet another stack for me to attend to. However I was able to report that everything else was in hand.

"Have you addressed a card to your Mama?" she asked.

"I'm summoning my strength," I said. Because of the Baccarat business, I was not in the best odour with the Queen. I confess to some relief that we wouldn't be required to show our faces at Balmoral over Christmas. Mama deplores gambling of any sort, even on horses, and she was incensed that I might be required to appear as a witness. I wasn't too sanguine at the prospect myself.

A week passed. The Christmas preparations went well. The magic lantern was found and tested. Hammond did his digging and the tree was erected in the ballroom. It took six men to lift it onto a trolley and trundle it through the house. We had immense fun with the stepladder used to hang the decorations, or, rather, I did, telling Alix I could see up to her knees and beyond when she was standing above me – which was true. She almost fell off through trying to adjust her skirt. She refused to go up again, so I invited one of her ladies-in-waiting to take her place and the girl turned as red as a holly berry and Alix was not at all amused. And then we had a jolly conversation of *double-entendres* about the pretty sights on view. I thought it jolly, anyway. I know a few ladies who would have thought it exceedingly funny.

A card arrived from Mama thanking me for mine and wishing me the blessings of Our Lord and a New Year of duty and decorum. She never gives up. I'm told she was full of fun in her youth. It's hard to imagine.

The one small anxiety in our arrangements was that the jewellery hadn't arrived by the end of December 22nd. I know Mr Garrard had promised to deliver by the day following, but in previous years he had always managed to get the consignment to us a day or so early. That evening I spoke to Knollys. He, too, was getting worried.

"Just to be sure, I'll send a telegraph," he said.

Oh, my stars and garters, what a shock awaited us! Next morning Mr Garrard wired back the following message:

Items were despatched December 21st. Cannot understand what has happened. Am coming personally by first available train.

Notwithstanding three inches of overnight snow, he was with us by midday, and I have never seen a man so discomposed. Quivering like a debutante's fan, he was practically in tears. "I had my people working day and night to complete the order, Your Royal Highness," he informed me. "It was all done, every item boxed up. I checked it myself, three times."

"You can look me in the eye, Garrard," I said. "I believe you. I've never had reason to doubt you before. Tell me, what arrangements did you make for the consignment to be delivered to Sandringham?"

"A personal messenger, sir. A young man who has worked for me for two years and whom I trust absolutely. He happens to live in Norfolk and wanted to visit his parents for Christmas, so I entrusted him with the valise containing the jewellery."

"Where precisely in Norfolk?"

"Oh, he was coming here first, sir. That was my firm instruction."

"Where, Mr Garrard?"

"A village called Holkham Staith, not fifteen miles from here, but that's hardly the point."

"I'll be the judge of what is the point," I said. He didn't know it, and not many do, but I've had a certain amount of success as an amateur detective. My investigative skills are known only to my intimates. "I know Holkham." I also knew a limerick about a young fellow of Holkham, but this wasn't the moment to speak it. "What's the young man's name?"

"Digby, sir. Horace Digby."

"It sounds respectable."

"He's of good family, sir. He's related to the Digbys of Denbighshire."

"It doesn't always follow that good blood will out. What were your instructions to Digby?"

"To take the train to Lynn, never letting go of the valise, and then hire a cab to convey him here."

"You saw him depart on the 21st?"

"I did, sir. I watched him get into a cab outside my shop in the Haymarket."

"Well, gentlemen," I said with all the authority of an experienced investigator, "we'll not solve the mystery by standing here. We must drive out to Lynn and see if Digby arrived."

Garrard rather undermined my announcement. "Sir, I already spoke to the stationmaster when I got in this morning. He confirmed that a young man answering Digby's description alighted at the station at noon on the 21st and hailed a four-wheeled cab."

"And what is the description Digby answers to?"

"Tall, very tall, about six foot three, lean, and wearing a Norfolk jacket with a distinctive green and yellow tweed design."

"Sounds hideous. Hat?"

"A brown bowler, sir."

"Well, if he hailed a cab at Lynn and it didn't get here, where would he have gone?"

"Holkham?" Knollys suggested.

"My thought exactly. Let's track the quarry to his lair."

In no time we were in one of my two-horse carriages gliding through the snowy landscape. In any other circumstances it would have been a delightful drive, with a clear blue sky above. My driver knew the route to Holkham and so do I, for that's where the Earl of Leicester resides and he's a shooting man. We once bagged upwards of 1,600 fowl there in a single day – sixteen guns, that is.

This time we weren't bound for Holkham Hall unfortunately. Far from being of good family, as Garrard claimed, Digby's people were in trade, as horse dealers. I didn't much care for them and I don't think they cared for me, even when Knollys told them who I was.

"We 'aven't seen 'un in weeks," was the reply to my question.

"Your Royal Highness," Knollys prompted the man.

"Months," the man added. "When was it we last saw 'Orace, Betty?"

" 'Orse fair," the mother said.

"We 'aven't seen 'un since 'orse fair," the man said.

"Your Royal Highness," Knollys said.

"Not that we don't trust you, but we'd like to look around your property," I said. "Your son has disappeared with a substantial amount of jewellery and a silver inkstand."

"What would we be doing with a silver inkstand?" the man said.

"What would anybody be doing with a silver inkstand?" the woman said.

Knollys was about to say his piece again, but I flapped my hand.

I started a cigar before going inside. You never know what vapours you will encounter in such a household. Without being uncivil to the Queen's humble subjects, I have to say that this wasn't Holkham Hall. The only good thing about it was that there weren't more rooms. We searched the kitchen and front room and looked inside two bedrooms. There were no signs of a recent visitor, nor of the missing valise. They had five pathetic horses standing in the snow at the back.

"They need blankets," I said.

"Where would we get blankets?" the man said insolently.

"I'll have some sent over before the day is out. See to it, Francis."

"You're a gent," the woman said unnecessarily.

"See that you put them over the horses and not your own bed," I said. "Come, gentlemen. We must pursue the trail elsewhere."

In sombre mood, we got back into the carriage.

Garrard cleared his throat. "Your Royal Highness, the class and manners of those people shocked me to the quick and I apologise profoundly for putting you through such an ordeal. It's apparent that Digby misinformed me as to his origins. I shall take it up with him as soon as he is found."

"Save your breath," I told him. "That's of small account compared to the loss of the Christmas presents."

Knollys said, "It suggests that the fellow is a blackguard."

"Not at all," I said. "You can't know the wine by the barrel. I'm not judging him until we find him with the booty in his hands."

"But how shall we trace him?"

"We must find the cabman who picked him up from the station. He'll know where he put him down."

"Brilliant!" Garrard said.

We drove to Lynn by the shortest route, still a cold journey of some fifteen miles. The snow scene was starting to lose its charm.

"How many cabs ply their trade at Lynn station, would you say?" I asked the others.

"Upwards of thirty. Fifty, even," Knollys said, betraying some despondency. He has never had much faith in my investigations. "I've seen the line in the station yard."

"But not all of them are four-wheelers, as this was," Garrard said. "Most are hansoms. We're not looking for a hansom."

"Good thinking," I said.

At the station, we lost no time in finding the station master. He must have seen my coat of arms on the carriage, for he'd donned his silk hat, which he now doffed with a flourish and a bow.

"You are the principal witness," I told him. "You saw a tall man carrying a large valise and wearing a loud Norfolk jacket arrive here two days ago, on the 21st."

"I spoke to him, Your Majesty," he said.

"Royal Highness," Knollys corrected him.

"You spoke? That's interesting. What did he have to say?"

"That he was bound for Sandringham with a valuable cargo and didn't want the inconvenience of standing in a queue for a cab, Your Royal – "

"Definitely our man," I said. "You summoned a four-wheeler?"

"The cleanest on the stand, Your – "

"Ah! So you can identify the driver, no doubt."

"His name is Gripper."

"And is he here this morning?"

"No longer, Your – "

"What do you mean by that?"

"He was here twenty minutes ago. He picked up a fare, a gentleman from London. They'll be well on their way to Sandringham by now."

"To *Sandringham*?" I said. "I'm expecting no visitors today. Describe this traveller."

"Middle-aged, brown suit and matching bowler, a rather military bearing and clipped manner of speech."

"He spoke to you?"

"He wanted to know about the man you're interested in, the tall man with the valise."

"Did he, by Jove! Back to the carriage, gentlemen. I sense a kill."

When we arrived at Sandringham, I was alarmed to see the four-wheeler on the drive in front of the main door with no sign of the driver or his mysterious passenger. I jumped out and rushed inside. A footman came to greet me.

"Where are the visitors?" I demanded.

"Sir, there's a gentleman in the ballroom with Her Royal Highness."

Fearful for Alix, I dashed in that direction, pursued by Knollys and Garrard. The moment I entered the ballroom I saw my darling wife standing in front of the Christmas tree with a brown-suited fellow holding a bowler hat.

"Don't move, my man!" I shouted. "Alix, step away from him at once."

To my amazement and confusion she simply laughed and said, "Oh, Bertie, don't make an exhibition of yourself. This is Sergeant Cribb, the famous detective. Come and shake his hand."

"What's a detective doing in my house?"

"Detecting," she said. "I invited him here. The presents for the servants haven't arrived and I thought we should find out why. I was just explaining about the tree and our custom of giving presents on Christmas Eve."

"Fine tree, sir," Sergeant Cribb said.

Ignoring him, I crossed the room and addressed my wife. "You invited this man here without consulting me? I don't want a police investigation. That's the last thing we want after the year we've had."

"He's an ex-policeman, dear, and very discreet."

"Retired on a modest pension, sir," Cribb said. He didn't look old apart from a few silver hairs, but policemen retire younger than most.

"And he comes highly recommended by the Chief Constable," Alix said. "We have to deal with this matter expeditiously."

"But you didn't speak to me about this."

"Because you were off doing other things. It's such a busy time."

I looked at Francis Knollys and rolled my eyes. "Well, Sergeant Cribb, what do you have to tell us apart from the fact that we have a fine tree?"

"I'd like to speak to the estate manager, sir."

"To Hammond? He's got nothing to do with it."

There was a silence that would have done for a lying-in-state.

Eventually Cribb glanced towards Alix. She gestured to the footman. "Find Mr Hammond and tell him he's wanted here."

I said, "It's the missing jewellery we're exercised about, not the damned Christmas tree."

"There may be a connection, sir," Cribb said.

"And I'm a Dutchman."

Presently Hammond made his entry. He was looking mightily perturbed, and I was perturbed, too, when I saw the state of his boots. Containing my displeasure, I gestured to Cribb to ask his questions.

"Fine tree," he parroted.

"Thank you, sir," Hammond said.

I told him he had no need to address Cribb as if he was a gentleman.

"I think it's the biggest I've seen," Cribb said.

Alix intervened to say it was a living tree still attached to its roots.

"Capital, ma'am," Cribb said, and turned back to Hammond. "When I was being driven through the grounds I noticed a small group of evergreens not far from the carriage path. Was this tree dug from there?"

"Yes."

"A home-grown tree. How charming."

Alix lavished a sweet smile on Cribb. I was starting to doubt her loyalty.

"And now, Mr Hammond," Cribb said, "I'm going to ask you to show me precisely where the tree was growing."

"I can do that."

"You'll ruin your shoes," Alix said. "The snow's quite deep. Bertie, have you got some galoshes to protect Sergeant Cribb's shoes?"

What next? I thought. Gritting my teeth, I clicked my fingers and sent a flunkey for enough overshoes for the four of us men. Alix elected not to come. She hates the cold.

Suitably attired, we left the house, Hammond leading. Before we'd gone a few yards Cribb left the party and trotted over to the cab still waiting near the entrance. Attached to the front below the driver's seat was a spade.

"You might care to look at this, sir," Cribb called out.

The insolence of the man. I know what a spade is. I've turned enough first sods in my time. But the other two went to look, so I joined them, not wishing to seem churlish.

Cribb said, "A necessary tool for a cabman in the depths of winter, a spade. You never know when you'll need to dig yourself out."

Then he held it horizontally towards me as if he was passing across a stuffed salmon for my inspection. "Take a close look at the dried mud attaching to the shoulder. I'll pick some off for you."

He scraped some off and I found myself constrained to look at fragments of dried mud lying in his palm.

"Do you see the pine needles?"

Now that he mentioned the fact, I did. I gave a nod.

"That's all right, then," Cribb said, taking back the spade and shouldering it like a rifle. "We'll have a use for this, I think."

Hammond had by now got some way ahead. We stepped out and caught up with him a short distance from the evergreen copse.

"Now, Mr Hammond," Cribb said, "kindly show us precisely where the Christmas tree was growing."

Hammond started to point and then drew back his hand and scratched his head instead. "Well, I'll be jiggered."

To borrow the words of the carol, the snow lay *deep and crisp and even*.

Even was the operative word.

"You dug out a large tree," Cribb said to him, "so where's the large hole?"

"Caught out, Mr Hammond," I said. "In spite of all the instructions to the contrary, you sawed the thing off at the base."

"I swear I didn't, sir. It took six of us a morning and an afternoon to dig under the roots."

"Perhaps you filled in the hole?" Knollys suggested.

"I wouldn't do that. Not when the tree has to be put back after Twelfth Night. May I borrow that spade?"

He started scraping away the layer of snow. Below it, the ground was even, but the soil was soft. "Someone else filled it in."

"Keep at it, Mr Hammond," Cribb said. "Dig out the soft stuff."

Hammond went at it with a will. We all had to stand back as the spadefuls of earth flew about us.

Cribb said, "Wait. What's that dark material?"

"It's fabric." Hammond bent down and scraped with his fingers and unearthed a brown bowler hat.

"Just the beginning," Cribb said. "Dig some more, Mr Hammond."

In only a few minutes Hammond exclaimed, "Oh, my Lord."

He'd uncovered a human hand and part of a sleeve of yellow and green tweed.

"Horace Digby, poor fellow," Garrard said.

In the warmth of the house I treated them to hot punch. We'd left some gardeners outside to warm themselves by extracting the rest of the corpse from the hole.

I waited for Alix to join us, and then said, "This is all very remarkable, Sergeant Cribb, but it hasn't brought back the missing jewels unless they're in the hole as well."

"No, they're not, sir. I recovered them earlier. Excuse me a moment." He left the room.

We were lost for words. We simply stared at each other until he returned carrying a valise and a large silver object that I recognised as an inkstand, Alix's Christmas present.

"What's that ugly thing?" Alix said.

"The murder weapon, ma'am," Cribb said.

All my good intentions dashed in a couple of sentences.

"Then who is the murderer?"

"Gripper, the cabman," Cribb said. "I have him cuffed, hand and foot. He's quite secure, lying on the floor of his own cab. It was a crime of opportunity and it happened on the 21st, before the snow came. Digby got into his cab at Lynn station and said he wanted to be driven to Sandringham. It was pretty obvious that the valise contained something valuable. All the way here the cabman planned the robbery. Inside the gates where it was quiet, he stopped and told Digby to hand over the booty. Digby put up a fight, but the cabbie grabbed something heavy – and I think it was that silver object – and brained him with it. He may not have intended murder, but that's what it became. It was his good luck that a hole big enough for a grave had been dug nearby. He dropped the body in and used his own spade to cover it with the excess soil beside the hole. That's how he got the pine needles in the mud. And there was more good luck for him when the snow came, levelling everything."

"But bad luck when you came along," Alix said, her voice overflowing with admiration.

"Yes, I got the gist of the story from the stationmaster at Lynn. It was a risk using the same cab, but I fancy the killer thought he'd got away with it. And he wasn't likely to attack me with nothing in my hands. I arrested him on suspicion as soon as I got here."

"You're a brave man, as well as a fine detective," Alix said, actually clapping her hands. "Isn't he a brave man, Bertie?"

"Where were the stolen jewels?" I asked.

"In the box seat he sits on."

"Speaking of boxes, do we have a Christmas box for Sergeant Cribb?" Alix asked.

She looked to me, I looked to Knollys and he sniffed, sighed and took a couple of gold sovereigns from his pocket.

"And there's his fee, of course," Alix said. "Twenty-five pounds, I suggest."

Cribb looked as if his Christmas was just beginning.

As for me, I've never felt the same about Christmas trees. Before Papa made them popular, we had something rather better. The custom was to hang up a bough entwined with mistletoe, holly, ivy and other evergreens, candles, apples and cinnamon sticks. It was called the kissing bough and when I'm King I intend to reinstate it.

If the Queen allows.

SAY THAT AGAIN

We called him the Brigadier with the buggered ear. Just looking at it made you wince. Really he should have had the bits surgically removed. He claimed it was an old war wound. However, Sadie the Lady, another of our residents, told us it wasn't true. She said she'd talked to the Brig's son Arnold who reckoned his old man got blind drunk in Aldershot one night and tripped over a police dog and paid for it with his shell-like.

Because of his handicap, the Brigadier tended to shout. His "good" ear wasn't up to much, even with the aid stuck in it. We got used to the shouting, we old farts in the Never-Say-Die Retirement Home. After all, most of us are hard of hearing as well. No doubt we were guilty of letting him bluster and bellow without interruption. We never dreamed at the time that our compliance would get us into the High Court on a murder rap.

It was set in motion by She-Who-Must-Be-Replaced, our so-called matron, pinning a new leaflet on the notice board in the hall.

"Infernal cheek!" the Brig boomed. "They're parasites, these people, living off the frail and weak-minded."

"Who are you calling weak-minded?" Sadie the Lady piped up. "There's nothing wrong with my brain."

The Brig didn't hear. Sometimes it can be a blessing.

"Listen to this," he bellowed, as if we had any choice. " 'Are you dissatisfied with your hearing? Struggling with a faulty instrument? Picking up unwanted background noise? Marcus Haliburton, a renowned expert on the amazing new digital hearing aids, will be in attendance all day at the Bay Tree Hotel on Thursday, 8th April for free consultations. Call this number now for an appointment. No obligation.' No obligation, my arse – forgive me, ladies. You know what happens? They get you in there and tell you to take out your National Health aid so they can poke one of those little torches in your ear and of course you're stuffed. You can't hear a thing they're saying from that moment on. The next thing is they shove a form in front of you and you find you've signed an order for a thousand pound replacement. If you object they drop your NHS aid on the floor and tread on it."

"That can't be correct," Miss Martindale said.

"Completely wrecked, yes," the Brigadier said. "Are you speaking from personal experience, my dear, because I am."

Someone put up a hand. He wanted to be helped to the toilet, but the Brigadier took it as support. "Good man. What we should do is teach these blighters a lesson. We could, you know, with my officer training and George's underworld experience."

I smiled faintly. My underworld links were nil, another of the Brig's misunderstandings. One afternoon I'd been talking to Sadie about cats and happened to mention that we once adopted a stray. I thought the Brig was dozing in his armchair, but he came to life and said, "Which of the Krays was that – Reggie or Ronnie? I had no idea of your criminal past, George. We"ll have to watch you in future."

It was hopeless trying to disillusion him, so I settled for my gangster reputation and some of the old ladies began to believe it, too, and found me more interesting than ever they'd supposed.

By the next tea break, the Brigadier had turned puce with excitement. "I've mapped it out," he told us. "I'm calling it Operation Syringe, because we're going to clean these ruffians out. Basically, the object of the plan is to get a new super-digital hearing aid for everyone in this home free of charge."

"How the heck will you do that?" Sadie asked.

"What?"

She stepped closer and spoke into his ear. "They're a private company. Those aids cost a fortune."

The Brig grinned. "Simple. We intercept their supplies. I happen to know the Bay Tree Hotel quite well."

Sadie said to the rest of us, "That's a fact. The Legion has its meetings there. He's round there every Friday night for his g&t."

"G&t or two or three," another old lady said.

I said, "Wait a minute, Brigadier. We can't steal a bunch of hearing aids." I have a carrying voice when necessary and he heard every word.

" 'Steal' is not a term in the military lexicon, dear boy," he said. "We requisition them." He leaned forward. "Now, the operation has three phases. Number One: Observation. I'll take care of that. Number Two: Liaison. This means getting in touch with an inside man, Cormac, the barman. I can do that also. Number Three: Action. And that depends on what we learn from Phases One and Two. That's where the rest of you come in. Are you with me?"

"I don't know what he's on about," Sadie said to me.

"Don't worry," I said. "He's playing soldiers, that's all. He'll find out it's a non-starter."

"No muttering in the ranks," the Brigadier said. "Any dissenters? Fall out, the dissenters."

No one moved. Some of us needed help to move anywhere and nobody left the room when tea and biscuits were on offer. And that was how we were recruited into the snatch squad.

On Saturday, the Brigadier reported on Phases One and Two of his battle plan. He marched into the tea room looking as chipper as Montgomery on the eve of El Alamein.

"Well, the obbo phase is over and so is the liaison and I'm able to report some fascinating results. The gentleman who wants us all to troop along to the Bay Tree Hotel and buy his miraculous hearing aids is clearly doing rather well out of it. He drives a vintage Bentley and wears a different suit each visit and by the cut of them they're not off the peg."

"There's money in ripping off old people," Sadie said.

"It ought to be stopped," her friend Briony said.

The Brig went on, "I talked to my contact last night and I'm pleased to tell you that the enemy – that is to say Marcus Haliburton – works to a predictable routine. He puts in a fortnightly appearance at the Bay Tree. If you go along and see him you'll find Session One is devoted to the consultation and the placing of the order. Session Two is the fitting and payment. Between Sessions One and Two a box is delivered to the hotel and it contains up to fifty new hearing aids – more than enough for our needs." He paused and looked around the room. "So what do you think is the plan?"

No one was willing to say. Some might have thought speaking up would incriminate them. Others weren't capable of being heard by the Brigadier. Finally I said, "We, em, requisition the box?"

"Ha!" He lifted a finger. "I thought you"d say that. We can do better. What we do is requisition the box."

There were smiles all round at my expense.

"And then," the Brigadier said, "we replace the box with one just like it."

"That's neat," Sadie said. She was beginning to warm to the Brigadier's criminal scheme.

He'd misheard her again. "It may sound like deceit to you, madam, but to some of us it's common justice. They called Robin Hood a thief."

"Are we going to be issued with bows and arrows?" Sadie said.

"I wouldn't mind meeting some merry men," Briony said.

The Brigadier's next move took us all by surprise. "Check the corridor, George. Make sure no staff are about."

I did as I was told and gave the thumb-up sign, whereupon the old boy bent down behind the sideboard and dragged out a flattened cardboard box that he rapidly restored to its normal shape.

"Thanks to my contacts at the hotel I've managed to retrieve the box that was used to deliver this week's aids." No question: he intended to go through with this crazy adventure. In the best officer tradition he started to delegate duties. "George, your job will be to get this packed and sealed and looking as if it just arrived by courier."

"No problem," I said to indulge him. I was sure the plan would break down before I had to do anything.

"That isn't so simple as it sounds," he said. "Take a close look. The aids are made in South Africa, so there are various customs forms attached to the box. They stuff them in a kind of envelope and stick them to the outside. What you do is update this week's documents."

"I'll see what I can manage."

"Then you must consider the contents. The instruments don't weigh much, and they're wrapped in bubblewrap, so the whole thing is almost as light as air. Whatever you put inside must not arouse suspicion."

"Crumpled-up newspaper," Sadie said.

"What did she say?"

I repeated it for his benefit.

Sadie said, "Briony has a stack of *Daily Mails* this high in her room. She hoards everything."

I knew that to be true. Briony kept every postcard, every letter, every magazine. Her room was a treasure house of things other people discarded. She even collected the tiny jars our breakfast marmalade came in. The only question was whether she would donate her newspaper collection to Operation Syringe. She could be fiercely possessive at times.

"I might be able to spare you some of the leaflets that come with my post," she said.

Sadie said, "Junk mail. That'll do."

"It doesn't incriminate me, does it?" she said. "I want no part of this silly escapade."

"Excellent," the Brigadier said, oblivious. "When the parcel is up to inspection standard, I'll tell you about the next phase."

The heat was now on me. I had to smuggle the box back to my room and start work. I was once employed as a graphic designer, so the forging of the forms wasn't a big problem. Getting Briony to part with her junk mail was far more demanding. You'd think it was bank notes. She checked everything and allowed me about one sheet in five. But in the end I had enough to stuff the box. I sealed it with packing tape I found in Matron's office and showed it to the Brigadier.

"Capital," he said. "We can proceed to phase four: distracting the enemy."

"How do we do that?"

"We inundate Marcus Haliburton with requests for appointments under bogus names."

"That's fun. I'll tell the others."

Even at this stage, it was still a game, as I tried to explain later to the police. Some of us had mobiles and others used the payphone by the front door. I think a couple of bold souls used the phone in Matron's office. I don't know if we succeeded in distracting Haliburton. He must have been surprised by the number of Smiths, Browns, Jones and Robinsons who had seen his publicity. The greedy beggar didn't turn any away.

And so the day of the heist arrived. Almost everyone from the Never-Say-Die had been talked into joining in and clambered onto the bus the Brigadier had laid on. Half of them were so confused most of the time that you could have talked them into running the London Marathon. The notable exception was Briony. She wanted no part of it. She stayed put, guarding her hoard of newspapers and marmalade jars. The Brigadier called her a ruddy conchie when he found out.

In their defence, few of them knew the finer points of the battle plan. But they still amounted to a formidable squad as they alighted from the bus and listened to the Brigadier's Agincourt-style speech.

"There are senior citizens all over Britain who will think themselves accursed they were not here with us. We few, we happy few, deaf but not downtrodden, stand on the brink of victory. Onward, then."

So began the main assault, as the Brigadier called it. Four old ladies crossed the hotel foyer walker to walker, a vanguard forging a route for the main party, twelve more on sticks and crutches, with two motorised chairs like tanks in the rear. Inexorably they headed for the suite used by Marcus Haliburton for his consultations. Their task: to block all movement in the corridor.

Because of my supposed underworld connections I had been selected for a kind of SAS role, along with the Brigadier himself. At some time in the first hour, while all the new patients were being documented, tested and examined, a security firm would deliver the latest box of hearing aids to the hotel. One of the staff was then supposed to bring it to the suite for Haliburton to begin handing out the aids to people who had placed orders on his previous visit. Thanks to the congestion in the corridor this would not be possible.

The next part was clever, I must admit. The Brigadier had booked the room two doors up and he and I were waiting in there with our own box filled with crumpled-up junk mail. The porter was bound to come past with the box containing the expensive digital aids.

We waited three-quarters of an hour and it was a nervous time. I had my doubts whether two elderly gents were capable of intercepting a burly hotel porter, but the Brigadier was confident.

"We"re not using brute strength. This is our strength." He tapped his head.

"But if it doesn't work?"

To my horror he took a gun from his pocket and gave a crocodile grin. "My old service revolver."

"That would be armed robbery," I said, aghast. "Don't even think of it."

He misheard me, of course. "From another pocket he produced a flask of brandy. "You need to drink a bit? Take a swig, old boy. It stops the shakes, I find."

Before I could get through to him I heard the squeak of a trolley wheel in the corridor outside. The moment of decision. Should I abort the whole operation? Unwisely, disastrously as it turned out,

I decided to go on with it. I stepped into the corridor, right in the path of the trolley, and said to the porter pushing it, "Mr Haliburton said to lock the parcel in here for the time being. He'll collect it when the people waiting have been dealt with."

He said, "I can't do that. I'm under firm instructions to hand it to Mr Haliburton in person."

I winked and said, "I work with him. It's as good as done." I pressed a five-pound note into his sweaty palm.

Persuaded, he wheeled the parcel into the room and left it just inside the door. The Brigadier meanwhile had stepped out of sight into the bathroom. The porter had the impression he was locking the parcel in an empty room. The idea was that the Brigadier would then emerge from the bathroom with our box of junk mail and make the switch, returning to the bathroom with the box containing the aids, where he would lock himself in for an hour.

My job was to shepherd the Never-Say-Die residents as quickly as possible out of the corridor and back to the bus. I was starting to do so when a man in a grey pinstripe suit came marching up and said, "What's the trouble here? I'm Buckfield, the hotel manager."

"No trouble, Mr Buckfield," I said. "The system can't cope, That's all. Some of these old people have been waiting an hour for an appointment with the ear specialist. I'm suggesting they come back next time. We've got transport outside."

He looked at me with some uncertainty. "Are you their warden?"

"Something like that."

"One of the bellboys tells me he delivered a box of valuable hearing aids to Room 104. Was that at your bidding?"

I said, "Yes. I think you'll find it's still there."

He had a pass key and opened the door and picked up the parcel that was waiting there. I gave all my attention to ushering the old ladies towards the foyer and the waiting bus. Most of them were pleased to leave and didn't understand what we had achieved. A few genuine customers for the hearing aids were just as confused, and when we got to the bus I had difficulty persuading two of them that they weren't in the Never-Say-Die party.

Finally everyone except the Brigadier was on board. It was my job to see that all was clear and help him out of Room 104 with the parcel we had requisitioned, the most dangerous part of Operation Syringe.

Trying to look like any other guest, I crossed the foyer and stepped along the corridor. It was now empty of people. I tapped on the door of 104 and immediately realised that there was a fatal flaw in our plan. How would the Brigadier hear my knocking? I tried a second time.

No response.

Along the corridor, the door of Haliburton's suite opened and an old man came out. I tried to ignore him, but he said, "Are you waiting for a consultation? It's that room I just came out of."

I thanked him, but I don't think he heard. I took off a shoe and tried hammering on 104 with it.

At last the door opened and there was the Brigadier with the parcel in his arms. For the first time since I'd known him he looked concerned. "Take this to the bus and tell the driver to put his foot down."

"Aren't you coming?" I said.

"Cunning? Far from it," he said. "I'm a silly arse. Left my service revolver on the bed and some beggar in a pinstripe picked it up."

"Leave it," I shouted into his ear. "Come with me."

"Can't do that," he said and made a little speech straight out of one of those war films when the doomed Brit showed his stiff upper lip. "That revolver is my baby. Been with me all over the world. I'm not surrendering, old boy. I'll get back to base. See if I don't."

I said, "I'm leaving with a heavy heart."

He said, "Don't be so vulgar."

No use trying to talk sense into him. He really had need of a decent hearing aid.

I carried the parcel to the bus. Everyone cheered when they saw it. Then Sadie said, "Where's the Brigadier?"

I didn't want them to know he'd brought a gun with him, so I said he was hiding up until it was safer to leave.

The bus took us back to the home and we tottered off to our rooms for a nap after all the excitement. We'd agreed not to open the box before the Brig returned.

All evening we waited, asking each other if anyone had heard anything. I was up until ten-thirty, long past bedtime. In the end I turned in and tried to sleep.

Some time after midnight there was a noise like a stone being thrown at my window. I got out of bed and looked down. There in the grounds was the Brigadier blowing on his fingers. He shouted up to me, "Be a good fellow and unbolt the front door will you? I just met a brass monkey on his way to the welder's."

In twenty minutes every inhabitant of the house except the Matron and her two night staff assembled in the tea room. The nightwear on display is another story.

"Open it, George," the Brig ordered.

They watched in eager anticipation. Even Briony had turned out. "Ooh, bubblewrap," she said. "May I have that?"

"You might as well, because you're not getting a hearing aid, you conchie," the Brigadier said.

I unwrapped the first aid. It was a BTE (behind the ear), but elegance itself. I offered it to the Brigadier. He slotted it into his ear. "Good Lord!" he said. "I can hear the clock ticking."

Everyone in the room who wanted a replacement aid was given one, and we still had a few over. The morale of the troops couldn't have been higher. Even Briony was happy with her stack of bubblewrap. We all slept well.

At breakfast, the results were amazing. People who hadn't conversed for years were chatting animatedly.

Then the doorbell chimed. The chime of doom. A policeman with a megaphone stood in the doorway and announced, "Police.

We're coming in. Put your hands above your heads and stay where you are."

Sadie said, "You don't have to shout, young man. We can all hear you."

We were taken in barred vans to the police station and kept in cells. Because there was a shortage of cells some of us had to double up and I found myself locked up with the Brigadier.

"This is overkill," I said. "We're harmless old people."

"They don't think so, George," he said in a sombre tone. "Marcus Haliburton was shot dead in the course of the raid."

"Shot? I didn't hear any shots."

"After you left, it got nasty. They'll have me for murder and the rest of you for conspiracy to murder. We can't expect all our troops to hold out under questioning. They'll put up their hands, and we're all done."

He was right. Several old ladies confessed straight away. What can you expect? The trial that followed was swift and savage. The Brigadier asked to be tried by a court martial and refused to plead. He went down for life, with a recommendation that he serve at least ten years. They proved that the fatal shots had been fired from his gun.

I got three years for conspiracy to murder – in spite of claiming I didn't know about the gun. Sadie was given six months. The Crown Prosecution Service didn't press charges against some of the really frail ones. Oddly, nobody seemed interested in the hearing aid heist and we were allowed to keep our stolen property.

The Never-Say-Die Retirement Home had to carry on without us. But there was to be one last squirt from Operation Syringe.

One morning three weeks after the trial Briony decided to sort out her marmalade jars and store them better, using the bubblewrap the aids had been kept in.. She was surrounding one of the jars with the stuff when there was a sudden popping sound. One of the little bubbles had burst under pressure. She pressed another and it made a satisfying sound. Highly amused, she started popping every one. She continued at this harmless pastime for over an hour. After tea break she went back and popped some more. It was all enormous fun until she damaged her fingernail and had to ask She-Who-Must-Be-Replaced to trim it.

"How did you do that?" Matron asked.

Briony showed her.

"Well, no wonder. There's something hard inside the bubble. I do believe it's glass. How wicked."

But it didn't turn out to be glass. It was an uncut diamond, and there were others secreted in the bubblewrap. A second police investigation was mounted into Operation Syringe. As a result, Buckfield, the manager of the Bay Tree Hotel, was arrested.

It seemed he had been working a racket with Marcus Haliburton, importing uncut diamonds stolen by workers in a South African diamond mine. The little rocks had been smuggled to Britain in the packing used for the hearing aids. Interpol took over the investigation on two continents.

It turned out that on the day of our heist Buckfield the manager suspected something was afoot, and decided Haliburton might be double-crossing him. When he checked Room 104 he found the Brigadier's revolver on the bed and he was certain he was right. He took it straight to the suite. Haliburton denied everything and said he was only a go-between and offered to open the new box of aids in the manager's presence. We know what it contained. Incensed, Buckfield pointed the gun and shot Haliburton dead.

After our release, we had a meeting to decide if we would sue the police for wrongful imprisonment. The Brigadier was all for it, but Sadie said we might be pushing our luck. We had a vote and decided she was right.

The good thing is that every one of us heard each word of the debate. I can recommend these new digital aids to anyone.

POPPING ROUND TO THE POST

Nathan was the one I liked interviewing best. You wanted to believe him, his stories were so engaging. He had this persuasive, upbeat manner, sitting forward and fixing me with his soft blue eyes. Nothing about him suggested violence. "I don't know why you keep asking me about a murder. I don't know anything about a murder. I was just popping round to the post. It"s no distance. Ten minutes, maybe. Up Steven Street and then right into Melrose Avenue."

"Popping round to the post?"

"Listen up, doc. I just told you."

"Did you have any letters with you at the time?"

"Can't remember."

"The reason I ask," I said, "is that when people go to the post they generally want to post something."

He smiled. "Good one. Like it." These memory lapses are a feature of the condition. Nathan didn't appreciate that if a letter had been posted and delivered it would help corroborate his version of events.

Then he went into what I think of as his storyteller mode, one hand cupping his chin while the other unfolded between us as if he were a conjurer producing a coin. "Do you want to hear what happened?"

I nodded.

"There was I," he said, "walking up the street."

"Steven Street?"

"Yes."

173

"On the right side or the left?"

"What difference does that make?"

According to Morgan, the detective inspector, number twenty-nine, the murder house, was on the left about a third of the way along. "I'm asking, that's all."

"Well, I wouldn't need to cross, would I?" Nathan said. "So I was on the left, and when I got to Melrose – "

"Hold on," I said. "We haven't left Steven Street yet."

"I have," he said. "I'm telling you what happened in Melrose."

"Did you notice anything in Steven Street?"

"No. Why should I?"

"Somebody told me about an incident there."

"You're on about that again, are you? I keep telling you I know nothing about a murder."

"Go on, then."

"You'll never guess what I saw when I got to Melrose."

That was guaranteed. His trips to the post were always impossible to predict. "Tell me, Nathan."

"Three elephants."

"In *Melrose*?" Melrose Avenue is a small suburban back street. "What were they doing?"

He grinned. "Swinging their trunks. Flapping their ears."

"I mean, what were they doing in Melrose Avenue?"

He had me on a string now and he was enjoying himself. "What do you think?"

"I'm stumped. Why don't you tell me?"

"They were walking in a line."

"What, on their own?"

He gave me a look that suggested I was the one in need of psychotherapy. "They had a keeper with them, obviously."

"Trained elephants?"

Now he sighed at my ignorance. "Melrose Avenue isn't the African bush. Some little travelling circus was performing in the park and they were part of the procession."

"But if it was a circus procession, Nathan, it would go up the High Street where all the shoppers could see it."

"You're right about that."

"Then what were the elephants doing in Melrose?"

"Subsidence."

I waited for more.

"You know where they laid the cable for the television in the High Street? They didn't fill it in properly. A crack appeared right across the middle. They didn't want the elephants making it worse so they diverted them around Melrose. The rest of the procession wasn't so heavy – the marching band and the clowns and the bareback rider. They were allowed up the High Street."

The story had a disarming logic, like so many of Nathan's. On a previous trip to the post he'd spotted Johnny Depp trimming a privet hedge in somebody's front garden. Johnny Depp as a jobbing gardener. Nathan had asked some questions and some joker had told him they were rehearsing a scene for a film about English suburban life. He'd suggested I went round there myself and tried to get in the film as an extra. I had to tell him I'm content with my career.

"It was a diversion, you see. Road closed to heavy vehicles and elephants."

Talk about diversions. We'd already diverted some way from the double murder in Steven Street. "What I'd really like to know from you, Nathan, is why you came home that afternoon wearing a suit that didn't fit you."

This prompted a chuckle. "That's a longer story."

"I thought it might be. I need to hear it, please."

He spread his hands as if he was addressing a larger audience. "There were these three elephants."

"You told me about them already."

"Ah, but I was anticipating. When I first spotted the elephants I didn't know what they were doing in Melrose. I thought about asking the keeper. I'm not afraid of speaking to strangers. On the whole, people like it when you approach them. But the keeper was in charge of the animals, so I didn't distract him. I could hear the sound of the band coming from the High Street and I guessed there was a connection. I stepped out to the end of Melrose."

"Where the postbox is."

"What"s that got to do with it?"

"When you started out, you were popping round to the post."

"Now you've interrupted my train of thought. You know what my memory is like."

"You were going towards the sound of the band."

He smiled. "And I looked up, and I saw balloons in the sky. Lots of colours, all floating upwards. They fill them with some sort of gas."

"Helium."

"Thank you. They must have been advertising the circus. Once I got to the end of Melrose Avenue I saw a woman with two children and each of them had a balloon and there was writing on them – the balloons, I mean, not the children. I couldn't see the wording exactly, but I guessed it must have been about the circus."

"Very likely." In my job, patience isn't just a virtue, it's a necessity.

"You may think so," Nathan said, and he held up his forefinger to emphasise the point. "But this is the strange thing. I was almost at the end of Melrose and I looked up again to see if the balloons in the sky were still in sight and quite by chance I noticed that a yellow one was caught in the branches of a willow tree. Perhaps you know that tree. It isn't in the street. It's actually in someone's garden overhanging the street. Well, I decided to try and set this balloon free. It was just out of reach, but by climbing on the wall I could get to it easily. That's what I did. And when I got my hands on the balloon and got it down I saw that the writing on the side had nothing to do with the circus. It said *Happy Birthday, Susie*."

Inwardly, I was squirming. I know how these stories progress. Nathan once found a brooch on his way to the post and took it to the police station and was invited to put on a Mickey Mouse mask and join an identity parade and say "Empty the drawer and hand it across or I'll blow your brains out." And that led on to a whole different adventure. "Did you do anything about it?"

"About what?"

"The happy birthday balloon."

"I had to, now I had it in my hands. I thought perhaps it belonged to the people in the house, so I knocked on the door. They said it wasn't theirs, but they'd noticed some yellow balloons a couple of days ago tied to the gatepost of a house in Steven Street."

"Steven Street?" My interest quickened. "What number?"

"Can't remember. These people – the people in Melrose with the willow tree – were a bit surprised because they thought the house belonged to an elderly couple. Old people don't have balloons on their birthdays, do they?"

"So you tried the house in Steven Street," I said, giving the narrative a strong shove.

"I did, and they were at home and really appreciated my thoughtfulness. All their other balloons had got loose and were blown away, so this was the only one left. I asked if the old lady was called Susie, thinking I'd wish her a happy birthday. She was not. She was called something totally unlike Susie. I think it was Agatha, or Augusta. Or it may have been Antonia."

"Doesn't matter, Nathan. Go on."

"They invited me in to meet Susie. They said she'd just had her seventh birthday and – would you believe it? – she was a dog. One of the smallest I've ever seen, with large ears and big, bulgy eyes."

"Chihuahua."

"No, Susie. Definitely Susie. The surprising thing was that this tiny pooch had a room to herself, with scatter cushions and squeaky toys and a little television that was playing *Lassie Come Home*. But the minute she set eyes on me she started barking. Then she ran out, straight past me, fast as anything. The back door of the house was open and she got out. The old man panicked a bit and said Susie wasn't allowed in the garden without her lead. She was so small that they were afraid of losing her through a gap in the fence. I felt responsible for frightening her, so I ran into the garden after her, trying to keep her in sight. I watched her dash away across the lawn. Unfortunately I didn't notice there was a goldfish pond in my way. I stepped into it, slipped and landed face down in the water."

"Things certainly happen to you, Nathan."

He took this as a compliment and grinned. "The good thing was that Susie came running back to see what had happened and the old lady picked her up. I was soaking and covered in slime and duck-weed, so they told me I couldn't possibly walk through the streets like that. The old man found me a suit to wear. He said it didn't fit him any more and I could keep it."

"All right," I said, seizing an opportunity to interrupt the flow. "You've answered my question. Now I know why you were wearing a suit the wrong size."

He shrugged again. He seemed to have forgotten where this had started.

It was a good moment to stop the video and take a break.

Morgan the detective watched the interview on the screen in my office, making sounds of dissent at regular intervals. When it was over, he asked, "Did you believe a word of that? The guy's a fantasist. He should be a writer."

"Some of it fits the facts," I pointed out. "I believe there was a circus here last weekend. And I know for certain that the cable-laying in the High Street caused some problems after it was done."

"The fact I'm concerned about is the killing of the old couple at twenty-nine, Steven Street, at the approximate time this Nathan was supposed to be on his way to the post."

"You made that clear to me yesterday," I said. "I put it to him today and he denies all knowledge of it."

"He's lying. His story's full of holes. You notice he ducked your question about having a letter in his hand?"

"Popping round to the post is only a form of words."

"Meaning what?"

"Meaning he's going out. He needs space. He doesn't mean it literally."

"I'd put a different interpretation on it. It's his way of glossing over a double murder."

"That's a big assumption, isn't it?"

"He admitted walking up the left side of Steven Street."

"Well, he would. It's on his way to the High Street."

"You seem to be taking his side."

"I'm trying to hold onto the truth. In my work as a therapist that's essential." I resisted the urge to point out that policemen should have a care for the truth as well.

"Are those his case notes on your desk?" Morgan said.

"Yes."

"Any record of violence?"

"You heard him. He's a softie."

"Soft in the head. The murders seem to have been random and without motive. A sweet old couple who never caused anyone any grief. In a case like this we examine all the options, but I'd stake my reputation this was done by a nutter."

"That's not a term I use, Inspector."

"Call him what you like, we both know what I mean. A sane man doesn't go round cutting people's throats for no obvious reason. Nothing was taken. They had valuable antiques in the house and over two hundred pounds in cash."

"Would that have made it more acceptable in your eyes, murder in the course of theft?"

"I'd know where he was coming from, wouldn't I?"

"What about the crime scene? Doesn't that give you any information?"

"It's a bloody mess, that's for sure. All the forensic tests are being carried out. The best hope is that the killer picked up some blood that matches the old couple's DNA. He couldn't avoid getting some on him. If we had the clothes Nathan was wearing that afternoon, we'd know for sure. He seems to have destroyed everything. He"s not so daft as he makes out."

"The suit he borrowed?"

"Went out with the rubbish collection, he says. It didn't fit, so it was useless to him, and the old man didn't want it back."

"Makes sense."

"Certainly does. We"re assuming the killer stripped and took a shower at the house after the murders and then bundled his own clothes into a plastic sack and put on a suit from the old man's wardrobe. Very likely helped himself to some clean shoes as well."

"I'm no forensic expert, but if he did all that, surely he must have left some DNA traces about the house?"

"We hope so. Then we'll have him, and I look forward to telling you about it."

"What about the other suspect?"

There was a stunned silence. Morgan folded his arms and glared at me, as if I was deliberately provoking him.

"Just in case," I said, "you may find it helpful to watch the video of an interview I did later this morning with a man called Jon."

I knew Jon from many hours of psychotherapy. He sat hunched, as always, hands clasped, eyes downturned, a deeply repressed, passive personality.

"Jon," my unseen voice said, "how long have you lived in that flat at the end of Steven Street?"

He sighed. "Three years. Maybe longer."

"That must be about right. I've been seeing you for more than two years. And you still live alone?"

A nod.

"You manage pretty well, shopping and cooking, and so on. It's an achievement just surviving in this modern world. But I expect there's some time left over. What do you enjoy doing most?"

"Don't know."

"Watching television?"

"Not really."

"You don't have a computer?"

He shook his head.

"Do you get out of the house, apart from shopping and coming here?"

"I suppose."

"You go for walks?"

He frowned as if straining to hear some distant sound.

"Just to get fresh air and exercise," I said. "You live in a nice area. The gardens are full of flowers in spring and summer. I think you do get out quite a bit."

"If you say so."

"Then I dare say you've met some of your neighbours, the people along Steven Street, when they're outside cleaning their cars, doing gardening or walking the dog. Did you ever speak to the old couple at number twenty-nine?"

He started swaying back and forth in the chair. "I might have."

"They have a little toy dog, a Chihuahua. They're very attached to it, I understand."

"Don't like them," Jon said, still swaying.

"Why's that? Something they did?"

"Don't know."

"I think you do. Maybe they remind you of some people you knew once."

He was silent, but the rocking became more agitated. Momentarily his chin lifted from his chest and his face was visible. Fear was written large there.

"Could this old couple have brought to mind those foster parents you told me about in a previous session, when we discussed your childhood, the people who locked you in the cupboard under the stairs?"

He moaned a little.

"They had a small dog, didn't they?"

He covered his eyes and said, "Don"t."

"All right," I said. "We"ll talk about something else."

"You'll get thrown out of the union, showing me that," Morgan said. "Isn't there such a thing as patient confidentiality?"

"In the first place, I don't belong to a union," I said, "and in the second I'm trying to act in the best interests of all concerned."

"Thinking he could kill again, are you?"

"Who are we talking about here?" I asked.

"The second man. Jon. He seems to have a thing about old people. He's obviously very depressed."

"That's his usual state. It doesn't make him a killer. I wanted you to look at the interview before you jump to a conclusion about Nathan, the other man."

"Nathan isn't depressed, that's for sure."

"Agreed. He has a more buoyant personality than Jon. Did you notice the body language? Nathan sits forward, makes eye contact, while Jon looks down all the time. You don't see much of his face."

"That stuff about the foster parents locking him in the cupboard. Is that true?"

"Oh, yes, I'm sure of it. I'd be confident of anything Jon tells me. He doesn't give out much, but you can rely on him. With Nathan I'm never sure. He has a fertile imagination and he wants to communicate. He"s trying all the time to make his experiences interesting."

"Falling into the pond, you mean? Did you believe that?"

"It"s not impossible. It would explain the change of clothes."

"I was sure he was talking bollocks but now that you've shown me this other man I'm less confident. I'd like to question Jon myself."

"That won't be possible," I said.

He reddened. "It's a bit bloody late to put up the shutters. I've got my job to do and no one's going to stand in my way."

"Before you get heavy with me, inspector, let me run a section of the second interview again. I'm going to turn off the sound and I want you to look closely at Jon. There's a moment when he sways back and the light catches his face."

I rewound the tape and let it play again, fast forwarding until I found the piece I wanted, the moment I'd mentioned the old couple and Jon had started his swaying, a sure indicator of stress. "There." I used the freeze-frame function.

Jon's face was not quite in focus but there was enough to make him recognizable.

"Christ Almighty," Morgan said. "It's the same guy. It's Nathan."

I let the discovery sink in.

"Am I right?" he asked.

I nodded.

"Then what the hell is going on?"

"This may be hard for you to accept. Nathan and Jon are two distinct identities contained in the same individual, a condition we know as Dissociative Identity Disorder. It used to be known as Multiple Personality Disorder, but we've moved on in our understanding. These so-called personalities are fragments of the same identity rather than self-contained characters. Jon is the primary identity, passive and repressed. Nathan is an alter ego, extrovert, cheerful and inventive."

"I've heard of this," Morgan said. "It's like being possessed by different people. I saw a film once."

"Exactly. Fertile material for Hollywood, but no entertainment at all if you happen to suffer with it. The disturbance is real and frightening. A subject can take on any number of personality states, each with its own self-image and identity. The identities act as if they have no connection with each other. My job is to deconstruct them and ultimately unite them into one individual. Jon and Nathan will become Jonathan."

"Neat."

"It may sound neat, but it's a long process."

"It's neat for me," he said. "I wasn't sure which of the two guys is the killer. Now I know there's only one of them, I've got him, whatever he calls himself."

"I wouldn't count on it," I said.

He shot me a foul look.

"The therapy requires me to find points of contact between the alter-personalities. When you came to me with this double murder, I could see how disturbing it would be for Jon. He carries most of the guilt. But this investigation of yours could be a helpful disturbance. It goes right back to the trauma that I think was the trigger for this condition, his ill-treatment at the hands of foster-parents who happened to own a dog they pampered and preferred to the child."

"My heart bleeds," Morgan said, "but I have a job to do and two people are dead."

"So you tell me. Jon thinks he may have murdered them, but he didn't."

"Come off it," he said.

"Listen, please. Nathan's story was true. He really did have that experience with the balloon and the little dog and falling in the pond. For him – as the more positive of the identities – it was one more entertaining experience to relate. But for Jon, who experienced it also, it was disturbing, raising memories of the couple who fostered him and abused him. He felt quite differently, murderous even."

"Hold on," Morgan said. "Are you trying to tell me the murders never happened?"

"They happened in the mind of Jon and they are as real to him as if he cut those old people's throats himself. But I promise you the old couple are alive and well. I went to Steven Street at lunch time and spoke to them. They confirmed what Nathan told me."

"I don't get this. I'm thinking You're nuts as well."

"But it's important that you do get it," I told him. "There's a third identity at work here. It acts as a kind of conscience, vengeful, controlling and ready to condemn. It, too, is convinced the murders took place and have to be investigated. Recognizing this is the first step towards integration. Do me a favour and have another look at Jon's face. It's still on the screen."

He gave an impatient sigh and glanced at the image.
"Now look at this, inspector."
I handed him a mirror.

WINDOW OF OPPORTUNITY

"There is a window in your life. All you have to do is open it and let the sunshine in."

Nikki listened, fascinated. She'd come here expecting a con, but the man spoke like a prophet. He had his audience enthralled. He was a brilliant speaker. Looks, perfect grooming, charisma. He had it all.

"How many times have I heard someone say, 'You should have been here yesterday. It was glorious'?" He smiled. "A comment on our English weather, but it sums up our attitude to life. You should have been here yesterday. My friends, forget about yesterday. We are here *today*. Seize the day. Open that window and let the sunshine in."

The applause was wild. He'd brought them to a pitch of excitement. And this wasn't evangelism. It was about being effective in business. The setting was Lucknam Park in Wiltshire, where the government held its think-tank sessions. Companies had paid big bucks to send their upcoming executives here. Lives were being changed for ever. Not least, Nikki's.

This was her window of opportunity. She'd been sent here for the weekend by the theatrical agency to help with the role play. Inspired by what she had heard, she was about to act a role of her own. She stepped to the front, scythed a path through the admirers and placed a hand over his arm. "If you don't mind, Julian, there's someone you should meet upstairs, in your suite." To his adoring fans she said, "He'll be back, I promise."

It worked. In the lift, he said, "Who is it?"

"Me."

His amazing blue eyes widened. "I don't understand."

"I've seized the day."

The moment he laughed, she knew she'd succeeded. He was still high on the reception he'd got. When they entered the suite, she put the *do not disturb* sign over the doorknob. The sex was sensational.

They had a weekend in Paris and a Concorde trip to New York. Nikki found herself moving in circles she'd never experienced before. Royal Ascot. Henley. Her drama school training came in useful.

They married in the church in rural Dorset where her parents lived. She arrived with Daddy in a pony and trap and after the reception in Dorchester's best hotel, she and Julian were driven to the airport in a stretch limo. The honeymoon was in Bermuda. Julian paid for almost everything. Daddy couldn't have managed to spend on that scale.

"It's no problem," Julian said. "I'm ridiculously well off. Well, *we* are now."

"You deserve to be, my darling," Nikki said. "You've brought sunshine into so many lives."

They bought a huge plot of land in Oxfordshire and had their house built to Julian's design. As well as the usual bedrooms and reception rooms, it had an office suite, gym, games room and two pools, indoors and out. A tennis court, stables and landscaped garden. "I don't want you ever to be bored," Julian said. "There are times when I'll be away."

Nikki was not bored. True, she'd given up her acting to devote more time to homemaking, but she could not have managed both. When Julian was at home, he was forever finding new windows of opportunity, days to seize. His energy never flagged. He got up at five-thirty and swam a mile before breakfast and made sure she was up by seven. Even in her drama school days she hadn't risen that early. Actors work to a different pattern.

He had each day worked out. "We'll plant the new rockery this morning and clear the leaves out of the pool. This afternoon I'll need

your help fitting the curtains in the fourth bedroom. This evening
the Mountnessings are coming for dinner and I want to prepare an
Italian meal, so we'll need to fit in some shopping."

Nikki suggested more than once that most of these jobs could be
done by staff. They could afford to get people in.

"That goes against my principles," Julian said.   "There's
immense satisfaction in doing the jobs ourselves."

"One day I'd like to sit by the pool we keep so clean," she said.

"Doing what, my love?"

"Just sitting – or better still, lying."

He laughed. He thought she was joking.

In bed, he showed no sign of exhaustion. Nikki, twelve years
younger than he, was finding it a trial to match this energy.

At such a pace, it didn't take long for the house to be in perfect
shape, all the curtains and carpets fitted, the pictures hung. Nikki
had looked forward to some time to herself when the jobs were
done, but she hadn't reckoned on maintenance.

"Maintenance?"

"Keeping it up to the mark," Julian explained. "We don't let the
grass grow under our feet."

In the middle of their love-making the same night, the thought
occurred to her that he regarded this, too, as maintenance. From that
moment, the magic went out of their marriage.

What a relief when he went to America for a week on a lecture
tour. He left her a maintenance list, but she ignored it and lounged
by the pool every day watching the leaves settle on the surface and
sink to the bottom.

When he returned he was as energised as ever. Jet-lag was unknown to Julian's metabolism. "So much to attend to," he said. "If
I didn't know better, I'd almost think you'd ignored that list I gave
you."

He was as active as usual in bed. And up before five next
morning. He'd heard some house martins building a nest under the

eaves above the bedroom window. They made an appalling mess if you didn't do something about it.

When Nikki drew back the bedroom curtain she saw his sun-tanned legs right outside. He'd brought out his lightweight aluminium ladder. His feet, in gleaming white trainers and socks, were on one of the highest rungs. She had to push extra hard to open the window and force the ladder backwards, but she succeeded. And let the sunshine in.

THE CASE OF THE DEAD WAIT

A Christmas at home wasn't ever in Laura Thyme's plans. Where was home? She'd hurled a large stone through the front window of her last one. Her two-timing cradle-snatcher of a husband Nick had blighted all the nice memories of that place. She tried to think of herself these days as a free spirit. *Tried*, because deep inside she hadn't entirely got the man out of her system. He still had the capacity to hurt.

Well, she was sure of one thing. She wouldn't dump herself on either of her grown-up children. They would have plans of their own, and quite right, too. If Matthew or Helena looked forward to pulling anything on Christmas Day it wasn't a cracker with their mum. They really were free spirits, long past the stage when Laura made it her business to know who they were sleeping with.

As for Rosemary – her gardening oppo, Dr Rosemary Boxer, the ex-academic with the happy knack of finding wealthy clients with ailing plants – she'd be the perfect company for a festive lunch, but she had an elderly mum living alone. Last weekend Rosemary had called to wish Laura a merrier time than she was expecting for herself.

The result: Laura was house-sitting.

She was alone in The Withers, a large Jacobean house in Wiltshire. Two of her oldest and richest friends, Jane and Michael Eadington, were having three weeks in the Canaries. A call at the end of November had set it up. "We're in such trouble, Laura. You know we've got these silly orchids that are Mike's latest hobby? Our daughter Maeve – the model – was going to look after them and now

190

she's got a chance to do a series of shows with Calvin Klein in New York. Could you, would you, *will* you, please, be our fairy godmother?"

Sorted.

Even after discovering that the house had another resident – Wilbur, the rescue greyhound.

She'd driven the Land Rover down there on Christmas Eve. For all its mechanical uncertainties the ancient four by four was ideal transport for the country. She overheated only once, and the car didn't overheat at all. She was just in time to see the Eadingtons off. A quick introduction to the orchids, six trays of them in the conservatory under banks of fluorescent tubing. Hurried instructions about the central heating, persuading Wilbur to wear a coat for winter walks and what to do in a power failure. Firm orders not to be in the least concerned if anything broke or went wrong."It's all replaceable, darling. We're just so pleased to have you here. Treat it like your own home. Raid the freezer, watch the DVDs, drink the wine in the cellar, have an orgy if you want."

For a few minutes after they'd driven up the lane Laura wondered if she'd done the right thing. The house seemed bigger than she remembered from the last visit. She'd never once set foot upstairs. The orchids were in flower, but didn't look pleased at being handed over to her care. Winter was supposed to be the flowering season, but some of them were wilting. Mike had talked about misting and humidity levels and feeding. She didn't want any casualties. She returned to the vast space the Eadingtons used as the living room.

A sudden movement at the window gave her a wicked shock. The greyhound had emerged from behind the curtain, where he'd been sitting on the sill. Yes, a greyhound on a window sill. It was that kind of room, that kind of window, that kind of curtain. "I'm in charge now, Wilbur," she told him, wagging a finger, "and if the two of us are going to survive you'd better not play any more tricks like that."

Treat the place like your home, they'd said, so she took out her Christmas cards and started setting them up. The cards triggered mixed feelings. It was good to hear from old friends, but it could hurt when the envelopes came addressed to Nick and Laura with messages along the lines of "How are you two getting along? Give us a call and let's all meet up in 2005."

Wilbur jumped back on his sill and knocked down most of the cards.

"Making some kind of point, are we?" Laura said. But she moved them to the grand piano.

When the doorbell rang a moment later, the rest of the cards dropped out of her hand. It was a chiming bell and her charming friends had set it to the opening bar of *God Rest Ye, Merry Gentlemen*, which can be pretty startling when you don't expect it. Wilbur barked, so she had to shut him in the conservatory first.

A tall – six foot tall, at least – thin-faced woman with deep-set, accusing eyes was on the doorstep with a plate covered with a cloth. "And who the devil are you?" she said.

Laura did her best to explain, but it didn't make much impact.

"Where's young Maeve? She ought to be looking after the house," the woman said.

"Yes, but she"s dashed off to New York. A last minute change of plans."

"What do I do with these, then? I made them for the family." She lifted the cloth briefly to reveal a batch of underdone mince pies.

"I don't know," Laura said, adding with tact, "They smell delicious. I'm sorry, but you didn't say who you are."

"Gertrude Appleton from next door. We always exchange mince pies at Yuletide. Have you made yours?"

"I just arrived."

That didn't count with Gertrude Appleton. She clicked her tongue and looked ready to stamp her foot as well. "I must have one of yours, or I'll get bad luck for a year."

"Why?"

"It's Wiltshire custom, isn't it? You eat a pie on each of the twelve days of Christmas, and every one has to be baked by a different friend. Then if the Lord is merciful you'll survive to see another Christmas. Bless my soul, there isn't anyone else I can ask."

"You'd better step inside a moment," Laura said, not wanting to panic this woman and playing for time while she thought about ways to resolve the problem.

"No, I won't come in," Gertrude Appleton said, and those fierce eyes were suddenly red at the edges and starting to water. "I don"t know you from Adam. Couldn't call thee a friend."

"Let's be friends. Why not? It's the season for it," Laura said, dredging deep to sound convivial. "Listen, Gertrude, why don't I do some baking right now and make some pies for you?"

"But you won't have mincemeat."

"I'm positive all the ingredients must be in the kitchen. Jane adores cooking, as you know."

Gertrude raised her chin in a self-righteous way. "Mine was made with the puddings four weeks ago, the week after Stir-up Sunday."

"Stirrup what?"

"Stir-up Sunday. Haven't you heard of that? The last Sunday before Advent. That's when you make your puddings and mince, after the collect for the day; 'Stir up, we beseech thee, O Lord, the wills of thy people.' "

This was getting more and more weird.

"In that case, Jane may have made hers already," Laura said. "I'll check. One way or another, you'll get a mince pie from me, Gertrude. Depend upon it."

"Take these, then." Gertrude thrust the plate towards her. "You'll need some for the waits."

Laura had a mental picture of old-fashioned kitchen scales, with her mince pie being weighed against Gertrude's and found wanting.

"The carollers. They come round every Christmas Eve, and they always want a bite to eat and mulled wine, too, the boozy lot. I must be off. I have seasonal jobs to do. There's greenfly and aphids in the greenhouse."

"You're a gardener?" Laura said with interest.

"Ha!" She tossed her head. "Am I a gardener? I wouldn't bother to go on without my garden. It's the saving of me."

"I do some gardening, too. What are you going to do about the aphids – spray them?"

Gertrude looked shocked. "I don't hold with chemicals. No, I'll smoke the varmints out, like I always do."

"Fumigation? Effective, I expect, though I've never tried it," Laura said.

"I've got these magical smoke things, like little strips of brown paper. Had them for years. Just close up all the windows and seal the cracks and set light to they strips. Let it blaze for a while, and then I stamp it out so they can smoulder. Soon as the smoke appears I'm out of there quicker than hell would scorch a feather and shut the door behind me. When I go in again, there's not a greenfly left to say it ever happened."

Laura refrained from mentioning that the magical smoke things undoubtedly contained chemicals of some kind. "Good luck with it, then. And I won't forget the mince pies. Which direction do you live?"

She was glad to have a task, although she could think of better ones than this. After closing the door she carried the plate to Jane's enormous kitchen, plonked it on the table and checked the walk-in larder for jars of mincemeat.

No joy. If you were planning to spend Christmas in Lanzarote, she reflected, you wouldn't feel obliged to make mincemeat. Even on Stir-up Sunday.

She checked the freezer. Well stocked, but not with seasonal items.

She thought of the supermarket in Bradford on Avon. A bought mince pie wouldn't suffice of course. Those eyes like calculators would spot a Mr Kipling at fifty paces. The pastry, at the very least, would have to look home made.

Then Laura had her inspiration. She'd save herself the toil, tears and sweat by recycling some of Gertrude's own mince pies and simply making new lids for them. She picked a sharp knife and prised the lid off one. A neat dissection. The trick would be to spread a little jam over the mincemeat to seal the replacement.

She found all the ingredients she needed and switched on the oven.

When the phone on the wall rang she was up to her elbows in flour.

"You'll just have to leave a message after the tone," she said to it.

"This is Calvin Klein's office in New York. Mr Klein was hoping to speak to Maeve about the trip. We'll call back."

Laura said, "Calvin Klein! I could be speaking to Calvin Klein and I'm sifting ruddy pastry?"

She was adding the egg yolk and water when the phone went again. This time she grabbed it with a floury hand. In a come-hitherish tone she said, "Hi, how can I be of service?"

"Laura?"

She knew that voice and it wasn't Calvin Klein"s. "You! I thought you were someone else. Oh, never mind. It's good to hear from you."

"It's a miracle," Rosemary said. "I used one of those directory enquiry numbers and I'm sure it was someone in Calcutta, but she seemed to know the Eadingtons. You're installed in deepest Wilts, then?"

"In deepest sums it up. I haven't been here an hour and I'm already making pastry for the locals. What's with you?"

"A change of plans, actually. Mother forgot to tell me. When I got here she was all packed up to leave. You know she does competitions? She won a trip for two to the Bahamas, courtesy of Cadbury's, or Kelloggs, or someone."

"How marvellous! But what are you going to wear? I bet you didn't pack your bikini."

"Oh, she isn't taking me." Rosemary said as if that went without saying. "You know what mother's like. She's taking some old gent called Mr Pinkerton from the Tai Chi group. I'm high and dry, Laura. I was wondering if – well – if there's a spare bed in this stately pile you're looking after."

Laura took a step back and there was a yelp from Wilbur, who had got too close. "That wasn't me. Do I have a spare bed? Dozens. That's brilliant."

"I could get a train to Bath tonight."

"You've made my Christmas. I"ll be waiting on the platform."

She had fitted the fresh lids on those pies, twelve of them, and very appetizing they looked. She'd used a beaten egg glaze that gave them a lovely amber finish to leave no doubt that they were different from Gertrude Appleton's insipid-looking offerings. Rosemary was due on a late train at 10.50, so it was likely that the carollers would get their treats. Would eleven pies be enough? She needed to put one aside, of course, for Gertrude, to help her survival plan. If twelve or more carollers came, Laura told herself, it was a sure bet that some wouldn't want another pie if they'd been eating them all around the village. The mulled wine simmering in a saucepan was another matter.

About eight-thirty, Wilbur howled and Laura heard muted singing. She shut Wilbur in the kitchen and opened the front door. She needn't have worried about the catering. A mere four men stood under a lantern. Three wore cardboard and tinsel crowns and were giving an uneven rendering of *We Three Kings*. The fourth, holding up the lantern, was the vicar unless his collar was from a carnival shop, like the crowns. He looked too young to be a clergyman. Just like policemen, Laura thought.

When they started on the solo verses, Melchior's reedy voice almost faded away. For a fat man he was producing a very thin sound. Caspar, with "Frankincense to offer have I" was marginally better, and Balthazar, "Myrrh is mine, its bitter perfume", lost the tune altogether. She was thankful when they got to the last chorus. She popped a two-pound coin into the box and invited them inside.

"Muddy feet," said the vicar. "We'd better not."

Melchior had already taken a step forward and needed restraining by his companions. Too much mulled wine already, Laura suspected. But she still fetched the tray from the kitchen with the jug of wine and the pies.

"I may have over-catered here. I was expecting more of you," she said as she invited them to help themselves. The man who'd sung the part of Caspar handed round the plate of mince pies, but it was obvious that they'd eaten well already. Only Melchior took one. The wine was more popular.

"We would have had two shepherds as well," Balthazar said, "but one didn't show up and the other dropped out at Long Farm."

"It's quite a trek," the vicar said.

"He was legless," Balthazar said.

"You don't live here, do you?" Caspar asked Laura. "You're not a burglar, by any chance?"

"Giving us mulled wine and the finest mince pie I've had all night? You must be joking," Melchior said to his friend.

A slightly dodgy mince pie, Laura almost confessed. They seemed likeable men, even if their singing wasn't up to much. She introduced herself and explained about the house-sitting. They told her their names but she soon forgot them. They were the vicar and Caspar, Melchior and Balthazar tonight, and she'd probably never see them again, so why think of them as anything else?

"What do you do when you're not house-sitting?" the tuneless one, Balthazar, asked.

"Gardening, mainly."

"So do I. Not a lot of gardening to be done this time of year," little Caspar said.

"You're wrong about that," Laura said. "There are no end of jobs. I'll be out there tomorrow."

"Cutting some holly and mistletoe?" the vicar said.

"Good suggestion. The house could do with some, as you see."

"Christmas roses? You've got some in the front."

"If you mean the *helleborus niger*, they're not such good specimens. The ones you buy in florists come so much taller and whiter, thanks to forcing," Laura said, thinking Rosemary would have been proud of that bit of expertise.

"Nasty things. Poisonous," Melchior said, slurring his words even more.

"Mistletoe berries are poisonous, too," Balthazar said.

The vicar decided not to go down that route. "We'd better drink up, gentlemen. Three more houses and a long walk to go."

"Have you been to Gertrude Appleton?" Laura asked.

"The house afore you. Stingy old mucker," Melchior said.

"That"s a bit unseasonal, isn't it?" the vicar said.

"We all know Gertrude," Caspar said. "Before we get a glass or a bite to eat from her, we have to promise to take *her* a mince pie after Christmas."

"And if we forget, she'll come hammering on our doors," Balthazar said.

Laura was about to explain that it was a superstition, but stopped herself. These villagers didn't miss a thing. They'd know all about Gertrude.

"Thanks for these, good lady," Caspar said as he returned the plate, with ten of the eleven pies remaining. "Sorry we couldn't all do justice to them."

Melchior said without warning, "I need to sit down. I'm feeling dizzy."

"You'd better come in," Laura offered. "I was wondering about you."

"And It's not the wine," said Balthazar. "He's a teetotaler."
Laura gave Balthazar a second look, but he seemed to be speaking in all seriousness. She noticed Melchior didn't have a glass in his hand.

"Would you mind, Mrs Thyme?" the vicar said. "I don't think he's capable of continuing." He picked the crown off the fat man's head. "I'll have to be Melchior now." Judged by the speed of the change he'd wanted a starring role all evening.

Laura took a grip on Melchior's arm and steered him inside to an armchair. Then she said something she was to regret. "Why don't you gentlemen finish your round and come back for him?"

"He farms just up the lane," Caspar said, and Laura thought she detected a suggestion that they might not, after all, return for their companion. "Blackberry Farm. It can't be more than three hundred yards."

They waved goodnight.

After closing the door, Laura glanced at her watch. There was still ample time before she needed to collect Rosemary.

Melchior had slumped in the chair and was snoring softly.

"Strong coffee for you," Laura said.

He made a sound she chose to take as appreciation. It could have been a belch.

In the kitchen, Wilbur was round her feet. She found the store of dog food and opened a tin. She said, "Consider yourself lucky, Wilbur. I've got other demands on my time."

When she took the coffee to Melchior his snoring was heavier and his chin was buried in his chest. This wasn't good. She didn't want this overweight man settling into a deep sleep and being immovable just when she needed to drive to Bath. She checked the time again. She really ought to be leaving in less than an hour. She wasn't certain how long it would take to drive to the station.

"Coffee?"

No response.

"Have some coffee. It'll brighten you up."

Wishful thinking. He didn't make a murmur that wasn't a snore.

In a louder voice she said, "I made the coffee."

This was becoming a predicament. She'd have to touch the man's face or hands to get a response, but she'd only just met him.

Didn't even know his real name. How do I get myself into situations like this? she thought.

She put down the coffee and stood with her arms folded wondering how to deal with this. Wilbur came in and sniffed at the mud on the boots.

Fresh air, she decided. She flung open a couple of windows and an icy blast of December ripped through the room.

Wilbur streaked upstairs, but Melchior didn't move a muscle.

"Come on, man!" Laura said. She found the remote and switched on the television. The Nine Lessons and Carols at full volume. Switched the channel to the Three Tenors.

No result.

In frustration Laura brought her two hands together and slapped her own face quite hard. She'd have to overcome her innate decorum and give him a prod. Alone with a strange bloke in someone else's house, but it had to be done.

First she switched off the three of them belting out *Nessun Dorma*. Her nerves couldn't take it.

Tentatively she put out a finger and touched the back of Melchior's right hand, resting on the arm of the chair. It remained quite still. She placed the whole of her hand across it and squeezed.

There was a slight reaction, a twitch of the eyelids, but they didn't open. Laura leaned closer and blew on them. Nothing. She drew a deep breath and patted his fat face.

He made a sound, no more than "Mm" – but a definite response.

"Wake up, please," she said. "I don't want you asleep."

A triumph. The eyes opened and stared at her.

"It's no good," she told him. "You can't sit here for ever. Let's see if you can walk to the car and I'll drive you home. Blackberry Farm, isn't it?"

At the mention of his address, Melchior made a definite effort to move. He rocked forward and groaned. Laura thrust her hand under his armpit and encouraged the movement. Out of sheer determination she got him to his feet. He was still unsteady, but she wrapped his arm around her shoulders and hung onto it and kept him upright.

"The car's outside. Come on. Start walking."

It was slow progress and a huge physical effort, but she kept him on the move, talking all the time in the hope that it would keep him conscious. Getting down the two small steps at the front door was hard enough, but the real challenge was hoisting him onto the passenger seat of the Land Rover.

She swung the door open with her free hand. "I'm going to need your help here, Melchior. One giant leap for mankind."

He moaned a little, maybe at Laura's attempt to be cheerful.

To encourage him, she curled her hand under his knee and lifted his right leg up to the level of the vehicle floor. It felt horribly limp. She found places for his hands to grip. "On the count of three," she said, "and I'll probably end up with a slipped disc. One, two, three!"

If he made some gesture towards the performance it wasn't obvious. Laura found herself making a superhuman effort. Dignity abandoned, she put her shoulder under his rump and inched him upwards. All those hours of heavy gardening paid off. He got one buttock onto the seat and she rammed him like a front-row forward until he was in a position where she could snap the safety belt across.

She ran back to the house and closed the windows and door. Wilbur was inside, but did she have the key? She hoped so.

The Land Rover, bless its antiquated ignition system, started first time.

Blackberry Farm. Which way? Her passenger was in no condition to say. Laura swung right and hoped. The lanes were unlit, of course. Her full beam probed the hedgerows ahead. Can't be more than three hundred yards, Caspar had said. She'd gone that distance already. She continued for another two minutes, then found a gate entrance. Nothing so helpful as a sign. She reversed into the space and retraced her route. Maybe she should have turned left coming out of The Withers.

Then she saw the board for Blackberry Farm fixed to a drystone wall. Drove into the yard and sounded the horn. She'd need help getting Melchior down. It would be useful if he had a couple of hefty sons.

From one of the farm buildings came a wisp of a woman wearing overalls and wellies. She was about Melchior's age, Laura judged. Two sheep dogs came with her, barking.

"I've brought the farmer home," Laura said, competing to be heard. "He's rather tired. Is there anyone who can help get him down?"

The little lady spread her hands. "There's only me, my love."

Laura got out and opened the passenger door. "We'll have to manage together then. Is he your husband?"

"Yes, and I don't like the look of 'un,' the little lady said. "Douglas, you gawpus, what's the matter with 'ee?"

Laura looked. Her passenger had taken a definite turn for the worse. He was making jerky movements with his head and left leg. Change of plan. "I think we should get your husband to a doctor fast," she said. "Jump aboard."

"I can't come with 'ee," the farmer"s wife said. "I've got a cow in calf."

"But I'm a stranger here. I don't know where to take him," Laura almost wailed.

"Horse piddle."

"What?"

"Royal United, Bath. Agzy-dennal Emergissy."

Laura understood now. "Which way?"

"Left out of the yard and straight up the lane till you reach the A36. You'll pick up the horse piddle signs when you get close to the city."

"Can you call them and say I'm on the way with a man having convulsions?"

"After I've seen to the cow."

Laura swung the Land Rover towards the gate, scattering the dogs, and started up the lane. "Don't worry," she said to Melchior, or Douglas, "you'll be getting help very soon." The only response was a vomiting sound.

"Please! Not in the Land Rover," she muttered.

She was forced to concentrate on the drive, trusting in the Lord that she wouldn't meet anything as she belted along the lane. Passing points seemed to be unknown in this part of Wiltshire. The beam picked out the scampering shape of a badger up ahead. It saved itself by veering off to the left.

Then she spotted headlights descending a hill and guessed she was close to the main road. Right or left? She'd have to make a guess. Her instinct said right.

Forced to stop at the intersection, she glanced at her passenger. His face was still twitching and looked a dreadful colour in the passing lights. This was much more serious than over-indulgence in mulled wine.

Now was when she could do with an emergency light and siren. Out on the A36, with a long run into Bath – and a sign told her she *had* taken the right direction – she was overtaking like some teenage joyrider in a stolen Merc. Other drivers flashed their lights at her and one idiot got competitive and tried to force her to stay in the wrong lane. But there came a point when she was high on the downs and the city lights appeared below her. At any other time she would have been enchanted by the view. All she could think was where is the hospital?

At the first traffic lights she wound down the window and asked. Of course it had to be on the opposite side of the city. Another hair-raising burn-up through the streets and she found seriously helpful signs at last.

A&E. She drew up behind an ambulance. Someone was rolling a stretcher on wheels towards the Land Rover. The farmer's wife must have alerted them. The passenger door was opened.

"Is this the man with convulsions?"

Laura took this to be one of those inane questions people ask in times of crisis. Of course he had convulsions. He'd been convulsing all the way to the hospital.

But when she turned to look at him, he'd gone still.

They checked his heart. The doctor shook his head. They unstrapped Melchior and transferred him to the stretcher and raced it inside.

Nothing had been said to Laura. She could only conclude that she'd brought in a man who was dead. Maybe they'd revive him. She moved the Land Rover away from the entrance and went in to find out.

She was twenty minutes late collecting Rosemary. It was such a relief to see her.

"I'm so sorry."

"My dear, you look drained. Whatever has happened?"

Rosemary insisted on taking the wheel and Laura told her story as they headed out of the city.

"So couldn't they revive him?" Rosemary said.

"What's the phrase? Dead on arrival. They worked on him, but it was no use."

"What was it – heart?"

"No one would say. They'll do an autopsy, I suppose. I told them all I could. It seemed to happen very suddenly. He said he felt dizzy and asked to sit down. I thought it was the mulled wine, but it turned out he hadn't had a drop all evening. He's TT. Then he fell asleep, a really deep sleep. I got him into the car – I don't know how – he was pretty far gone – and his wife noticed the convulsions, which was when I knew he needed medical help."

"Dizziness, anaesthesia and convulsions. Was he vomiting?"

"Trying to, anyway."

"It sounds more like poisoning to me," Rosemary said.

"Poisoning?"

"Did he eat anything?"

"One of the mince pies I handed out. That's all."

"That's all right then," Rosemary said. "No problem with that, if you were the cook."

Laura clapped her hand to her mouth.

Rosemary said, "What's wrong?"

"I did something dreadful. I may have killed him."

"Hold on." Rosemary pulled into a layby and turned off the engine. "Laura, get a grip and tell me just what you're talking about."

Laura's voice shook as she explained what she had done with Gertrude Appleton's pies. "If there was anything in them I'll never forgive myself."

From a distant field came the triple bark of a dog-fox, answered by a vixen sounding eerily like a woman screaming. Rosemary shivered. "We'll face this together."

It was close to midnight when they drove up the lane to The Withers. Christmas morning, almost.

In a effort to lighten the mood, Rosemary said, "If you look in that bag at your feet you'll find I packed a bottle of bubbly. Let's open it as soon as we get in, shall we?"

"You're a star," Laura said. "Some Christmas cheer in spite of everything." But her voice trailed away.

A police car was on the drive.

"Is one of you ladies Mrs Laura Thyme?" the officer asked. "You're about to see in Christmas at the police station."

It was the day after Boxing Day, and still Laura was troubled by guilt.

"What upset me most was the way that detective put his hand on my head and pressed down when I got in their car, just like they do with murderers."

"That didn't mean a thing," Rosemary said.

"Well, he didn't do it to you." Laura"s voice shook a little. "Is it possible those pies were poisoned?" \

"Possible, I suppose."

"Think of what goes into mincemeat – all those rich flavours, the fruits, the spice, the peel. You could add almost any poison and it wouldn't be obvious."

"If they were poisoned, we've still got eleven of them sitting in the fridge."

"Ten. I handed the singers a plate with eleven and ten came back. The farmer took one and ate it. That's certain."

"There are eleven in the fridge. I counted," Rosemary said in her precise way.

Laura snapped her fingers. "You're right. I kept one back for Gertrude, the neighbour. She asked specially."

"Gertrude," said Rosemary. "She's the one the police should be questioning. I wonder if she'd eat that pie if you offered it. She wouldn't know it's one of hers with a new lid." ·

"I don't want another death on my hands."

"This is all supposition anyway," Rosemary said. "We'll probably find the poor man died of natural causes."

"Listen, if Gertrude is a poisoner, those pies were meant for my friends Jane, Michael and Maeve. Was she in dispute with them? You know what neighbours can be like."

"Neighbourly, in most cases."

"What could she have used?"

"You said She's a gardener. You and I know that a garden is full of plants capable of poisoning people."

"Christmas roses!" Laura said. "We've got some in the front."

"Let's not leap to any conclusions," Rosemary said, trying to remain calm. "Besides, your carol singers had been round most of the village eating mince pies and drinking wine before they got to you. If he was poisoned, it could have been someone else's pie that did it."

Laura refused to think of anyone else except Gertrude as responsible. "I'd dearly like to know if she was having a feud with Jane and family."

"Why don't we ask someone?"

"In a village? Who do you ask?"

"The vicar. He ought to be discreet."

The vicarage was ten minutes away, at the end of a footpath across the frost-covered fields. If nothing else, they'd be exercising Wilbur the greyhound. With difficulty they got him into his coat.

They passed Gertrude's garden on the way. Laura grabbed Rosemary's arm. "Look, she's got a patch of Christmas roses."

"She's also got white bryony in her hedge and a poinsettia in her window, both of them potential killers, but it doesn't make her a murderer," Rosemary said to curb Laura's imagination. "She may have mistletoe inside the house. Death cap toadstools growing in her compost. I see she has a greenhouse. There could be an oleander in there."

But Laura was unstoppable. "I didn't tell you about the greenhouse. She told me she was fumigating it for pests, and I don't know what she was using, but it sounded primitive and hazardous as well. Would you believe burning shreds of paper that she had to stamp on to produce the smoke?"

Rosemary winced. "Out of the ark, by the sound of it. Well, out of some dark shed. Old gardeners used flakes of nicotine. Highly dangerous, of course, and illegal now. What's wrong with a spray?"

Laura tapped the side of her nose. "Chemicals."

"Fumes are eco-friendly, are they? Isn't that the vicarage ahead?"

They shouted to Wilbur, who must have scented fox or rabbit. He raced back, tail going like a mainspring, and got no reward for obedience. He was put on the lead and no doubt decided it's a dog's life.

The vicarage was surrounded by a ten-foot yew hedge that Rosemary mentioned was another source of deadly poison. Laura gave her a long look. "You wouldn't be winding me up, would you?"

She smiled. "Encouraging a sense of proportion."

The vicar, in a Bath Rugby Club sweatshirt, was relaxing after his Christmas duties. He sounded genuinely disturbed about the death of Melchior, and guilt-stricken, also. "If I'd had any idea he was so ill, I wouldn't have asked you to take him in," he said to Laura. "You acted splendidly, getting him to hospital."

"I couldn't tell the police much about him," Laura said. "Didn't even know his surname."

"Boon. Douglas Boon. His family have farmed here for generations. Blackberry Farm is the last of the old farms. I suppose his wife inherits. There aren't any children. She'll have to sell up, I should think."

"What do you mean by the last of the old farms?"

"Traditional. Cattle and sheep. Everyone's switching to flowers and bulbs since that foot and mouth epidemic. We didn't have an outbreak here, thank the Lord, but other farmers didn't want the risk and sold up. Much of the land has been put under glass by Ben Black, known to you as Balthazar."

"The tall man?" Laura said.

"A giant in the nursery garden business and a very astute businessman. Lay chairman of the Parochial Church Council as well, so I have to work closely with him. He's from London originally. To the locals, he's an incomer, but he gives them a living."

"So he'll be interested in Blackberry Farm if it comes on the market?" Rosemary said.

"No question." The vicar sighed. "I happen to know he made Douglas a handsome offer last week, far more than it's worth, and I heard that Douglas was willing at last to sell."

"Every man has his price," Laura remarked.

"Yes, and it is also said that gold goes in at any gate except the gate of heaven. As it turns out, Ben will get the farm for a fraction of that offer if Kitty Boon wants to sell." He looked wistful. "I'll be sorry if the cows go. They hold up the traffic when they're being driven along the lane for milking, but rows of daffodils wouldn't be the same at all."

Laura had a vision of rows of daffies holding up the traffic.

"Do you mind if I ask about someone else?" she said. "On Christmas Eve Gertrude Appleton called with some mince pies."

"Gertrude?" The vicar had a special smile for this member of his flock. "That's one of her many superstitions. Something about exchanging pies to avoid bad luck. False worship really. I don't approve, but we all indulge her because she's such a formidable lady."

"Harmless?"

"We have to hope so."

"Is she on good terms with my friends, Jane and Michael Eadington?"

"As far as I know."

"No boundary disputes? Complaints about the greyhound? Excessive noise?"

"I've never heard of any. Why do you ask?"

Rosemary said quickly, "It's a joke. Those pies she brought round aren't the most appetising."

The vicar smiled. "Now I understand. Did you try one?"

She shook her head. "It's the look of them, paler than Hamlet's father."

His eyes twinkled at that. "I'm afraid not one of the carollers could face one the other night."

"And will you indulge her, as you put it, and exchange mince pies?"

He smiled, "The annual batch of pies for Gertrude is one more parochial duty for me. I don't have a wife to cook for me, unfortunately."

"Your pies are delicious, I'm sure," Laura said, liking this young clergyman.

Rosemary said in her no-nonsense voice, "The third of the Three Kings was Caspar, right?"

"Little Colin Price the other night," the vicar said. "He's my tenor, at the other end of the scale from Ben Black."

"As a singer, do you mean?"

"I was thinking of his situation. Colin's up against it financially. He was a dairy farmer like Douglas, but less efficient. He lost a big contract with the Milk Marketing Board a couple of years ago and Douglas bought him out. He's reduced to work as a jobbing gardener these days."

Laura exchanged a wry smile with Rosemary. "There are worse ways to make a living."

"True. But I have to object when he does it on Sundays sometimes and misses Morning Service. Colin just smiles and quotes those lines 'One is nearer God's heart in a garden than anywhere else on earth.' That isn't scripture, I tell him, It's a bit of doggerel."

The vicar came out to see them off and Rosemary admired the yew hedge and asked if he clipped it himself.

"Every twig," he said. "Can't afford a gardener on my stipend. Some people seem to have the idea that yew is slow-growing. From experience I can tell you that's a myth."

"What do you do with the clippings – burn them?"

"No, I bag them up and send them away to be used in cancer treatment."

"For the taxol in them," Rosemary said. "Very public-spirited."

"I must admit they pay me as well," the vicar said with a fleeting smile at Laura.

Their return across the frost-white fields was spoiled by a blue police light snaking through the lanes. Laura said, "I just *know* it's going to stop at The Withers."

She was right.

When they got there the inspector was looking smug. "You might be thinking the forensics lab was closed over Christmas, but I happen to know one scientist who is a perfect Scrooge, can't stand the parties and the eating and only too grateful to earn double overtime. It's bad news for you, I'm afraid, Mrs Thyme. The late Douglas Boon was poisoned. My scientist found significant amounts of taxin in his body."

"Toxin?" Laura said.

"Taxin. It comes from the yew," Rosemary murmured. "Just like taxol, only this is no help to anyone, not to be taken in any form."

"You're well informed," the inspector said.

"I'm a plant biologist."

"And Mrs Thyme? Are you also an expert?"

"Only an amateur," Laura said.

About as amateur as a million-pound-a-week footballer, if the inspector's look was anything to go by. "I've got a warrant to search this house."

"Here? What are you looking for?" Rosemary asked.

"We know from the stomach contents that the last food Mr Boon ingested was a mince pie. In your statement of Christmas Eve, Mrs Thyme, you admitted administering a pie to the deceased."

"*Administering*?" said Rosemary. "She handed round a plate of pies, that's all."

"And we'd like to have them examined, if they aren't already destroyed."

This was a defining moment for Laura. Should she confess to changing the lids on Gertrude's pies? She glanced towards Rosemary, who nodded back. "Inspector," she said, "there's something I ought to tell you, something I didn't mention last time."

The inspector raised both hands as if a wall was about to collapse. "Don't say another word. I'm going to issue an official caution and you're going to accompany me to the police station."

"Oh, what nonsense," Rosemary said. "The pies were made by someone else, and that's all there is to it."

"Don't put ideas in her head, Miss Boxer. She's in enough trouble already."

As Laura got into the police car, Wilbur whimpered. The hand pressing down on the back of Laura's head felt like an executioner's this time. They kept her waiting more than an hour while the house was searched. The plate of mince pies, wrapped now in a polythene evidence bag, was carried from the kitchen in triumph.

Rosemary watched in silence, sickened and infuriated by this turn of events. She could see Laura's troubled face through the rear window of the patrol car as they drove away. She thought about following in the Land Rover, and then decided they wouldn't let her near the interview room. She'd be more useful finding out precisely what had been going on in this sinister village.

By asking around, she tracked Colin Price (the little man Laura knew as Caspar) to the garden behind the village hall. He was up a ladder pruning a huge rambler rose. The clippings were going into a trailer he'd wheeled across the lawn.

"What's that – an albertine?" Rosemary asked, seeing how the new shoots sprouted from well up the old stems.

"Spot on."

"Late pruning, then?"

"It's a matter of getting round to these jobs," he said. "I can only do so much. It's mostly grass-cutting through the summer and well into autumn. Other jobs have to wait."

She introduced herself and mentioned that she was Laura Thyme's friend. "Laura had the unpleasant job of driving poor Mr Boon to hospital on Christmas Eve. You met her earlier, of course."

"That's correct," he said. "And now she's been picked up by the police, I hear."

"Word travels fast," Rosemary said.

"Fields have eyes, and woods have ears, as the saying goes." He got down from his ladder. "But all of us can see a police car with the light flashing. What do you want to ask me?"

"It's about the man who died, Douglas Boon. Could anyone have predicted that he'd take one of the mince pies my friend offered round?"

He shrugged. "Doug liked his food. Everyone knew that. I've rarely seen him let a plate of pies go by."

"So he had one at every house that evening?"

"Every one except Miss Appleton's."

"Gertrude's? Was there a reason for that?"

A slow smile. "Have you met the lady?"

"No."

"Have you sampled her cooking?"

"No."

"If you had, you'd understand." He closed the pruning shears in a way that punctuated the remark.

She said, "I thought you all exchanged pies with her."

"We do, but we don't have to eat them. My wife always makes a batch and I prefer hers any day."

Rosemary ventured into even more uncertain territory. "Did Douglas have any enemies around here?"

He mused on that for a moment. "None that I heard of."

"His dairy farm was the last in the village, I heard. What will happen to it now?"

"Kitty isn't capable of running it alone. Likely it'll be bought for peanuts by Ben Black and turned into another nursery. That's the trend."

"Sad to see the old farms disappearing," Rosemary said. "It happened to yours, I was told."

"Bad management on my part," Colin said without hesitation. "I've no one to blame but myself. Doug acquired the herd and my three fields."

"Would you buy them back if they came on the market?"

"I'm in no position to. Ben is the only winner here."

She asked where Ben was to be found.

"This time of day? I wouldn't know. Last I saw of him was yesterday morning."

She decided instead to call on the village Lucretia Borgia.

The cottage could have done with some new thatching, but otherwise it looked well maintained. Gertrude Appleton must have seen Rosemary coming because the door opened before she reached it.

Tall, certainly. She had to dip her head to look out of her door. And she was holding a meat cleaver.

"What brings you here?" she asked Rosemary. The eyes fitted Laura's description of them as about as sympathetic as wet pebbles.

"I'm staying next door."

"You think I don't know that? What do you want?"

A little Christmas cheer wouldn't come amiss, Rosemary thought. "My friend Laura has been taken to the police station for questioning about the death of Mr Boon."

"So?"

"So she can't keep her promise to bring you a mince pie. We had some left, but the police have seized them."

Those cheerless eyes widened a little. "She baked me a pie?"

Rosemary sidestepped that one. "She was saying it mattered to you, something about good luck for next year."

Gertrude's face lightened up and she lowered the cleaver to her side. "Did she really?"

"She said you generously made her a present of some pies of your own, and advised her that the carol singers were coming round."

Abruptly, the whole look reverted to deep hostility. "Was it one of my pies she fed to Douglas Boon?"

"I believe it was."

"And now They're saying he was poisoned? Are you accusing me?" Suddenly the cleaver was in front of her chest again.

Rosemary swayed out of range. "Absolutely not."

"You said the police seized some pies. Were any of mine among them?"

"Actually, yes."

Gertrude took in a sharp breath. "I've made pies for twenty years and more, and never a word of complaint."

"So we've got to find out how some taxin – that's from a yew bush or a tree, the seeds, the foliage or the stems – found its way into that pie, which apparently killed him."

"One of mine? How could it?"

"Can you remember making the mincemeat? Did anyone come by while you were mixing the fruit?"

"Not a living soul."

"Could anyone have interfered with it since?"

"Impossible. This isn't open house to strangers, you know. No one crosses my threshold."

That much Rosemary was willing to believe. "You don't have a yew bush in your garden, I suppose?"

"I wouldn't. It's the tree of death. It kills horses, cattle, more animals than any other plant."

"Yes, but this was deliberate. Human deaths from taxin are rare. Someone added seeds of yew, or some part of it, to the mincemeat Douglas Boon consumed on Christmas Eve. Don't you see, Gertrude? We've got to discover how this happened. I'm certain Laura is innocent."

"They'll pin this on me," she said. "That"s what they'll do, and everyone in the village will say the old witch deserves it."

"Will you do something for Laura's sake? For your own sake?" Rosemary said. "Will you think about everything connected with the making of the mincemeat? The chopping of the fruit, the source of all the ingredients, sultanas, currants, raisins, peel, nuts – whatever went into it. Go over it in your mind. Did anyone else contribute anything?"

"No."

"Please take time to think it over."

Gertrude sniffed, stepped back and closed the door.

Late that afternoon, Wilbur's barking brought Rosemary to the front door before Laura emerged from the police car that returned her to The Withers.

"What a relief," Rosemary said. "Have they finished with you?"

"I wouldn't count on it," Laura said as she scratched behind Wilbur's ears. He'd given her a delightful, if slobbery, welcome.

Over a fortifying cup of tea, she told her tale. She had been interviewed three times and kept in a room that wasn't quite a cell, but felt like one. She'd told the detectives everything she knew and provided a written statement. "I'm sure they would have charged me with murder if it wasn't for Gertrude's pies. They had them analysed and got the results back this afternoon."

"Poisoned?"

"No." Laura smiled. "They were harmless, all of them."

Rosemary pressed her fingers to her lips. "I find that hard to believe."

"So did the inspector. You should have seen his face when he told me I was free to leave."

"That's amazing. Gertrude is innocent."

"And so am I." Laura glanced across the room. "What's he eating? Wilbur, what have you got in your mouth? No, Wilbur, no!" She dashed across and forced open the dog's jaws. A small piece of mincemeat fell into her palm. "Rosemary, look. There are crumbs on the carpet. I think he's had a mince pie."

Rosemary was already at her side fingering the pastry crumbs. "It can't have come from inside the house. The police spent over an hour searching the place."

"The garden, then," Laura said. "He must have found it in the garden."

They went to the front door. "Let him show us," Rosemary said. "Find it, Wilbur. Good dog."

Wilbur knew what was wanted. He went straight to a lavender bush and lifted it with his nose. A brownish conical thing was exposed.

"A death cap," Rosemary said.

"Do you mind?" Laura said. "That's pastry. That's one of my lids." She picked it up and turned it over. "How on earth did this get here?"

The question hung in the air unanswered. Wilbur's co-operation could only go so far.

"Should we get him to a vet?" Laura said.

"Let's give him water first."

Rosemary filled his bowl and brought it to him. He lapped it obediently.

"He doesn't seem to be suffering," Laura said. "The onset was rapid with Douglas Boon."

"Taxin is one of the quickest of all the plant poisons," Rosemary said. "I doubt if we'd get him to a vet in time."

"He looks all right."

Wilbur licked her hand and wagged his tail.

"I think he wants some more."

An hour later, he was still all right.

Rosemary and Laura allowed themselves the luxury of fresh tea. They didn't get to drink it because Wilbur unexpectedly barked several times and ran to the door. Someone was outside holding a flashlight.

Laura looked out. The evening had drawn in and she had difficulty seeing who it was.

The voice was familiar. "You'd better call the police," Gertrude Appleton said. "I've gone and killed another man."

"This can't be true," Laura said. "You're in the clear. Your pies were analysed today and there's nothing toxic in them."

With a stare like the condemned woman in a silent movie, Gertrude said, "Follow me," and started towards the gate.

Laura looked at Rosemary. They'd been in dangerous situations before. Rosemary shrugged. At least Gertrude wasn't wielding that cleaver. They went after her.

She paused at her garden gate and turned the flashlight beam on Rosemary and Laura to check that they were behind her. Then she led them to her greenhouse and unlocked the door.

The place would have been creepy even in daylight, with a huge overhanging vine that still had some of its leaves, brown and contorted. Other skeletal plants in pots had been brought in for the winter. Gertrude edged around a raised flowerbed in the centre and directed the flashlight at a dark shape on the floor.

A man's body.

"I killed him," Gertrude said with a stricken sigh. "I never looked here when I smoked out the pests on Christmas Eve. I just put down the stuff and set light to it."

"He is dead, I suppose?" Laura said.

Rosemary leaned over for a closer look. "Well dead, I would say."

Gertrude was still reliving the experience. "I made sure it was smouldering and got out, locking the door behind me. Opened it an hour ago and found him. I can only suppose he was drunk and crept in here to sleep it off." She paused. "Will I go to prison?"

"Let me have the flashlight," Laura said. She edged past Gertrude for a closer inspection. "I can't say I know him intimately, but isn't this one of the carol singers, the tall one, Balthazar?"

"Ben Black? It is!" Gertrude said in despair. "God forgive me. What have I done?"

"Unless I've got my facts muddled, you haven't done anything at all," Laura said. "You fumigated on Christmas Eve after visiting me, am I right?"

Gertrude nodded.

"That was in the afternoon? You locked the door and didn't open up until today? You left the key in the lock?"

Another nod from Gertrude.

"Think about it," Laura said. "Ben was alive and singing carols that same evening. He couldn't have been trapped in here. See, there's dried blood on the back of his scalp. It looks as if someone hit him over the head and dumped the body in here. Yes, we will call the police, but I don't think you're in any trouble."

Over cocoa that night, with the dog asleep in front of a real log fire, Rosemary summed up the case. "What we have are two impossible crimes. One man poisoned by a harmless mince pie and another bludgeoned to death in a locked greenhouse."

"The second crime isn't impossible," Laura said. "The key was in the door. Obviously the killer could get in and out. They put the body in there and locked it again thinking it might not be found for some time."

"They?"

"Could be a man or a woman. That's all I mean."

"Then are we agreed that there's only one killer?" Rosemary said.

"Let's hope so."

"So why was Ben Black bumped off?"

"Because he knew something about the first crime?"

"Very likely. And why did the first crime take place?"

"The death of Douglas Boon? It could have been a mistake," Laura said. "Maybe he ate a poisoned pie intended for Ben Black."

"I don't think so," Rosemary said. "Remember, Douglas was a gannet. He was guaranteed to take any pie that was offered except one of Gertrude's."

"Hers were on the heavy side," Laura recalled.

"So if we assume Douglas's death was planned and carried out in cold blood, what did Ben find out that meant he had to be murdered as well?"

"It's got to be something to do with the mince pie Wilbur found under the lavender bush," Laura said.

"Another harmless pie?"

They were silent for some time, staring into the flames. "Do you think that young vicar is all he seems?" Rosemary said.

Laura frowned. "I rather like him."

"A bad sign usually," Rosemary said. "Let's go and see him tomorrow."

"Won't the police say we're interfering?"

"They're going to be ages getting to the truth, if they ever do. For them, it's all about analysing DNA evidence, and we know how long that takes. A good old-fashioned face-to-face gets a quicker result."

O vernight it snowed and they both slept late.
"It's the total silence, I think," Laura said. "I always get a marvellous sleep when there's a snowfall."

"Whatever it is," Rosemary said,"I've had a few ideas about these deaths and I'd like to try them out on you."

After breakfast they put on wellies and took Wilbur for his longest walk yet. He was more frisky than ever, bounding through the snow regardless of that mince pie the day before. People might spurn Gertrude's cooking, but this hound had thrived on it. Along the way, they kept a look out for yew trees, and counted five in and around the village, and three yew hedges. Over a pre-lunch drink in a quiet corner of the pub, Rosemary unfolded her theory to Laura and it made perfect sense. They knew from experience that theories are all very well, but the proof can be more elusive. They decided to go looking for it late in the afternoon.

" A re we clear about what each of us does?" Rosemary said.
"All too clear," Laura said. "You get the inside job while I wait out here with Wilbur and freeze."

"He'll be fine. He loves the snow and he's got his coat on. Just stroll around as if you're exercising him."

They had parked outside the village church.

Rosemary went in and found the vicar slotting hymn numbers into the frame above the pulpit.

"Busy, I see."

He almost dropped the numbers. "You startled me. I have a choir practice shortly."

"I know. We had a walk this morning, and I saw the church notice board."

"We meet earlier when the schools are on holiday."

"A smaller choir now."

"Sadly, yes. Plenty of trebles and altos, but only one tenor remaining. I'm going to miss Ben and Douglas dreadfully."

"Would you mind if I stay and listen?"

He looked uneasy. "I don't know what sort of voice they'll be in after Christmas. There's always a feeling of anticlimax."

"If it's inconvenient, vicar, I'll go." She watched this challenge him. He was supposed to welcome visitors to his church.

After a moment, he said, "Stay, by all means. But I must go and turn up the heating. I don't insist they wear vestments for practice, but I don't like to see them in coats and scarves."

"Of course."

Little boys started arriving, standing around the vestry on the north side, chattering about their Christmas presents. The choirstalls gradually filled. Two women choristers appeared from the vestry and so did Colin Price. He recognised Rosemary and smiled.

The practice was due at four. Some were looking at their watches. It was already ten past. The organist played a few bars and stopped. Everyone was in place except the vicar.

There was a certain amount of coughing. Then, unexpectedly, raised voices from the direction of the vestry. The vicar was saying, "Outrageous. I can't believe you would be so brazen."

A female voice said, "I'll be as brazen as I like. I've got what I came for and now it's up to the police." It was Laura.

"We'll see about that," the vicar said.

"Get your hands off me," Laura said.

Rosemary got up from the pew where she was sitting and walked quickly around the pulpit to the vestry. The door was open. Inside, the vicar was grappling with Laura, pressing her against the hanging coats and scarves.

Rosemary snatched up a brass candlestick and raised it high.

Over the vicar's shoulder Laura said, "No, Rosemary!"

Distracted, the vicar turned his head and Laura seized her chance and shoved him away. He fell into a stack of kneelers.

He shouted to Rosemary, "Don't help her. She's a thief. I caught her going through people's clothes."

Laura said, "You were right, Rosemary. There were pastry crumbs in his pocket. Oh, get out of my way, vicar. I'm going to make a citizen's arrest."

She dodged past him and ran into the main part of the church in time to see a small figure making an exit through the west door.

Rosemary, some yards behind her, called out, "Laura, that man is dangerous."

"So am I when roused," Laura said.

She dashed up the aisle and out of the church to the car park. There, the runaway, Colin Price, was standing by his pick-up truck. But he'd shied away from the door because a dog was baring its teeth in the driver's seat.

"Wilbur, you're a hero," Laura said when she'd recovered enough breath. Before going in to search the vestry, she'd noticed the door of the pickup was unlocked, so she'd installed Wilbur in the cab as a back-up.

Colin wasn't going to risk opening that door and he knew he wouldn't get far through the snow on foot. He raised both hands in an act of surrender.

To the delight of the choirboys, the practice was abandoned, and they were sent home. In the warmth of the vestry, Colin seemed not just willing to talk, but eager. "I've been an idiot. I should never have killed twice. It was meant to turn out differently."

"Why kill at all?" the vicar said. He'd dusted down his clothes and was a dignified figure again.

"I hated Douglas Boon," Colin said. "We were rivals in the old days, both of us dairy farmers, but he was so damned successful and I was failing on the paperwork. I couldn't compete. Lost my contract and had to sell up, and of course there was all the humiliation of selling to him – and for less than it was worth. He had me over a barrel. So I was reduced to odd jobs. I'd see my beautiful herd every day when I was on my way to mow another lawn. The resentment festered. And then I learned that Ben Black had made him an offer for the land, a huge offer, and he was selling up, for millions. He could retire and live in luxury and my cows would go for slaughter. The anger boiled over."

"But they weren't your cows any more," the vicar pointed out. "You'd sold them."

"You don't understand about animals, do you?" he said. "I raised them from calves. They were a dairy herd, not for beef."

"So you made up your mind to kill him," Rosemary said, "and you chose poison as the method. The yew, because its dangers are well known to all farmers, and the mince pie because it was part of the tradition here."

"And Boon was a glutton," he said. "He was certain to take it."

"Your wife had made a set of pies, knowing Gertrude would be round at some stage," Rosemary went on. "You added seeds of yew to one of them and had it with you on Christmas Eve. When you got to The Withers you took the plate as if to hand it round, but you passed your poisoned pie to Douglas."

Colin glared at her. "How do you know that? You weren't even there."

Laura said, "Pastry crumbs in your pocket, the obvious place to hide the killer pie. Our dog Wilbur found a pie in the garden and ate it. He survived, so it must have been a harmless one of ours that you chucked under a bush. I checked your coat for crumbs just now. That was what all the fuss was about. The vicar thought I was a thief."

Rosemary said to Colin, "Thanks to Laura getting the poor man to hospital, the police were alerted. News of the poisoning went quickly around the village and at some point over Christmas, Ben Brown got suspicious enough to come and see you. He threatened to tell the police. You panicked, cracked him on the head and killed him."

Laura said, "And transferred the body to Gertrude's greenhouse in your pick-up and trailer. She was under suspicion, so you thought you'd add to it. While you were in church just now I checked under the tarpaulin in the trailer. Bloodstains. The police will match them to Ben's blood group."

Colin's shoulders sagged. All the fight had gone out of him.

In all the excitement, Laura hadn't given a thought to her main reason for being in the house. Over supper that evening, she dropped her knife and fork and said, "The orchids. I've completely forgotten about them."

She had visions of dead and drooping plants in their dried-up trays.

"What am I going to say to Mike?" she said as she raced to the conservatory.

But the orchids were doing fine, better than when she'd taken over. The droopy ones were standing tall.

"They benefited from being left alone," Rosemary said. "He's a novice at this. The roots of an orchid are covered by a spongy material that holds water."

"Like a camel's hump?"

"Well ...I'm saying he must have overwatered them."

That evening Wilbur was rewarded with a supper of chopped turkey and baked ham. After he'd curled up in front of the fire, Rosemary and Laura slipped out of the front door to make a call on a neighbour.

Gertrude invited them in and poured large glasses of sherry.

"I'm so grateful to you both," she said. "I must have had calls from half the village saying how sorry they are for all I've been through. I kept telling them you two are the heroes."

"Far from it," Rosemary said with modesty.

"But you are. And you, Laura, being mistaken for a thief and wrestling with the vicar."

"That wasn't so bad."

Rosemary said, "He's rather dishy. She enjoyed getting into a clinch."

They all laughed.

"And now," Gertrude said, looking happier than they'd seen her, "another Christmas tradition. To ensure good fortune for us all in the new year, I insist that you have a slice of my home made Christmas cake. You can make a wish." She went out to the kitchen.

Rosemary said in confidence, "I'm going to wish that I survive this."

Laura said, "I'm so glad I wore this cardigan. It's got pockets."

MYSTERY NOVELS
AND SHORT STORIES
BY PETER LOVESEY: A CHECKLIST

I. NOVELS

(In the following list, the publisher of the first British edition is followed by the publisher of the first United States edition.)

Wobble to Death. Macmillan, 1970; Dodd, Mead, 1970.
    Sergeant Cribb series.
The Detective Wore Silk Drawers. Macmillan, 1971; Dodd, Mead, 1971.
    Sergeant Cribb series.
Abracadaver. Macmillan, 1972; Dodd, Mead, 1972.
    Sergeant Cribb series.
Mad Hatter's Holiday: A Novel of Mystery in Victorian Brighton.
    Macmillan, 1973; Dodd, Mead, 1973.
    Sergeant Cribb series.
Invitation to a Dynamite Party. Macmillan, 1974; as *The Tick of Death.*
    Dodd, Mead, 1974.
    Sergeant Cribb series.
A Case of Spirits. Macmillan, 1975; Dodd, Mead, 1975.
    Sergeant Cribb series.
Swing, Swing Together. Macmillan, 1976; Dodd, Mead, 1976.
    Sergeant Cribb series.
Waxwork. Macmillan, 1978; Pantheon, 1978.
    Sergeant Cribb series.
The False Inspector Dew: A Murder Mystery Aboard the SS Mauretania.
    Macmillan, 1982; Pantheon, 1982.

Keystone. Macmillan, 1983; Pantheon, 1983.

Rough Cider. Bodley Head, 1986; Mysterious Press, 1987.

Bertie and the Tinman: From the Detective Memoirs of King Edward VII. Bodley Head, 1987; Mysterious Press, 1988.

Bertie series.

On the Edge. Century Hutchinson, 1989; Mysterious Press, 1989.

Bertie and the Seven Bodies. Century Hutchinson, 1990; Mysterious Press, 1990.

Bertie series.

The Last Detective. Scribners, 1991; Doubleday, 1991.

Peter Diamond series.

Diamond Solitaire. Little, Brown, 1992; Mysterious Press, 1992.

Peter Diamond series.

Bertie and the Crime of Passion. Little, Brown, 1993; Mysterious Press, 1993.

Bertie series.

The Summons. Little, Brown, 1995; Mysterious Press, 1995.

Peter Diamond series.

Bloodhounds. Little, Brown, 1996; Mysterious Press, 1996.

Peter Diamond series

Upon a Dark Night. Little, Brown, 1997; Mysterious Press, 1998.

Peter Diamond series.

The Vault. Little, Brown, 1999; Soho Press, 2000.

Peter Diamond series.

The Reaper. Little, Brown, 2000; Soho Press, 2000.

The House Sitter. Little, Brown, 2003; Soho Press, 2003.

Peter Diamond series.

The Circle. Time Warner, 2005; Soho Press, 2005.

Hen Mallin series.

The Secret Hangman. Sphere, 2007; Soho Press, 2007.

Peter Diamond series.

The Headhunters. Sphere, 2008; Soho Press, 2008.

Hen Mallin series.

II. NOVELS UNDER THE PSEUDONYM PETER LEAR

Goldengirl. Cassell, 1977; Doubleday, 1978.
Spider Girl. Cassell, 1980; Viking, 1980.
The Secret of Spandau. Michael Joseph, 1986.

III. SHORT STORY COLLECTIONS

Butchers and Other Stories of Crime. Macmillan, 1985; Mysterious Press, 1987.
The Staring Man and Other Stories. Helsinki: Eurographica. 1989. A signed limited edition containing four stories from *Butchers and Other Stories of Crime.*
The Crime of Miss Oyster Brown and Other Stories. Little, Brown, 1994.
Do Not Exceed the Stated Dose. Crippen & Landru, 1998; Little, Brown. 1998.
The Sedgemoor Strangler and Other Stories of Crime. Crippen & Landru, 2001; Allison & Busby, 2002.
Murder on the Short List. Crippen & Landru, 2008.

III. COLLABORATIONS

The Rigby File. Hodder & Stoughton, 1989.
The Perfect Murder. HarperCollins, 1991.

IV. EDITED ANTHOLOGIES

The Black Cabinet: Stories based on True Crimes, unlocked by Peter Lovesey. Xanadu, 1989.

3rd Culprit: A Crime Writers' Annual, edited by Liza Cody, Michael Z. Lewin and Peter Lovesey. Chatto & Windus, 1994.

The Verdict of Us All: Stories by the Detection Club for H.R.F. Keating, edited by Peter Lovesey. Crippen & Landru, 2006; Allison & Busby, 2006 .

V. SHORT STORIES

"The Bathroom." *Winter's Crimes 5.* Macmillan, 1973; *Ellery Queen's Mystery Magazine* [hereafter *EQMM*], August 21, 1981, as "A Bride in the Bath." Collected in *Butchers and Other Stories of Crime.*

"The Locked Room." *Winter's Crimes 10.* Macmillan, 1978; *EQMM*, March 1979, as "Behind the Locked Door." Collected in *Butchers and Other Stories of Crime.*

"A Slight Case of Scotch." Collaborative story. *The Bell House Book.* Hodder & Stoughton, 1979.

"How Mr Smith Chased His Ancestors." *Mystery Guild Anthology.* Book Club Associates, 1980; *EQMM*, November 3, 1980, as "A Man with a Fortune." Collected in *Butchers and Other Stories of Crime.*

"Butchers." *Winter's Crimes 14.* Macmillan, 1982; *EQMM*, Mid-July 1982, as "The Butchers." Collected in *Butchers and Other Stories of Crime* and in *The Staring Man and Other Stories.*

"Taking Possession." *EQMM*, November 1982. Collected in *Butchers and Other Stories of Crime* and in *The Staring Man and Other Stories* as "Woman and Home."

"The Virgin and the Bull." *John Creasey's Mystery Crime Collection.* Gollancz, 1983; *EQMM*, July 1983, as "The Virgoan and the Taurean." Collected in *Butchers and Other Stories of Crime.*

"Fall-Out." *Company Magazine*, May 1983; *EQMM*, June 1984. Collected in *Butchers and Other Stories of Crime.*

"Belly Dance." *Winter's Crimes 15.* Macmillan, 1983; *EQMM,* March 1983, as "Keeping Fit." Collected in *Butchers and Other Stories of Crime.*

"Did You Tell Daddy?" *EQMM,* February 1984. Collected in *Butchers and Other Stories of Crime.*

"Arabella's Answer." *EQMM,* April 1984. Collected in *Butchers and Other Stories of Crime.*

"Vandals." *Woman's Own,* December 29, 1984; *EQMM,* December 1985. Collected in *Butchers and Other Stories of Crime.*

"The Secret Lover." *Winter's Crimes 17,* Macmillan, 1985; *EQMM,* March 1988. Collected in *Butchers and Other Stories of Crime.*

"The Corder Figure." *Butchers and Other Stories of Crime.* Macmillan, 1985; *EQMM,* January 1986. Collected in *Butchers and Other Stories of Crime* and in *The Staring Man and Other Stories.*

"Private Gorman's Luck." *Butchers and Other Stories of Crime.* Macmillan, 1985; *EQMM,* July 1985. Collected in *Butchers and Other Stories of Crime.*

"The Staring Man." *Butchers and Other Stories of Crime.* Macmillan, 1985; *EQMM,* October 1985. Collected in *Butchers and Other Stories of Crime* and in *The Staring Man and Other Stories.*

"Trace of Spice." *Butchers and Other Stories of Crime.* Macmillan, 1985. Collected in *Butchers and Other Stories of Crime.*

"Murder in Store." *Woman's Own,* December 21, 1985. Collected in *Do Not Exceed the Stated Dose.*

"Curl Up and Dye." *EQMM,* July 1986. Collected in *The Crime of Miss Oyster Brown and Other Stories.*

"Photographer Slain." Contest story. *The Observer,* November 30, 1986.

"Peer's Grisly Find: Butler Dead in Bath." Contest story. *The Observer,* December 7, 1986. Printed as a separate pamphlet, under the title "The Butler Didn't Do It," to accompany Crippen & Landru's limited edition of *The Sedgemoor Strangler and Other Stories of Crime.*

"Brighton Line Murder." Contest story. *The Observer*, December 14, 1986.

"The Poisoned Mince Pie." Contest story. *The Observer*, December 21, 1986.

"The Royal Plot." Contest story. *The Observer*, December 28, 1986.

"The Curious Computer." *New Adventures of Sherlock Holmes.* Carroll & Graf, 1987. Collected in *The Crime of Miss Oyster Brown and Other Stories.*

"Friendly Yachtsman, 39." *Woman's Own*, July 18, 1987; *EQMM*, May 1988. Collected in *The Crime of Miss Oyster Brown and Other Stories.*

"The Pomeranian Poisoning." *Winter's Crimes 19.* Macmillan, 1987; *EQMM*, August 1988, as "The Zenobia Hatt Prize." Collected in *The Crime of Miss Oyster Brown and Other Stories.*

"Where is Thy Sting." *Winter's Crimes 20.* Macmillan, 1988; *EQMM*, November 1988, as "The Wasp." Collected in *The Crime of Miss Oyster Brown and Other Stories.*

"Oracle of the Dead." *EQMM*, Mid-December 1988; *Best*, March 3, 1989.

"A Case of Butterflies." *Winter's Crimes 21.* Macmillan, 1989; *EQMM*, December 1989. Collected in *The Crime of Miss Oyster Brown and Other Stories.*

"Youdunnit." *New Crimes.* Robinson, 1989; *EQMM*, Mid-December 1989. Collected in *The Crime of Miss Oyster Brown and Other Stories.*

"The Haunted Crescent." *Mistletoe Mysteries.* Mysterious Press, 1989. Collected in *The Crime of Miss Oyster Brown and Other Stories.*

"Shock Visit." *Winter's Crimes 22.* Macmillan, 1990; *EQMM*, February 1990, as "The Valuation." Collected in *The Crime of Miss Oyster Brown and Other Stories.*

"The Lady in the Trunk." *A Classic English Crime.* Pavilion, 1990. Collected in *The Crime of Miss Oyster Brown and Other Stories.*

"Ginger's Waterloo." *Cat Crimes.* Donald L. Fine, 1991. Collected in *The Crime of Miss Oyster Brown and Other Stories.*

"Being of Sound Mind." *Winter's Crimes* 23. Macmillan, 1990; *EQMM*, July 1991. Collected in *The Crime of Miss Oyster Brown and Other Stories*.

"The Christmas Present." *Woman's Own*, December 24, 1990; *EQMM*, Mid-December 1991, as "Supper with Miss Shivers." Collected in *The Crime of Miss Oyster Brown and Other Stories* as "Supper with Miss Shivers."

"The Crime of Miss Oyster Brown." *Midwinter Mysteries* 1. Scribners, 1991; *EQMM*, May 1991. Collected in *The Crime of Miss Oyster Brown and Other Stories*.

"The Man Who Ate People." *The Man Who . . .* Macmillan, 1992; *EQMM*, October 1992. Collected in *The Crime of Miss Oyster Brown and Other Stories*.

"You May See a Strangler." *Midwinter Mysteries* 2. Little, Brown, 1992. Collected in *The Crime of Miss Oyster Brown and Other Stories*.

"Murder By Christmas Tree." Contest story. *The Observer*, December 20, 1992. Printed as a separate pamphlet to accompany Crippen & Landru's limited edition of *Do Not Exceed the Stated Dose*.

"Pass the Parcel." *Midwinter Mysteries* 3. Little, Brown, 1993; *EQMM*, Mid-December 1994. Collected in *The Crime of Miss Oyster Brown and Other Stories*.

"Murder in the Library." Contest story. *Evening Chronicle*, Bath, October 6, 1993.

"The Model Con." *Woman's Realm Summer Special*, 1994. Collected in *The Crime of Miss Oyster Brown and Other Stories*.

"Bertie and the Fire Brigade." *Royal Crimes*. Signet, 1994. Collected in *Do Not Exceed the Stated Dose*.

"The Odstock Curse." *Murder for Halloween*. Mysterious Press, 1994. Collected in *Do Not Exceed the Stated Dose*.

"Passion Killers." *EQMM*, January 1994. Collected in *Do Not Exceed the Stated Dose*.

"The Case of the Easter Bonnet." *Bath Chronicle*, April 17, 1995; *EQMM*, April 1997. Collected in *Do Not Exceed the Stated Dose.*

"Never a Cross Word." *You, Mail on Sunday*, June 11, 1995; *EQMM*, February 1997. Collected in *Do Not Exceed the Stated Dose.*

"The Mighty Hunter." *Midwinter Mysteries 5.* Little, Brown, 1995; *EQMM*, January 1996. Collected in *Do Not Exceed the Stated Dose.*

"The Proof of the Pudding." *A Classic Christmas Crime.* Pavilion, 1995. Collected in *Do Not Exceed the Stated Dose.*

"The Pushover." *EQMM*, June 1995. Collected in *Do Not Exceed the Stated Dose.*

"Quiet Please—We're Rolling." *No Alibi.* Ringpull, 1995; *EQMM*, December 1996. Collected in *Do Not Exceed the Stated Dose.*

"Wayzgoose." *A Dead Giveaway.* Warner Futura, 1995; *EQMM*, May 1997. Collected in *Do Not Exceed the Stated Dose.*

"Disposing of Mrs Cronk." *Perfectly Criminal.* Severn House, 1996; *EQMM*, December 1997. Collected in *Do Not Exceed the Stated Dose.*

"A Parrot is Forever." *Malice Domestic 5.* Pocket Books, 1996. Collected in *Do Not Exceed the Stated Dose.*

"Bertie and the Boat Race." *Crime Through Time.* Berkley, 1996. Collected in *Do Not Exceed the Stated Dose.*

"The Corbett Correspondence" (with Keith Miles). *Malice Domestic 6.* Pocket Books, 1997.

"Because It Was There." *Whydunit? Perfectly Criminal 2.* Severn House, 1997. Collected in *Do Not Exceed the Stated Dose.*

"Ape." *Mary Higgins Clark Mystery Magazine*, Summer1998. Collected in *The Sedgemoor Strangler and Other Stories of Crime.*

"Showmen." *Past Poisons.* Headline, 1998; *EQMM*, March 2000. Collected in *The Sedgemoor Strangler and Other Stories of Crime.*

"The Four Wise Men." *More Holmes for the Holidays.* Berkley, 1999. Collected in *The Sedgemoor Strangler and Other Stories of Crime.*

"The Perfectionist." *The Strand Magazine*, April-July 2000. Collected in *The Sedgemoor Strangler and Other Stories of Crime.*

"The Word of a Lady." *EQMM*, July 2000. Collected in *The Sedgemoor Strangler and Other Stories of Crime.*

"The Sedgemoor Strangler." *Criminal Records.* Orion, 2000. Collected in *The Sedgemoor Strangler and Other Stories of Crime.*

"Interior, With Corpse." *Scenes of the Crime.* Severn House, 2000; *EQMM,* August, 2001. Collected in *The Sedgemoor Strangler and Other Stories of Crime.*

"Dr Death." *Crime Through Time III.* Berkley, 2000. Collected in *The Sedgemoor Strangler and Other Stories of Crime.*

"The Problem of Stateroom 10." *Murder Through the Ages.* Headline, 2000; *EQMM,* December, 2001. Collected in *The Sedgemoor Strangler and Other Stories of Crime.*

"The Amorous Corpse." *The Mammoth Book of Locked Room Mysteries and Impossible Crimes.* Robinson, 2000. Collected in *The Sedgemoor Strangler and Other Stories of Crime.*

"The Kiss of Death." Published as a separate pamphlet by Crippen & Landru, 2000. Collected in *The Sedgemoor Strangler and Other Stories of Crime.*

"Away with the Fairies." *Malice Domestic 10.* Avon, 2001. Collected in *The Sedgemoor Strangler and Other Stories of Crime.*

"Star Struck." *Death by Horoscope.* Carroll & Graf, 2001. Collected in *The Sedgemoor Strangler and Other Stories of Crime.*

"The Usual Table." *The Mysterious Press Anniversary Anthology.* Mysterious Press, 2001. Collected in *The Sedgemoor Strangler and Other Stories of Crime.*

"Murdering Max." *EQMM,* September-October 2001. Collected in *The Sedgemoor Strangler and Other Stories of Crime.*

"The Stalker." Previously unpublished. Collected in *The Sedgemoor Strangler and Other Stories of Crime.*

"Window of Opportunity." *Sunday Express Magazine,* 6-12 April, 2003; *EQMM,* November, 2004. Collected in *Murder on the Short List.*

"The Man Who Jumped for England." *Mysterious Pleasures.* Little, Brown, 2003; *EQMM,* June, 2005. Collected in *Murder on the Short List.*

'The Field." *Green for Danger.* The Do-Not Press, 2003; *EQMM*, September-October, 2004. Collected in *Murder on the Short List.*

"Second Strings." *The Strand Magazine,* June-September, 2004. Collected in *Murder on the Short List.*

"Razor Bill." *Sherlock,* Issue 60, 2004. Collected in *Murder on the Short List.*

"Bullets." *The Mammoth Book of Roaring Twenties Whodunnits.* Constable & Robinson, 2004. Collected in *Murder on the Short List.*

"The Case of the Dead Wait." *Daily Mail,* 24, 27 and 28, December, 2004; *EQMM,* January 2007. Collected in *Murder on the Short List.*

"Needle Match." *Murder is My Racquet.* Mysterious Press, 2005. Collected in *Murder on the Short List.*

"Say That Again." *The Ideas Experiment.* PawPaw Press, 2006; *EQMM,* March-April, 2007. Collected in *Murder on the Short List.*

"A Blow on the Head." *I.D. Crimes of Identity.* Comma Press, 2006. Collected in *Murder on the Short List.*

"Popping Round to the Post." *The Verdict of Us All.* Crippen & Landru, 2006; *EQMM,* November 2007. Collected in *Murder on the Short List.*

"Bertie and the Christmas Tree." *The Strand Magazine,* October-December, 2007. Collected in *Murder on the Short List.*

"The Best Suit." Previously unpublished. Collected in *Murder on the Short List.*

"The Homicidal Hat." Published as a separate pamphlet by Crippen & Landru for Malice Domestic Convention, 2008.